WINTER KILL

For Dorn HAZOL,

with my LovE,

Josephine / E. J!

X

WINTER
KILL

E J PEPPER

Troubador Publishing
Unit E2 Airfield Business Park,
Harrison Road, Market Harborough,
Leicestershire. LE16 7UL
Tel: 0116 2792299
Email: books@troubador.co.uk
Web: www.troubador.co.uk

ISBN 978 1805142 836

British Library Cataloguing in Publication Data.
A catalogue record for this book is available from the British Library.

Printed and bound in Great Britain by 4edge Limited
Typeset in 11pt Minion Pro by Troubador Publishing Ltd, Leicester, UK

For Joan Griffiths
In Loving Memory

ACKNOWLEDGEMENTS

M Y WARMEST THANKS TO THE FOLLOWING:
Fellow author Sarah Hegarty, for her invaluable recommendations and help in seeing the book through to the end.

Craig Hillsley, whose insights and critique greatly strengthened the MS.

Linda Anderson for reading and continuing encouragement.

The team at Troubador for their dedication and expertise.

To Andrew – for being there.

ONE

A<small>LL</small> N<small>OVEMBER THE RAIN CONTINUES, DRIPPING</small> from the bony knuckles of the pollarded limes, falling in slanting stitches against the streetlights, and pouring out of the swollen sky, as if upended from some giant container. In London, the Thames Barrier is permanently raised whilst in the countryside, fields that should be filled with overwintering sheep, are water-logged and deserted.

Not so long ago, forecasters in the north would have been expounding at length about the different types of snow – light, wet, powdery, graupel – but other than a few remote spots – Widdybank Fell, Kinbrace, Eskdalemuir – the varieties, like so many wildlife species, are all but gone.

The latest international climate conference has ended in its usual stalemate and thoughts of Christmas parties or get-aways to the Caribbean are overshadowed by domestic crises: dubious dealings in high places, a new virus that's filling the hospitals at an alarming rate, and the influx of illegal immigrants, as persistent as the rain.

In that climate-free zone, twenty-four metres or so below ground, a tube train grinds its way into Embankment Station. The doors ease open and, disgorged from the hot belly, several dozen passengers trudge towards the escalator that will bear them up, like so many pieces of luggage, into the rainswept afternoon.

But now – a disturbance. A man, dressed in the ubiquitous uniform of anorak, jeans and trainers, starts shoving his way along the narrow platform, leaving those around him to rub their arms and glare at his retreating back. 'Fuck's sake!' a thin, red-haired fellow shouts. 'Watch where you're –' Yet already the man is out of earshot.

Once in the open air, he goes up Villiers Street at a half-run, pausing at the top to catch his breath. He's youngish, narrow shouldered with spiky hair swept back from a high forehead and a panicked look in the dark eyes. You might put him down as something junior in IT or sales – a shade too eager to please and surely the last person to become embroiled in national scandal and murder. But then how hard it can be to spot the lawbreakers among us when they are so expert at camouflage – when we have our own secrets to hide.

The phone call came two days earlier. 'I'm nae hanging about for you, Oliver Moorhouse – or whatever you call yourself,' the voice on the other end of the line said.

A person used to getting his own way, then, although at least with that Scots accent he's unlikely to be one of those public-school tossers, who delight in reminding someone like State-educated Ollie of his humbler place in the scheme of things.

Ollie is also a cautious man so it's as well he has no idea of what he's about to get himself into – that the murder is just a few weeks away. If he did know, he would surely turn tail and head for home. But for now, all he can think about is his desperate need of the promised cash, both to settle his mountain of bills and to pacify his increasingly disgruntled girlfriend.

The night is drawing in as he sets off along The Strand. His train was twenty minutes late – they're properly up the creek these days – but this is not going to be another one of his cock-ups, he tells himself, reaching for his phone to check the venue, which should be somewhere just ahead of him.

Go back a few years and this street would have been prosperous and bustling, but now, with so many cafes and shops boarded up, what few shoppers there are scurry along the pavements, anxious to escape the wet.

Ollie has been hoping that the meeting would be held in one of the modern places, where the coffee is not too pricey and the bright lights give the illusion of sunnier days. But he sees to his disappointment that what's been chosen is somewhere to which he'd normally give a wide berth: a half-timbered coffee house with a beat-up wooden door and paint peeling off the window frames.

Some instinct makes him glance behind but the pavement is deserted. Of course, he's not being followed. Why on earth would he be? He pushes open the door and steps into a long, narrow room, filled with high-backed wooden booths – like bloody coffin lids, he thinks. What lighting there is comes from individual lamps, the scarlet shades throwing small pools of crimson onto the surface of the tables. To his left is the bar, its glasses and bottles winking in the mirror that runs along the opposite wall. Its reflection also catches the drops of rain running down the front window giving him the unsettling impression of being under water.

He walks forward, scanning the tables. The place isn't busy – two or three couples chatting together and a younger woman – a lawyer from the look of her navy outfit – busy on her laptop. Of a lone businessman, there is no sign, and he has a moment's panic. He's hungry for this. He *needs* this.

The instructions were for him to choose a seat in the window. He hovers, uncertain, patting his inner pocket to check the envelope is still there.

A short, fat waiter appears from behind the counter, a striped apron wrapped around his large stomach. 'Mr. Moorhouse? You'll be wanting that one.' He points to an empty table overlooking the street that Ollie realises he's walked straight past. 'How did you know who I –?' But the waiter has turned his back and Ollie slides into the seat, glancing at his watch. After all that panic, he's ten minutes early and could do with something to steady his nerves. He orders a large glass of Merlot. His stomach rumbles – it's been hours since his breakfast fry-up – but he makes do with a bowl of salted peanuts that he crams into his mouth in between gulps of wine.

He peers through the window. The passing traffic is spasmodic, with only the occasional bloom of headlights piercing the murky atmosphere. They sweep across a boarded-up shop on the opposite pavement and, as if in protest, a large black bundle gives a sudden shift. There are many such bundles in this city – in most of the cities in the country for that matter – and the few passers-by don't break their stride at what is probably just another victim of the recession. Although not as severe as the previous one, for those who, through sheer bad luck or some administrative blunder, have ended up on the streets, it is endless, fathomless misery.

Ollie however is not one to dwell on this. He has enough troubles of his own to cope with.

The woman lawyer is leaving, pausing in the doorway to put up her umbrella before stepping into the wet on spiky heeled shoes. Good legs, he notes. What is Amy doing now? He gulps his drink, picturing the wonderful curve of her arse as she turned from the shower and the way she kicked the door shut when she caught him watching. He'd like to text her, but suppose she has another go at him? Although it wasn't his fault that his pay has been cut yet again. *It never is, Ollie*, he can hear her saying. He wants to tell her how much she means to him, but the thought always seems too difficult to voice. Instead, he's promised to go easy on the booze. She'll come round in time. Understand that –

'Sorry tae keep you waiting.' A figure slides into the seat beside him and extends a hand. 'You ken what the trains are like.'

Ollie does a double take. From the briefing his editor gave, Ollie was expecting some middle-aged businessman

– all M & S suit, ironed shirt and aftershave. Whereas the person beside him is wearing a crumpled raincoat and battered hat. And he's *old* – in his eighties perhaps – with a lined face and small deep-set eyes.

The waiter is hovering. 'The usual, Hamish?'

'If you'd be sae kind, Andrei,' he says, placing a black briefcase on the seat beside him. 'And I trust you and that bonny wife of yours are keeping well?' He turns back to Ollie. 'Nae need to introduce myself.'

It's reassuring that the man is known in here, although what after all does that mean? And not for the first time, Ollie questions what on earth has made him agree to this assignment. It's just that on the phone Hamish – and it occurs to him to wonder if that *is* his real name – sounded so bloody plausible. And then there was that confident briefing from Ollie's editor. 'I know you're being asked to put money up front,' Jack had said. 'The paper's not in a position to fund you, but if you decide to pursue this, it should pay off big-time – could well be the scoop of the year.' He paused, taking a drag on his vape. 'And I imagine you'll manage to raise the cash.'

Now, as if reading Ollie's thoughts, Hamish says: 'Let's nae beat about the bush. You've brought the money?'

Ollie nods, noticing the contrast between the man's shabby appearance and the intelligence in the blue eyes– as if they belong to a schoolteacher or a librarian.

'Show me,' Hamish demands.

'I need to be sure you have the information.' Ollie tries to keep his voice steady, assertive. After all, he's the one being made to cough up.

He chuckles. 'Oh, I have it all right. In fact, even better, I'm about to take you to the person in question.'

Ollie hesitates. 'You're sure this is as big as my editor says because...' His voice tails away. He can't afford for it to go wrong, he thinks.

'I'm nae fooling around with you, laddie, and I suggest you don't do so with me.' His drink has arrived and he grips it, the veins in his hands standing out amongst the sprinkle of age spots. 'I take it you're the man for the job. So, do you still want it? Because I can't have you wasting my time.'

'Yes – yes I do.' But Christ! If he gets this wrong, he'll be out on his ear filling supermarket shelves.

'Understand that I can only give you an introduction. After that it's up to you.'

'But this *is* big?'

'It is, laddie.' The man's tone is persuasive, reassuring.

Ollie reaches into his inner pocket and draws out the envelope. The man takes it from him, licking a finger while he counts the notes inside. When he's finished, he gives a nod of satisfaction that Ollie wishes he could share. There on the table is the deposit towards a new boiler. Amy will kill him if she finds out. Won't be convinced, any more than he is now, when he tells her he'll be getting it all back in spades.

But it's too late to change his mind because, in a series of swift moves, Hamish has scooped up the notes, tucked them into the envelope and shoved it into the pocket of his grubby coat.

'Now, before I take you to him, let me tell you again that this could well be the turning point of your life. *If* you handle it right.'

At least this echoes what Jack has told him. 'I wonder' – again he hesitates – 'are there any pointers you can give me?'

'I've been connected with the newspaper business nigh on sixty years. They may have brought in all this fancy technology but let me tell you what never changes. This.' He taps his nose with a bent finger. 'When you're on the scent, laddie, follow it – wherever it takes you.' He pauses. 'And believe me, this is going to take you to places you've never dreamed of.'

'Yes,' Ollie says, his uncertainty fading under those penetrating eyes. A scoop like this will get him off that local rag – away from stories of out-of-control dogs and stolen bikes – and onto one of the nationals. And once there, the world will look at him differently, Amy will look at him differently. Will look at him with *respect*.

'So' – Hamish picks up the briefcase– 'Why do you think I asked you to sit in the window?'

'So I could see you coming?'

He shakes his head. 'So, you could use your bluidy eyes.' He swallows his drink in a few swift gulps. 'Now, sup up, laddie, and let's get going.'

TWO

OLLIE HAS EXPECTED THEM TO HEAD ALONG THE road, perhaps to the tube station, but instead Hamish gives a quick tug on his sleeve before darting across to the opposite side. The man may only come up to his ear, but he has the wiry build of a jockey and Ollie has to go at a half run to keep up.

Once over the road, Hamish looks up at him from under the battered hat. 'Ready?' He doesn't wait for a reply but moves towards the nearest doorway.

The building was once a gift shop, Ollie remembers, filled with London souvenirs – plastic models of the Houses of Parliament, biscuit tins with pictures of the Union Jack on the lid, miniature Beefeaters and red London buses. All the tat that the tourists, particularly the Yanks and the Japanese, are so keen on. But the overseas visitors are still sticking to their home territory and now the shop is boarded-up, the entrance piled with discarded food containers, scraps of paper and black bundles of God knows what.

Hamish approaches the nearest bundle– the same one, Ollie realises, that he observed from his seat in the wine bar. Hamish pokes it with his boot and Ollie gives a start of surprise as a pale hand reaches up. Hamish grasps hold of it. Ollie was right to think that the Scotsman is stronger than he looks for now, like some grotesque enactment of a birth, a figure is pulled slowly from the bundle and stands facing them in the grey light.

None of the three speaks and the silence is filled with the swish of a passing car and the steady drip of rain.

The figure is that of a boy, looking to be still in his teens, dressed in a thin, nylon jacket and filthy jeans. He's bony and gaunt, the matted hair and white face marking him out as just another homeless wretch. I've paid good money for *this*? Ollie thinks, with a fresh onrush of doubt.

Hamish grips the boy's wrist. 'Right, Jimmy. Let's get going.'

'Where to?' Ollie asks, but the Scotsman is striding out, the boy stumbling along beside him. They turn to their right, passing shuttered shop fronts, a handful of small businesses that have survived the recession – a hardware store, a pharmacy, a pizza parlour – and a bedraggled queue waiting hopefully at a bus stop. The Gothic structure of the Law Courts looms ahead and then they are moving on, turning down a series of side streets that lead towards The Embankment.

It's the start of the rush-hour and the pavements are busy with office workers heading for home or the nearest pub. Ollie watches as Hamish and the boy perform a series of swerving moves to avoid the passers-by – the Covid Dance, as he once heard someone describe it. A few minutes later they are in a narrow alley, tall buildings hemming them in on either side and at the far end a concrete block of flats with grimy windows and a battered-looking door. They pause outside while the boy fumbles in his jacket for a key. Once the door is unlocked, they follow him into a small hallway where the reek of cat piss hangs in the air. He clicks on a light to reveal scuffed lino and an old-fashioned phone, its grey flex dangling off the wall like a torn ligament. Hamish, once again moving at surprising speed, heads up a flight of narrow stairs. Ollie and the boy follow more slowly, stepping aside on the third-floor landing to allow a thin, stooped woman to pass. She's wearing a stained ankle-length skirt and carries a string bag filled with tins of food, a large book balanced precariously on the top.

She looks up at them with rheumy eyes. 'Good day to you, James. I see you have a new visitor accompanying you today.' The cut-glass accent, so at odds with her appearance, leaves Ollie staring in surprise.

'Yup,' the boy mumbles.

'Perhaps you would kindly perform the necessary introductions.'

He brushes past her. 'Not now, Amelia.'

'Has he come to help?' she calls, as they continue up to the next landing. 'Someone must be able to.' The words echo down the stairwell.

At the top floor, Hamish stands waiting by a closed door. The boy unlocks it, clicking on a light to reveal an attic room with a sloping roof and bare floorboards. The furniture consists of a battered looking table, two chairs, a mattress with blankets tossed across it and a sink piled with cardboard containers of congealed food. The room is stuffy, a sweet staleness hanging in the air. Ollie glances across to the small window, which is covered in grime. God knows when it was last opened. The whole place is a bloody petri dish, he thinks, hovering just inside the door.

'Are you going tae invite us in, Jimmy?' Hamish demands. He doesn't wait for an answer, stepping forward and taking out the envelope Ollie gave him earlier. He peels off several notes. 'A down-payment,' he says, laying them on the table. 'Should help with the gear you want.'

Of course, Ollie thinks, as the sweetish stink of the room takes him back to his journalism course at Southwark when he had his fair share of nose candy. Nowadays he tries to keep off the stuff. Amy has made her views on it very clear and anyway, his hard-earned cash goes further in the pub.

Jimmy pockets the money. 'I did that waiter job you arranged for me,' he says, as he shuffles over to the mattress.

'And the house?' Hamish asks.

'Posh place in Mayfair. About a hundred people. Couldn't move for all the furs and jewels.' He pauses. 'The papers were in the place you said they'd be.'

'Excellent. Let's have them then.'

The boy thrusts his hand under the mattress before straightening and holding out a brown folder.

Hamish takes it from him and turns to Ollie. 'Sit yourself down, laddie, so we can take a look at what we've got.'

Ollie edges reluctantly into the room and lowers himself onto the wooden chair. The table is made of rough deal, its cracked surface filled with pieces of bacon rind and congealed fat.

Hamish extracts the folder's contents and spreads them on the desk.

Ollie hasn't known what to expect, but it certainly isn't this collection of dog-eared documents, some hand-written, others typed. He experiences a rush of anger. Is this what he's given good money for? He twists in his seat, staring into the Scotsman's face. 'You said you had definite intel.'

'And here it is, laddie.' He jabs a finger at the piece of paper nearest Ollie. 'How often do I have to tell you to use your bluidy eyes?'

Ollie turns back to the table.

The first letter in front of him is written in faded blue ink and is dated a couple of years earlier.

My Dear Florin,

Following our recent talk, I am writing to tell you that this must be our last communication by post. Otherwise, we are left too open. Too open to what? *Ollie wonders. In future I will send you items via courier. Each to be used once and then discarded. I repeat – once only. Wait to hear from me. Meanwhile, do nothing.*

Your friend, M. C.

Ollie looks up. 'I still don't follow. And who the hell is M. C.?'

'Keep reading.'

There are several more handwritten letters that leave him none the wiser but one other, typed on headed notepaper, catches his eye. It consists of just a couple of lines.

'Dear Charlie,
   Further to yours of the 4th inst., I agree with you on the need for caution. Will you arrange our next little gathering? Or shall I?'
   Yours ever, Bill

Ollie stares. Stamped at the top of the letter is a crowned portcullis set against a red background – the emblem of the House of Lords.

His interest aroused, he turns to the other documents. There are several passports, the names and other details blocked out in black ink; three receipts itemising unspecified goods received in the sum of £920,000, £886,000, and £754, 000 respectively, and a list of names, none of which mean anything to him.

He looks up and catches the flash of impatience in Hamish's eyes.

'You still dinnae get it?'

'I'm afraid not.' And suppose, after all, this is just a clever con?

Hamish taps Ollie's shoulder – not softly enough to be a friendly gesture, but as if trying to force Ollie to concentrate. 'Brightwell ring any bells?'

Ollie frowns. 'That scandal to do with money laundering? If I remember right, it led to the latest tightening of controls. And didn't the Home Office Minister – Jefferies –resign over it?'

'He did, laddie, and his wasn't the only head to roll.'

'Yes, it certainly caused quite a stink.'

The Scotsman nods. 'One bloody great stink and' – another tap – 'play your cards right, you'll be stirring up an even bigger one.' He jerks his head towards the boy, who seems intent on staring out of the window. But something about the set of his shoulders signals that he's not missing a word. 'Let's talk it through away from here.' Hamish raises his voice. 'Walls have ears, isn't that right, Jimmy?'

'You'd know, wouldn't you?'

Hamish steps forward. 'What's that?'

'I've been thinking.' The boy runs his tongue over cracked lips. 'Maybe I'm worth more than you're paying.'

'Is that a fact?'

'How about what we agreed, with a bit extra on top.'

Hamish digs into his briefcase, taking out a small packet and placing it on the deal table. It could be tea but of course Ollie knows that it's not.

'Is that all?'

Hamish smiles. 'Like another?'

'Fair's fair.'

'How about I show you what's fair.'

In a move that makes Ollie gasp, Hamish delivers a swift punch to Jimmy's stomach before gripping him by the throat and kicking his legs from under him. The boy sinks to the floor and as the gloved hands tighten their grip, he begins wheezing and gasping for breath. Hamish shakes him – like a terrier with a rat, Ollie thinks – the boy's head jerking from side to side, the eyes bulbous.

Ollie steps forward. 'For God's sake – you'll kill him!'

'Maybe that would be the easiest way.' To Ollie's relief, he loosens his hold. 'Certainly it would be the cheapest. Isn't that right, Jimmy?'

The boy is on his hands and knees, retching, a thin yellow stream spewing onto the bare boards, the reek of vomit filling the air. He looks up at Hamish. 'I'll get you!' he croaks.

'Then maybe you need another lesson in respect.' Hamish raises one booted foot and kicks the boy full in the ribs. There's a cracking sound and he screams, collapsing to the floor and trying to shield himself from the further kicks that Hamish is delivering with speed and precision. Eventually he pauses, staring down at the boy, who cowers, trembling.

'Think yourself lucky I didn't spoil your pretty face.'

Ollie fights off a wave of nausea.

'We're all done here.' Hamish says, scooping up the packet

'Please' – Jimmy's voice is shaking– 'I'll do whatever you want but, for God's sake, leave me that.'

Hamish tosses the pack onto the table. 'As long as we understand one another.'

'I'll be in the usual doorway.'

'What it is to have more than one place of residence, eh?' Hamish moves to the door and next moment his steps recede down the stairs.

Ollie turns back to the boy, who's on his side, clutching his ribs. 'Can I get you anything?'

'No you fucking can't!'

He tries again. 'You have this room, so why sleep out in all the cold and wet?' Because surely even this sordid place was better than a shop entrance piled with litter.

'Nowhere to run to from up here, is there?' the boy says, in a tone that implies he's speaking to a complete idiot. 'You're all fucking well the same.' He crawls across the floorboards and hauls himself onto the mattress. 'But I hope that Scottish cunt gets what's coming to him!'

Ollie takes the stairs two at a time to find Hamish waiting outside, his briefcase tucked under his arm.

'Do you think Jimmy needs –?' Ollie begins.

'Let's not waste any more time on that wee Jessie.' He pulls on a pair of tan gloves, turning his collar up against the rain. 'Now – let's find somewhere out of the wet so we can go over what we've got.'

All Ollie wants is to be back in his own house, sitting in front of the TV with a can of beer. But he doesn't have the balls to protest and, at the realisation, is filled with a renewed sense of his own inadequacy.

To his relief, they don't return to the wine bar. Instead, Hamish chooses a modern cafeteria with mock wood tables and a cream tiled floor. After the squalor of the attic room, Ollie is glad of the clinical feel of the place. They order coffee that they drink facing one another across a table. There are only a handful of other customers, sitting in ones and twos, engrossed in their laptops and mobiles.

Hamish glances around before extracting a folder from his briefcase. It's not the tattered document Ollie saw earlier. This one is uncreased, with a blue cover. He catches Ollie's look. 'You didn't think I was going to trust you with the originals, did you?' He opens the folder and extracts several sheets of photocopied paper that he pushes across the table. 'You need to start with these. Take a look.'

The names, some fifty of them, are in alphabetical order. Ollie skims through the lists. Dan, Fischer, Stepanov, Mayer, Muller, Schmidt, Weber, Zamfir. He looks up. 'Are they German? Or Jewish maybe?'

Hamish ignores him. 'This next sheet,' he says, pushing it across, 'gives more details: dates of birth, addresses, mobile numbers, and so on.'

'And you want me to what? Trace these people – wherever they've got to?'

'Just the ones in the UK. Shouldn't be too hard.'

'And that letter on House of Lords notepaper? And those others?'

'Leave them to one side for the moment.'

Ollie studies the list. 'But why would anyone hang onto information if it incriminates them?'

Hamish treats him to a cool stare. 'Because, laddie, people are complacent, lazy, or just bluidy fools.'

Ollie gazes into the murky depths of his Americano. He only scraped three O-levels, for God's sake! Hamish must have seen him coming. He looks up to find the blue eyes fastened on him and, once again, feels his stomach churn.

'Not losing your nerve, are you?'

He hesitates. 'But the payment you promised?'

'I'll bring the first instalment when we next meet.' He smiles. 'One thousand, as agreed.'

After the assault he's just witnessed, he has no appetite for any of this. But where else would he get the amount of cash Hamish is offering? How else settle his debts and make it good with Amy? 'No, I'm in,' he murmurs.

'Excellent. Once you've made the links between those names and the payments, that's when the story begins.' His mobile buzzes. 'Have to go. We'll meet again very soon. I'll text you the date.' He gets to his feet, staring down at him. 'I'm no playing games with you, laddie. And remember this – the people you'll be investigating won't be either.' And, with a nod, he's gone.

Ollie sits on at the table. When he next sees Hamish, he must ask the questions he should have put to him already. For a start, why can't the man do this work himself? Draw out his own cash? And why has he chosen an obscure reporter from an obscure newspaper? And what in God's name was the point of that visit to Jimmy if Hamish already had the duplicate documents?

Yet as he heads back towards the Embankment and home, Ollie suspects that whatever answers the Scot may give will leave him no nearer to understanding what the hell he's getting himself into.

Not losing your nerve, are you? Hamish said. As Ollie recalls the pack of drugs tossed onto the table and the brutal assault on Jimmy, he thinks: Nerve doesn't come near it. The truth is the Scotsman fucking terrifies him.

THREE

MARYA BONDAR SITS BY THE AGA, SWINGING stockinged feet backwards and forwards in front of the warmth. From a distance you might mistake her for a child – she's just over five foot, thin and flat-chested, with a fringe of straight black hair. But as she glances up, awaiting the summons from upstairs, the face is that of a middle-aged woman, with round, staring eyes and lips clamped together as if fearful of letting some unwanted information slip. Not surprising given that in her sixty odd years she's seen more than enough to keep schtum about and only rarely will the set of her mouth relax into a smile.

The previous spring, for instance, she went on a coach party to one of those National Trust places with patterned ceilings, gilded chairs and portraits of long-dead nobility staring down on it all. There were tapestries everywhere, canopied beds and a long table laid with exquisite china, but Marya remained unmoved – until, that is, she followed the string of tourists down a stone staircase to the flag-stoned passage that ran the length of the lowest floor. Leading off from the passage were a series of rooms once used for storing cheese and butter, for polishing silver and boots, and for hanging the corpses of the wildlife the nobility shot with the callous sangfroid Marya admires so much.

However, it was only when she entered the large kitchen that she gave one of her rare smiles. 'Why, it's just like the one at the Hall!' she exclaimed. For there were the same whitewashed brick walls, the central table of scrubbed wood; the arrangement of copper pans above the range and on the wall opposite, the line of bells with underneath them the abbreviated description of the rooms to which they belonged: *draw-room; libry; din-room; mast bed; billrd room*, and then the numbers for the other bedrooms running from 1 to 12.

She was still trying to take it all in when an American voice behind her drawled: 'Gee, Hunter, I'd give my right arm to have lived back in them days.'

'Reckon you've been watching too much of that *Downton* programme, Honey.'

'But the glamour – all those banquets and balls.'

'All them silk dresses and fancy jewellery is what you're really thinking and…'

As the voices moved away, Marya felt like sitting them down on one of the wide window seats and explaining that she works somewhere far more satisfying than some TV series that she watches if only to compare it – somewhat smugly it must be said – with Athelford Hall. For a start, the Hall is a proper home with real people living real lives amongst the exotic surroundings. She thinks of the stone unicorns by the front steps looking as if any minute they'll kick up their heels and take flight across the manicured lawn; the gold leaf mantel clocks; the peacocks with their jewelled tails fanned out behind them strutting up and down the gravelled drive. When Marya first heard their screeches, she thought her heart would stop with terror. They seemed so much the cries of the tortured. But once she had calmed, she accepted that, as is so often the case, the very beautiful can have their less appealing side.

In another way also Athelford Hall is unlike Downton because there is no army of servants here – only Seamus Doyle, employed a year earlier as butler and chauffeur, and Mrs. Acheson, the cook, who comes in every day, along with Edna Cox, a middle-aged cleaning woman from the local housing estate. Enough people to stop Marya feeling isolated, but not too many to be pestering her with unwanted questions.

That Marya is here at all is of course down to the mistress of the house, who has insisted on keeping her by her side. After all, they share the same homeland.

'Darlink,' she drawls in that voice, which sounds in Marya's ears like honeyed gravel, 'you cannot seriously be suggesting...' And whatever it is she does suggest – including the dismissal of most of the staff – 'they will only get under our feet, darlink' – her husband agrees to without a murmur.

Marya, who has a strong romantic streak, is of the opinion that the plump and balding Lord Arnold Leebury is the only ersatz feature of the Hall – someone who has risen from obscurity and should return there as soon as possible. Some days she dreams of the time when the handsome young prince will come galloping up on his horse to rescue the beautiful maiden. Except it won't be a prince, it will be Marya in the Land Rover, prising her stunningly beautiful mistress from the marshmallow embrace of her podgy husband. Until this happens, the world is one that Marya gives thanks for every morning as she wakes in her room under the eaves to the murderous screech of the peacocks and the sound of a van bearing the latest Amazon delivery.

Now she looks up as the bell from the master bedroom gives an imperious jangle. In an instant, she is slipping into her shoes, stopping by the mirror to smooth her fringe and going up the narrow servants' stairs. In the flag-stoned hall, the cleaning woman, Edna, a grey-haired pensioner with swollen ankles bulging over her shoes, is flicking her duster over a marble bust. Marya is very conscious of her higher status in the household and the two women exchange a cool nod. Besides, she doesn't have time to hear, yet again, how Edna's bunions are killing her.

On Marya goes, up the staircase, carpeted in faded shades of rose and gold, flanked at the top by a pair of eighteenth-century Chinese urns, bought at Sotheby's by Lord Leebury's father. She walks along a wide corridor lined with family portraits. The women are an unexciting bunch, dressed in drab blacks and greens with the fat cheeks and double chins that obviously come from the same unfortunate gene pool. The men, resplendent in their scarlet and yellow unforms are more presentable and Marya glances at them approvingly. Unlike the dishevelled, khaki-clad fighters she has encountered, these ancestors look as if they might actually provide a buffer between civilisation and chaos. Then she is outside the door of the master bedroom, tugging down her skirt and giving a firm knock.

There is a delay before it is answered, causing Marya to draw in her breath. At last, the gravelly voice calls: 'Enter!'

Magdalena Leebury sits in a tapestry chair by the wide bow of the window overlooking the deer park. The same view that Marya has from her bedroom two storeys above. She closes the door behind her and moves closer.

Her mistress continues to gaze out, but this is not something that Marya resents because it gives her the chance of once more filling her eyes – her soul – with the sight before her.

What is it that makes one person merely pretty but turns the next into a ravishing beauty? How can it be, Marya wonders, that a random arrangement of nose and mouth, forehead and chin can have such a result? It's not just the face of course, although many people, men in particular, find themselves drawn to those limpid grey eyes. Now, as her mistress gets up from her seat and crosses to the dressing-table, that sinuous, sensuous way of moving satisfies a part of the brain that responds to grace and beauty, causing people in the street to turn and stare. Marya always feels this same effect – that moment when she is drawn to her mistress as irresistibly as a flower to the sun. Like all the planets, Lady Leebury is indifferent to the effect she has on others. Or maybe she knows all too well? Either way, Marya is not bothered. Just to be 'in the presence' is enough.

'Now, darlink,' Lady Leebury says, without turning her head. 'I call you here because I need to choose dress for function tonight. You will help – no?'

'Of course,' Marya says, crossing the room to the double wardrobe. It is made of walnut inlaid with ivory and matches the side table with its vase of pale pink peonies that Lord Leebury orders each week from a Chelsea florist. This morning, Magdalena's nails are painted the same colour as the flowers.

Marya opens the wardrobe and runs an experienced eye over Lady Leebury's gowns. The day-to-day clothes – cashmere sweaters, tailored trouser suits and designer sportswear – are stored on shelves and racks in the dressing-room next door.

'Which ones do you want to see?' Marya asks, absorbing the melange of silks, sequins and feathers and the faint but unmistakable smell of the musky perfume her mistress wears.

Lady Leebury waves a languorous hand. 'Put out black, green satin, red lace. Oh – and cream chiffon.'

As Marya spreads them over the four-poster bed, she has a brief fantasy of lying naked inside one of them, her body pressed against her mistress's tanned skin. Sometimes when her ladyship is out, Marya will pull back the covers and check for signs of sexual congress. For weeks now there have been no stains on the sheets – other than from her mistress's monthlies. This is both reassuring and heartening – His Lordship is obviously not up to much, which of course may also account for Magdalena's moods: spells of lethargy interspersed with a strange restlessness. What she needs is a dose of the right kind of loving. In other words, a good fuck that would –

'Marya?' There's a sharpness to the voice. 'Spread out skirts of the green.'

'Certainly.' She turns. 'You will be going to the usual place?'

She sighs. 'Just to please Arnie.'

Marya ignores the lie, aware of how much her mistress's world hinges on those moments when the spotlight of the great and the good is upon her.

'Mind you, it is filled with draughts and falling down around the ears. When I was last there, I saw plaster crumbling off the wall and a bucket to catch leaks.'

'Terrible,' Marya murmurs, thanking whatever lucky star that has brought her to the well-ordered solidity of the Hall.

Her Ladyship rises from her chair and drifts across the Aubusson carpet towards her. Together, they stand looking down on the selection on the bed. 'So –' she pauses, pressing a manicured nail against the fulness of her lower lip. 'Not black – too dreary in all this rain. Chiffon makes one think of Henley or croquet on the grass – no?'

Marya nods although she only has a vague idea of where Henley is and her one encounter with croquet was the time she tripped in one of the hoops, sending the tray she was carrying flying.

'And His Lordship won't want me wearing green. "A commons colour," he always says. Which leaves red lace.' She smiles. 'Should warm things up nicely.'

Marya hangs the discarded choices back in the wardrobe. 'I'll see it's pressed and will look out your bag and shoes.' She turns to go when a thought occurs. 'Did Seamus tell you that he took a call earlier? On the private line?'

'He did not. Was it man or woman?'

'A Scottish man, he said.'

'And did that *eedyot* of a chauffeur enquire how this person got hold of the number?'

'No, but he said he'd call again.'

Two faint lines appear on Magdalena's forehead. 'A salesman?'

'Seamus said definitely not. He sounded – how do you say? – business-like – official.'

But her ladyship's mood has undergone one of its sudden swings, because she begins pacing the room, biting her lower lip and running her fingers through her hair. Then she stops, staring across at her, the eyes hardening until they seem to Marya to resemble circles of grey stone. 'Get out *now!*' Magdalena shouts. 'And don't bring me any more of these *stupeed* messages.' She picks up a shoe and hurls it at Marya, who ducks out of the way, closing the door behind her.

Out on the landing she stands, surprised. Magdalena has always been on the tetchy side, but this outburst seems not just another tantrum. It seems to stem from something more panic driven – more serious.

And, as Marya makes her way down to the basement kitchen another thought occurs: how fear has a way of driving people to extremes.

FOUR

Lady Magdalena Leebury, in low-cut lace dress and black kitten-heeled shoes, stands gazing around at the crystal chandeliers, the gilt-framed pictures and the carpet with its rose motif. If she were just able to shut her ears to the babble of English voices, she could be back in one of the sumptuous palaces of her homeland. Not that she's ever seen the inside of one. The largest building in her town is the church – a red brick edifice sandwiched between a shoe factory and an electronics shop.

'Splendid, isn't it?' a voice beside her says. It belongs to a middle-aged bishop with a thin, anxious face. Under a dark jacket he wears a purple shirt with a large silver cross on a chain.

'And so very good for the soul,' she agrees.

He gives her a doubtful look before edging away and in seconds she has forgotten him. As more guests fill the room, she regrets that the days of smoking in public are gone, and she can no longer flourish her ivory cigarette holder containing one of the Sobranie Black Russians Arnie used to order for her from Old Bond Street. It would have helped soothe her nerves – take her mind off the phone call.

Her private number is rigorously guarded, so how has this stranger managed to get hold of it? But there must be a perfectly reasonable explanation, so she will stop this fretting and enjoy her evening. She takes a sip of champagne. Arnie, ever solicitous, has seen that her glass is filled but now, as so often happens at these events, he has been waylaid by a group of colleagues – men like himself, middle-aged and with third-trimester paunches protruding over their belts. They huddle together, no doubt sharing some tidbit of gossip – this place is full of it.

Magdalena has many talents, not least of which is the ability to monitor those around her without appearing to do so – a skill acquired early on as an essential for survival. Now she notes how, the usual introductory banter over, the men grouped around Arnie have begun a more earnest discussion, perhaps about their latest charitable enterprise or perhaps, from the set of their shoulders, something weightier. Arnie might not be much in the looks department, but since his recent marriage – the acquisition of a beautiful wife improves a man's standing no end – he is listened to with increasing respect.

On first meeting her future husband, Magdalena spotted at once that he was one of a rare and fast-disappearing breed – a man of total integrity and someone therefore who could provide that refuge of which she was in such desperate need. As she registers the way his bald head catches the light from the chandelier, she thinks how predictable the good are. They follow certain rules and codes of conduct, which is what makes living with them so safe. The inevitable downside of course is that it can also make life a little dreary. Events like this evening's dinner are highlights along the way and as she makes small talk with some cabinet minister's wife, she reminds herself that it is far better to die of boredom than fear. And to be on the side of the powerful.

She takes another sip of champagne, aware of eyes turning towards her. These men do not stare in open admiration as her fellow countrymen would have done, but instead glance sideways in that underhand British way. She will have a laugh about this with Marya later.

Arnie is back by her side and a string of greetings and introductions begins. Viscount this and Lady the other, a Cabinet Minister from somewhere in the West Country and the Under Secretary for Health and Social Reform. Magdalena's dress is cut low, with Arnie's recent anniversary present of rubies nestling just above the cleft of her breasts. The men who come up to chat can't take their eyes off them while the stocky, broad-hipped wives in their pearl chokers treat her to a series of stiff smiles. Why do English women have such an atrocious dress sense? It seems the higher up the social ladder they go, the worse it gets. The dumpy woman in front of her, introduced as a duchess of somewhere unpronounceable in the north of the country, is wearing an ankle-length dress of shiny brown fabric that makes her resemble a frankfurter.

An elderly waiter approaches and Magdalena holds out her glass for a refill.

Arnie coughs. 'Lord Rosser – I don't think you've met my wife?'

She gives a faint smile of apology as she realises that the man at her elbow isn't a waiter, although he could certainly pass for one. His black dinner jacket and trousers have a decidedly rumpled look – obviously there is no valet to see to his clothes. And he's so short – his nose is on a level with her breasts. If he were to sneeze the snot would go straight down her cleavage. A thought that makes her take a step back.

'So, Arnold – how's life in your wee neck of the woods?' the man is saying. His accent is very pronounced, and she strains forward to concentrate.

Her husband puts a plump arm around her, the touch warm, heavy, proprietorial. 'Couldn't be better. Isn't that so, Lena?'

She flashes a smile. 'Certainly is, darlink.'

'And how in the world did a fellow like you come to land such a braw lassie?' the man asks.

She frowns, turning to Arnie for translation.

He gives a laugh. 'Married three years in April and, yes – I believe I'm the luckiest chap in the world.' He gives her waist another squeeze. 'And he's just paid you a compliment, Lena.'

'He is from Ireland?' she asks, thinking of Seamus Doyle, their chauffeur, who no doubt will be whiling away the hours in some Westminster pub until it's time to drive them back to the Hall.

'How can she insult a man so?' The small man throws his arms wide in an appeal to Arnold, or to anyone within earshot. 'Can she nae tell that every bone in ma body is Scots?'

She assumes this is just another of those unfunny British jokes and that Arnie will give some kind of laughing riposte. But his expression remains serious. 'I swear no offence was intended, Hamish,' he says, and it is the Scot whose thin lips split into a smile that for a moment gives him an uncanny resemblance to one of the gargoyles on the Athelford roof.

'None taken,' he says, turning his gaze back to Magdalena. 'But I'd say, my lassie, that you've nae been in this part of the world for long?' His eyes, an intense blue, move from her cleavage to her face. Both the look and the question seem innocent enough, but some deep-seated instinct has her on the alert. 'Well –' she begins but is saved from having to expand on her reply by a sonorous clang. In the far doorway, gong in hand, is a black-clad figure with silver-buckled shoes and a froth of cream ruffles at the throat. He gives a deep bow. 'Your Royal Highness, Your Excellencies, My Lords, Ladies, Honoured Guests, dinner is served.'

Magdalena, relieved to escape the Scottish man's penetrating eyes, allows Arnie to lead her down a carpeted passage and into a dining-room, its floor carpeted in the same rose motif, the walls panelled in red and green fleur-de-lys and hung with portraits of well-fed statesmen. Dinner has been set up at three long tables and she will later describe to Marya the crisp, linen tablecloths, the gleaming silverware, and the cut glass. Marya shares her love of the ornate and, more to the point, an understanding that beneath this sumptuous skin the beast still lurks.

Husband and wife are shown to their seats halfway down the righthand side. She settles into a red leather chair gazing in satisfaction at her place name: *Lady Magdalena Leebury.* Arnie will be on her left and on her other side, the name tag reads: *The Honourable Virginia Stonehurst.* The name doesn't inspire confidence. A part of her was hoping for some interesting younger person to talk with – preferably a man. Still, it is good to know that Arnie is busy doing the networking he so much enjoys.

She eyes the fleur-de-lys pattern. The wallpaper would look well in the master bathroom and she must ask Arnie to source the supplier. She turns in her chair, but he is still on his feet, chatting to some ancient-looking peer of the realm. That is what can be a teeny bit depressing about these occasions. Everyone is so *old.* All the same, she settles back in her seat with a sigh of pleasure, adjusting the front of her gown and tapping manicured fingernails on the linen cloth.

'You've dressed to tone with the room, ma lassie,' a voice on the other side of her declares. 'And how well you blend in.' As the small, waiter-like figure slips in beside her, she experiences a twinge of annoyance. Clearly, this man from Scotland is not the Honourable Virginia Stonehurst, but she can hardly wave him away a second time.

'Hope you've nae objections?' he says, as if reading her mind. 'And I must say that red suits you. It's not every woman that can get away with the colour.'

She nods acknowledgement of the compliment.

'Mary Magdalene. Scarlet woman. But redemption for her at the end.'

The man's small talk is making her uneasy and she looks up at Arnie, who is standing directly behind her, still deep in conversation. She gives a small tug on his sleeve and he breaks off. He's always so good at knowing when she's struggling.

'I see you're still monopolising my wife, Hamish.'

The small Scotsman gets to his feet. 'And I mustn't do so a moment longer, gorgeous as she is.' He pauses. 'Though I'm still wondering what part of our globe she might belong to.'

A pained look crosses Arnie's face. 'Magdalena has full British citizenship.' He pauses. 'Best not to dwell on the early years, don't you think? Well, I wouldn't want to go round talking of *my* boyhood – Sussex prep school, Winchester – we all know the drill.'

Kind Arnie, who says he had the happiest of childhoods, but as always has come to her rescue.

'Of *course,* we do. And you know that wee proposition I put to you, Arnold? If you're still interested, I could maybe call on you to discuss it further. If that's all right with you?'

'More than all right, dear chap.'

With a nod, the Scotsman wanders off towards the top end of the table.

'I'm not surprised you mistook him for a waiter,' Arnie says, as he settles beside her. 'But although he doesn't look up to much, he has a lot of influence.'

'Terrible dress sense,' she agrees.

Arnie leans closer and whispers, his breath hot in her ear. 'Would you believe it, Lena, but he's talking of my being given a post in the government?'

'How splendid, darlink!' But she's only half concentrating, too caught up in wondering what on earth Mary Magdalene has to do with anything.

FIVE

Two days later, Greg Jacobs is pacing the hall of his Twickenham villa – past the standard lamp, switched on to counteract the afternoon gloom, past the grandmother clock, inherited from some cousin of Anne's, and past the front room, where he hesitates, tugging at his ear. The door has been left ajar and through the chink he catches the murmur of voices. One, deeper than the others, is doing most of the talking, the sentences punctuated by a treble, followed by another in a slightly lower register – notes in search of a common theme. Or so he hopes. From somewhere outside comes the rattle of rain against a window.

He resists the temptation to peer through the narrow gap for a glimpse of the people who are entering his life. Although everyone says how fortunate they are, he can't fool himself: He's the one who is desperate to find an incentive to get up in the morning – to blooming well keep on going.

He retraces his steps to the front entrance where the reflection from the stained-glass window throws splashes of orange and scarlet across the polished floor. *Like a winter sunset!* he can hear Anne saying. But still homesick for all they'd left behind, he never shared her enthusiasm for this three-storeyed Edwardian house with its white timber-framed gable, ceilings decorated with acanthus leaf cornices and large, square rooms. Even after all these months, it feels alien. His training was in land management, for God's sake – and what wouldn't he give now to be in the open air, repairing a stone wall or planning field drainage? Although the painful truth is that, long before they moved south, he'd lost the motivation for all that, sitting for hours, whisky glass in hand, staring into space, and no doubt driving Anne mad. But just as mad is the idea that a widower like him, old-fashioned and set in his ways, would be able to handle this new enterprise. *Remember what we agreed.*

From the kitchen comes a clash of pans. Mrs. Mehta will be preparing their meal so he'd best get on with it.

He retraces his steps and drawing in his breath, pushes open the door. He's hoped the newcomers will find the faded chintz covers, the wood burner's glow, and the jumble of books and papers on the side table relaxing. It'll certainly be very different from what they're used to.

As he steps inside, the burble of voices dies away and he forces his lips into a smile. 'Greg Jacobs. Welcome to Holly Lodge.' The oldest girl gets up and returns his handshake. He recognises her from the photo in her file. 'You must be Frances.' She's pleasant-looking, with brown skin, curling hair and eyes that seem too large for her face. He also knows that she'll be nineteen next birthday.

'This is very good of you, Mr. Jacobs.' Her voice is hesitant but there's an air of calmness about her. Anne would approve, he thinks. Aloud he says: 'It's fine just to call me Greg.' He turns to the other two. 'And of course, that goes for both of you.'

Photos often don't do justice to their subjects. A year younger than Frances, Jason and Poppy's blue eyes, ash blond hair and chiselled features, are far more attractive than their images. But what gives Greg a jolt of surprise is their resemblance to one another – they're like enough to be twins. Although he knows also from the reports that they aren't related, and that none of the three has met before.

Poppy's small hand, the nails bitten to the quick, rests briefly in his before being withdrawn. Her hair, piled on top of her head, is tied back with a green satin ribbon. Something about that colour gives him a sense of optimism. Perhaps there's hope for this project yet, he thinks, turning his attention to the boy.

'Name's Jason.' The gaze is defiant. 'Nice place you've got here, Greg.' A large, hooped ring hangs from one ear, the other is pierced with a series of metal studs and his hair stands up in short spikes. If he were a dog, he'd be snarling, Greg thinks, recalling a particularly vicious collie he and Anne once homed in the Yorkshire farmhouse. It wasn't with them long.

He coughs. 'The housekeeper, Mrs. Mehta, will be bringing our tea in a couple of minutes and will show you round the rest of the house later. I thought it best to keep the business side of things till the morning. Give you a chance to settle in.'

'Cool,' Frances murmurs as she and Poppy settle in armchairs. Jason remains sprawled across a sofa. Greg would like to ask the boy to take his feet off but doesn't want to risk a confrontation at this early stage. So he sits on the opposite sofa and moments later, Mrs. Mehta appears, carrying the tray of tea. Anne employed her when they first moved in and she's been a steadying influence in the turbulent times he's been through. A widow in her early fifties, she has a large nose in a long face, and untidy greying hair swept into a bun. Behind round, clear-framed glasses, the eyes are watchful.

'Anything you need on the domestic front,' she says, placing the tray on a side table, 'then please feel free to ask.'

Jason looks up. 'Any chance of, like, a beer?'

'Maybe with supper, Jason.' She looks across at Greg. 'If that's OK with you, Mr. Jacobs?' She insists on keeping things formal and he's given up trying to persuade her to be on first-name terms. A widow, originally from Mumbai, she never speaks of her family and he assumes she has none.

'Of course.' He can hardly ask these young people to lay off alcohol when he enjoys a drink himself. Although they've had the zero-drug tolerance spelled out.

As the door closes behind Mrs. Mehta, he turns to Frances. 'Will you be mother?' It's what he used to say to

Anne, but this girl gives him a blank look. 'No worries,' he says quickly. 'I'll pour.'

'Quite a spread,' Jason says, biting into a scone. A blob of jam drops onto the sofa, and he wipes it off with his sleeve.

'Mrs. Mehta always does us proud. Which brings me onto the practical side. Breakfast is between 8.00 and 8.30; lunch is at 1.00; afternoon tea such as we're having today, is only provided at weekends, and supper is at 7.30.'

He realises how out-dated these arrangements will sound but it's important to provide structure – at least at this early stage. 'Obviously,' he continues, 'mealtimes may change once the three of you are in work.'

'Thanks,' Poppy murmurs, but she doesn't meet his gaze, glancing around the room as if searching for a point of escape

Jason swivels round. 'Yeah, but when are you going to, like, tell us about our work?'

'As I said – in the morning. I want to spend time with each of you going over the details. You might like to be first up, Jason? My study at 9.00am? Mrs. Mehta will show you where to go.' He pauses and to his relief, Jason mutters. 'Yeah, great.'

'So, Poppy, you and I will meet an hour later, at 10.00, and Frances, I'll see you at 11.00.' He's left her till the end, because already he can tell that she is the most grounded of the three. 'Last but not least,' he adds, and sure enough, is rewarded with a smile that lights her grey eyes.

'So,' he continues, 'if there's nothing more you want to ask at this stage, we'll meet again at supper.' He shuts the door on them, thankful to have the first awkward introductions over.

His study, facing the back, overlooks a long, narrow stretch of lawn with flowerbeds on either side and, at the far end, a large willow, its lower branches trailing the grass. On bad days the sight of that tree helps lift his mood.

He looks at his watch. Time for his evening whisky. Since he ended up in A & E last year with alcohol poisoning– *what a pillock, Greg!* – he allows himself just the one glass before supper and sometimes a small amount of wine.

He pours his drink before lifting Anne's photo from the desk. It was the one taken at Arnold Leebury's wedding. She smiles out at him from the frame, strands of hair blowing across her face. 'Mud in your eye, my darling,' he murmurs.

Before he married and moved back to Yorkshire, he and Arnold shared a flat in Bayswater, Arnold working as a junior solicitor while Greg finished his training in land management. They've kept in touch over the years. Arnold, short and plump and unfailingly good tempered – an antidote perhaps to Greg's northern brusqueness – always struck Greg as sound. He never seemed to have any girlfriends, or if he did, they never lasted, so Greg had him down as a confirmed bachelor – or perhaps with a male lover tucked away somewhere – who knew these days? But then a few years ago Arnold astonished everyone by marrying – not your ordinary Home Counties girl, as you might have expected – but a woman from some mid-European country.

The wedding was a lavish affair, the reception held on a warm June evening at the family's stately pile, Athelford Hall, with boating on the lake, and acres of roses scenting the air. And, most memorable of all, the bride, waves of auburn hair framing a heart-shaped face, so stunningly beautiful, it was impossible to take your eyes off her. 'If you don't stop your gawping, Greg Jacobs,' Anne whispered, 'I swear I'll push you into the nearest fountain!' He nuzzled her ear and she added: 'Though I admit you have good taste – she is simply gorgeous.'

A string orchestra began to play a Mozart aria and she whispered: 'I can feel a headache coming on. Be a love and fetch me a mineral water.' It took him a while to elbow his way through the knot of guests, exchanging greetings with one or two acquaintances, and queuing at the bar. When eventually he returned, holding out her drink, she stared – as if she'd forgotten who he was. 'For God's sake,' she snapped. 'Why didn't you get it into your fucking head that I didn't want ice?'

The first time he'd heard her swear and the first appearance of the symptoms that were to lay waste to all their carefully laid plans.

SIX

A MONDAY IN MID-JANUARY – FIVE YEARS AGO. HE and Anne were at the kitchen table finishing lunch. The farmhouse kitchen was snug, the Aga pumping out heat, and snow smacking against the windows, as if struggling to get into the warm. Beyond it the moorland, carpeted in white, stretched into the distance, broken by the blurred outline of the Haystack Rock.

'Champion hotpot – just the thing in this cold.'

Anne raised an eyebrow.

'*What?*'

'Is this what we've come to, Greg? Never anything real to say to each other?'

'It's not *that* bad!' He reached for the wine bottle. 'Top up?' His willpower seemed to have evaporated and he tried not to think how long it was since they made love.

She leaned over the table, reaching for his hand. 'I've come to a decision. We must make use of this windfall, Greg. God! Most people would give their eye teeth for it.'

Unbelievable to think that six months ago she should have walked into that local newsagent and bought a lottery ticket – something neither of them had ever done – and that it should have turned out a winner.

'All those millions,' she continued. 'Of course we were doing OK– you in local government and me as a deputy head. But we've never been one of those couples who take early retirement in order to go on cruises or spend days on the golf course.' She paused. 'Or to sit cooped up at home driving one another crazy.'

She meant him of course. Despite all the pills and therapy, his depression still hung over him like an impenetrable blanket – over them both.

'We need to make a fresh start, Greg. This is no life – for either of us.' He caught the flash of anger in her eyes. 'You get up late, have a short walk, read the paper and the rest of the time sit around on your backside drinking. You show no interest in joining any of the local clubs or activities.' She squeezed his arm. 'I know this is hard for you, love, but we can't go on this way.' She paused. '*I* can't.'

If he didn't agree, how much longer would she put up with him? He tugged at his ear. 'So what are you suggesting?'

'We've always poured ourselves into our work and to be honest, I'm feeling pretty lost without mine. We've no kids' – they exchanged a look – 'so why not help some youngsters who've had none of our advantages?'

'By doing what?'

'Well, at our age adoption is obviously out, and I don't think we'd cope with long-term fostering, but we could offer help in the shorter term – maybe just for a handful of young adults. Those who've had a troubled start in life. Give them a roof over their heads and training for a decent job.'

'Not many of those around here.'

'My point exactly.' She paused. 'Which is why we need to move.'

He felt a moment's dizziness. 'Give up the farmhouse?'

She nodded.

He thought for a moment. 'How about York, or maybe a smaller town? Skipton? Richmond?' He could just about cope with those.

She shook her head. 'I was thinking more of the Richmond in the south.'

'You're not serious?'

She bit her lip. 'I've discussed it with some colleagues and the consensus is that it would really help our project if we were within easy reach of central London. And my cousin's nursing home is in Twickenham – it would be good to be near her for the remaining time she has left. After all, she's the only family we've got.'

He felt a sickening twist in his gut. Once his wife made up her mind to something, there was no stopping her. 'You've obviously been thinking this through for a while?'

She nodded. 'Things aren't going to happen overnight – there's a huge amount of organising to do. But I have a suggestion over what to call our charity.' She looked across at him. "The William Jacobs Foundation." What do you think?'

'Fine,' he whispered, although to hear the name spoken aloud made him ache inside.

The charity took two years to set up and, gradually, he found himself drawn in, the project providing a much-needed focus to his day.

They agreed to start small, with just three places on offer and, of course, were flooded with applications. Times continued to be very tough and many young people leapt at the opportunity of being offered board and lodging, an apprenticeship or training, and an allowance for as long as was needed. Anne used her work contacts to put the security vetting in place and to set up an independent panel of advisers. The final choice of applicants rested on several factors, including: were they alcohol and drug free? And did they have the determination – the *gumption,* as Anne put it – not to be defeated by the tough hand they'd been dealt?

Greg was moved by the number of people willing to help, including Arnold Leebury, who gave a generous donation. 'I know you've still got plenty in the coffers, Greg, but you'd be surprised by how quickly it goes. As this married man knows only too well.' His round face creased into a smile. 'But by God, isn't Magdalena perfect?'

It was good to see Arnold so happy and if his friend could change his life, Greg thought, then there was hope for him also. But it seemed it was tempting fate to think that way because, just as they were settling into their new life, Anne's illness struck: an inoperable brain tumour.

In one of their last lucid conversations, he sat by her

hospital bed, holding a hand that felt so thin and frail in his. Her hair had fallen out after the latest round of chemo and he reached across and stroked the bald head, briefly comforted by the look of gratitude in the faded eyes. 'Listen to me, Greg,' she whispered. 'You must keep going with our charity work, including this project. Don't do it for me,' she added. 'Do it for *you*.'

So all these months later, as Jason comes slouching into the study, Greg tells himself that of course he must and will carry on.

The lad slumps onto a chair by the door and Greg shakes his head. 'The rules were made very clear.' It's a struggle to keep the anger from his voice.

'How do you mean?' The tone is defiant as ever.

He leans forward. 'You reek of hash.' Which of course also accounts for the boy's glazed expression.

At least he has the good grace to look away. 'To help me to settle in, like.'

Greg hesitates, struck by the boy's pallor and the Adam's apple protruding from the thin neck. The report, locked away in the filing cabinet, reads like some bland end-of-term assessment, giving away nothing of what this young man has been through. *Despite a difficult start, Jason seems determined to make a success of his life. And with the right sort of backing, we are confident he will do so.*

Greg tugs at his ear. 'If you promise this won't happen again, then I'm prepared to overlook it this once.'

He hesitates, nods.

Is he caving in too easily? He flips open the folder in front of him. 'Let's run through the details of this job.'

The boy fiddles with his leather necklace. 'I've been thinking, Greg. Maybe I'd be better off, like, staying on benefit?'

'Then why, in God's name, are you here?' He'd expected gratitude from this young man. Was that too much to hope for? 'If you stick at it,' he continues, 'there's an excellent chance of promotion.'

'Yeah,' Jason says again. 'But I didn't, like, see my goal in life as managing some fucking supermarket.'

'So what *did* you see your goal as being?'

'Dunno,' he mumbles.

Greg struggles to reconcile the glowing words of that report with the stroppy, unappealing lad in front of him. Although maybe the fault is not the boy's. Maybe Greg lacks the ability to make the connection with him that Anne would have done. She was always so good with the young.

He tries again. 'The skills they'll give you will be transferable and you'll earn far more than you'd get on benefits.'

For the first time, the face registers a flicker of interest. 'How much more?'

'I can't tell you the exact figure, but obviously it's something that will be discussed with you.' He pauses. After all the work that's gone into setting up the project, it would be a humiliating blow were any of these young people to pull out now. 'At least give it a go? See how you get on.'

To his relief, Jason gives a slow nod.

'Excellent, You're to report to the manager at 7.30 tomorrow morning. Mrs. Mehta will give you an early breakfast and you'll have a key to the house so you can come and go as you please.' He walks round and hands him the paperwork. 'The details are all here.'

Jason shrugs. 'Whatevs.'

Little sod, Greg thinks, as he ushers him out.

Billie Boy's photo is tucked away in the desk. Greg still finds it unbearable to recall the shining confidence in that three-year-old face – the utter conviction that his Mum and Dad would kiss him better. However difficult a start Jason may have had, Greg thinks, at least he has his life in front of him.

Poppy is waiting in the hall with Jason slouched against the wall beside her. Once again, Greg is taken aback by the physical similarity between the two – the same fair hair and delicate features and that same wiry jumpiness.

As they break off their conversation, she gives the boy a timid smile and is treated to a wink that leaves her blushing.

Although she exhibits none of Jason's hostility, he finds her nervousness almost as difficult to handle. She sits on the edge of the chair, twisting her hands together and when he gives a smile, she looks down at the floor. *Give it time, Greg.* 'All set for the morning then, Poppy?' How brusque he sounds!

She gives a small nod.

'You're going in as a junior assistant.' He pauses. 'And I see from your file that one day you'd like to have your own salon?'

'Yes,' she says, putting a hand to her face. He notices again her bitten-down nails and now he has the chance to study her in daylight, the pinched, hunted look in her face. You can read every official report going, he thinks, but none of them will come near the emotional truth of it.

She keeps glancing towards the door, so after going over the remaining details, he hands her the paperwork, and she slips like a shadow out of the room.

Now there's only the meeting with Frances to get through.

'So' – he opens her folder. 'You're ready to start work?'

She smiles across at him. 'I can't wait.' He registers again that calm, modulated voice.

'Champion. You'll be doing shift work in the nursing home until St. Thomas's confirms your place.'

'I feel so lucky – to be getting the training I've always wanted.'

'You – and Jason and Poppy – deserve all the luck you can get.' He smiles back at her. 'You'll make an excellent nurse, Frances.'

'I'll certainly try to be. And I can't thank you enough.'

What would she think if she knew how often he's wanted to pull out of this whole project? 'Well, I think we're about done.'

She hesitates. 'There was one thing.'

'Yes?'

'About Jason.'

He tugs at his ear. Not more trouble.

'I hope it's OK to mention this. It's just he can get into a bit of a strop –but it's only because he's nervous.' She gives

51

a small laugh. 'We all have our ways of coping.'

After she's gone out, he wonders, briefly, what hers might be – and whether she knows about Jason's drug habit. But surely she must smell the hash? But if the lad has an ally in her, then he can't be beyond hope. Aloud, he says: 'Of course. Thanks for mentioning it.'

The interviews over, he's just settling to his emails when a series of thuds echo through the house. He's on his feet, pulling open the study door and staring at the scene in front of him. Frances is on her hands and knees gathering up grocery items – tinned food, apples and onions – and placing them into a string bag. A blast of damp air rushes in through the open front door and standing just inside, looking unusually flustered, is Mrs. Mehta, a large book clasped to her chest.

'What on earth's going on?'

'I'm sorry, Mr. Jacobs, I did try to stop her, but she pushed right on past.'

'Who do you mean?'

'Some old tramp. She came in through the kitchen entrance, bold as brass. I told her I'd call the police – obviously frightened the life out of her. So she ended up dropping her groceries as well as this.'

He walks over and takes the book from her. '*Digital Assets and the Law*'– Odd choice for a bag lady.'

'What do you suppose she wanted?' Frances asks.

'Goodness knows.' Mrs Mehta says. 'Apparently she's heard of you, Mr. Jacobs, through someone called Jimmy.'

Greg shakes his head. 'Name doesn't ring any bells. She's gone, I suppose?'

'The last time I looked, she was loitering by the gate.'

He peers past her. The drive is about thirty feet long, bounded on either side by large bushes of hebe and laurel, their leaves shining in the wet. And there, standing motionless at the far end is a thin, stooped figure.

'She's obviously not quite right in the head. We'd better just leave her to it.'

Frances is at his elbow. 'Shouldn't we try to give her back her book and groceries?'

He nods. 'Good idea. Would you mind doing it, Frances? If you're quick, you should catch her.'

'Of course.'

No time for Frances to collect her own coat, so he hands her Anne's mackintosh that hangs on the hook by the door. He still can't steel himself to get rid of it – having it here feels as if there's still a part of her in the house.

Frances pulls on the coat while he searches for one of his business cards. 'Give her this, would you, and tell her if she still wants a word to give a ring.'

Mrs. Mehta shakes her head at him, obviously thinking he's a soft touch. 'Can't do any harm,' he mutters, watching Frances run down the drive.

After a couple of minutes, she is back. 'She seemed really surprised, Greg, but she took the book and bag– and your card.'

'Thanks again. Well, I'd best get on with my paperwork.'

'Today's post is on your desk, Mr. Jacobs. Oh – and lunch is in ten minutes.'

Back in the study he sifts through the usual batch of circulars and charity appeals. As well as helping with the funding for a local food bank, he has linked up with the Samaritans and the Marie Curie foundation.

Nowadays, most personal communication is done by text or email, but one letter stands out: an envelope, stamped with the House of Lords crest. *Coming up in the world, aren't we?* Anne would be teasing, knowing full well that sort of thing cuts no ice with him.

The writing isn't Arnold's, and now hunger wins out over curiosity.

The letter can wait until he's eaten.

SEVEN

THREE DAYS HAVE GONE BY AND OLLIE HAS HEARD nothing from Hamish Rosser. *See you soon,* he recalls the man saying. But how soon is that? And when Ollie tries to call, why doesn't he bloody well pick up?

Sometimes he feels tempted to treat their whole encounter as a farce – until he remembers the grip of the mottled hands on Jimmy's throat and the boy's screams as he collapsed onto the floor of that stinking attic room.

If only he'd pressed Jack for more information when he had the chance. He thinks back to the meeting a couple of weeks earlier. Six of them round the table debating which stories to run in the next edition. Ollie was assigned a long-standing dispute over a barking dog, and the threatened closure of a Victorian swimming baths – his days of pressing for more meaty assignments were long gone.

And then, as they were walking out of the room, Jack put a hand on his shoulder. He always forgot how tall the man was – perhaps because he was used to seeing him behind his desk. Over six foot four, broad-shouldered, with thinning, sandy-coloured hair, he seemed to tower over him. 'Let's you and me have a quiet word,' he said, showing Ollie into his office.

'Got something here that should interest you.' Jack flipped open his notepad. And it was then that Ollie learned of a contact – the editor became rather vague at this point – whom Ollie should meet. 'Here's the fellow's details. Talk to him – see what he has to say for himself. And Ollie – if you want this to work, you'll need to go along with what he asks.' His mobile was ringing and with a wave of his hand Ollie was dismissed before he could establish who exactly this contact was, and why Ollie must agree with what was asked of him.

Did Hamish have some kind of a hold on Jack? Ollie thinks now. From what he's seen of the Scotsman, nothing would surprise him. His gut instinct is telling him to get out of this assignment while he still can. So he must get hold of Jack – see if it's possible for a colleague to take over. Someone who would be able to handle Rosser.

The newspaper is housed on the top floor of a former department store, closed down during the first pandemic in 2020, and now used by various businesses – estate agents, insurance firms, a hairdressing salon and a taxi company.

Ollie steps into the open-plan office. Plate glass windows run along one wall and the opposite side is taken up by printers, shredders and an ancient coffee machine. The windows are grimy, what light there is coming from the overhead strip, which picks up the scuffed lino and the dusty leaves of the yucca plant that, against all the odds, continues to survive. In the central space, colleagues study screens, scribble notes, or talk into their mobiles.

The door to Jack's room is open and Ollie knocks and enters. The air is stuffy, Jack's blue vape pen and a half-drunk mug of coffee resting amongst a pile of paperwork. He doesn't look up from his phone, leaving Ollie feeling like some recalcitrant schoolboy, summoned to the Head's study.

Jack clicks off his phone. 'So – what can I do you for?'

Ollie clears his throat. 'About that lead.'

'The swimming baths?'

'No – the one from Hamish Rosser.' He pauses, anxious to get across to Jack that he has been working on it. 'From what I've been able to gather, it involves the shipment of goods.'

Stan take a drag on his vape. 'Illegal?'

'Yes, and –'

'As I recall, the tip-off came from a researcher on *Panorama*.' He blows a stream of smoke into the air. 'And –'

'I want to hand the assignment over.'

Jack stares. 'I gave you the lead, Ollie, so you could use your bloody initiative.'

'But you said I have to go along with what Rosser asks.' He pauses. 'And the truth of it is, he's a nasty little shit, mixed up in God knows what.'

'In our line of business, we get into bed with some pretty unsavoury customers. And who sorts the shit, Ollie? You, or God?'

'But I'm not sure I can take this further. I mean –'

'You're being paid to wipe your own arse, Ollie – don't expect me to do it for you.' Jack jabs a thumb at the door. 'And shut that after you.'

Ollie retreats, chastened, into the main office. On leaving school, nearly twenty years ago, he'd been grateful for the offer of an apprenticeship here. It wasn't long though before he realised he wasn't cut out for the work – he lacked that killing edge necessary for good journalism. He'd stuck with it because he appreciated the flexibility and freedom of the job and because he couldn't think of anything else he'd prefer. Now he looks around the room, wanting to ask his colleagues how they would deal with Rosser. But Ollie's suggestion of a quick pint is met by blank stares. 'Too much on,' his pal, Nick says, offering Ollie a crisp. 'Later in the week?'

So now there's nothing for it but to head home in the hopes that Amy will be there. 'I'm going back to my mum's!' she yelled, after their latest row. 'At least *she'll* be in when she says. At least *she'll* pay for her own bloody takeaway!' Amy then went into one of her sulks, refusing to speak, while he slammed doors and, evicted from the bedroom – *his* bedroom, *his* house, he felt like saying – spent sleepless hours on the sofa, worrying about how she would react were she to discover that the money Hamish Rosser pocketed so casually was the down-payment for a new boiler.

Dusk is falling as he turns into his road. His earlier euphoria – the sense that his life was about to take an upward turn – has drained away.

The street, like so many thousand others, is filled with semi-detached houses – post-war, two-up, two-down – a gentrified version of the one in which he grew up. He always promised himself that by the time he was in his mid-thirties, he would have made his mark in journalism and be living on a nice little estate somewhere in Surrey, with all the trappings that went with his new status: a wife and kids – maybe even a Labrador, although he's never been much of a one for animals. It's Amy who is glued to all the wildlife shows, along with the detective series she never tires of watching.

He shifts his rucksack higher onto his shoulder, the bottles of her favourite Chardonnay, picked up from the supermarket, giving a reassuring clink. With any luck, the wine will do its usual job. After one bottle they will soften towards one another – he promising to bring in more money and she assuring him that the last thing she wants is to live permanently with her Mum, who is with a new partner and making a complete horse's arse of herself.

After getting through most of a second bottle he and Amy will make love. That's the frustrating part, he thinks, as he unlocks the front door – the sex is intense, satisfying, and as they lie afterwards, arms and legs wrapped around one another, the aching sense of loneliness inside him eases. They've been together nearly two years – longer than any of his previous relationships – but is the physical side enough to hold them together?

No doubt all this business with Hamish Rosser is contributing to his despondency. If only he could get the man out of his head. And as for Jimmy: Ollie has seen plenty of horrors in his time – body parts scattered over the motorway, women with faces smashed in by abusive partners. But that emaciated boy spewing vomit onto the floor and the garret room reeking of stale grease and cocaine, seem to him a graphic illustration of humanity at its lowest point.

He steps into the hall, his longing for Amy stronger than ever. All he wants is to bury his face in her hair and run his hand over her smooth skin. He loves the fact that she's a well-built girl – all curves and big breasts and bottom – and cheerful with it. He also admires her ability to organise. As manager in a big department store, she's never happier than when checking supplies and prices, while in the house she sorts shelves and cupboards – tinned food stacked in rows, jumpers and shirts folded into neat piles.

He wishes he could find the words to tell her how much she means to him. But for now he'll order a takeaway and, while they eat, he'll update her on this assignment. Although just the thought of the little Scotsman leaves him with a queasy feeling in his gut.

'Hello, Babe!' he calls. When there's no answer, he walks through to the lounge, the silence settling around him. He's been in this place five years. Newly decorated when he first moved in, the cream walls have since faded to a shabby off-white that shows every mark. He knows it could do with a fresh lick of paint but has neither the cash nor the energy to see to it. The room is small with a couple of prints on the walls, a pair of grubby sofas and the TV in the corner. Although he keeps most of his work on his laptop, still the printed documents keep coming, and unread newspaper articles and papers are spread over the carpet. He eyes the coffee table containing the remains of his breakfast: a half-eaten bowl of cereal and a couple of dirty mugs. Amy would usually have cleared them away, so she must still be really pissed off with him.

In the kitchen, the clock on the microwave glows green and the fridge emits a steady hum, like a young child trying to console itself. The emptiness of the place gets to him – too much a reminder of what it was like growing up, his father having buggered off when Ollie was a toddler, leaving his mum to get by as best she could, working first as a dinner lady at his school and then, as he grew older, in a pizza parlour that paid more but meant she was out most evenings. As a teenager, it felt shameful to admit how much he hated those long after-school hours spent on his own, especially as most of his friends, who went on about their mums' constant nagging, envied him. But Christ! he'd minded. As he still does – a thought that he pushes away.

The unwashed breakfast dishes are piled in the sink and propped on the draining-board is a note in Amy's looped writing: *Meeting Sharon in wine bar. Don't wait up.* Normally she would have texted him the information and now she doesn't even tell him which bar she's in. But at least he knows who she's with – *if* she's telling the truth. He couldn't blame her if she ditched him for someone else. Why should she be the one to pay the bills and clear up after him? As he reaches into the fridge for a beer, he realises how much he needs this assignment – must not allow Hamish Rosser to intimidate him.

He walks through to the front room and switches on the TV news. *New drug for Alzheimer's; scandal over MPs' expenses; sea levels at their highest.* The same old stuff. He picks up a folder. Somewhere in here is the makings of a scoop, so he must hold his nerve – not just for the sake of the promised cash, but because he needs to prove to Amy that he's not just an aimless loser.

He flips open the file. Surely there must be a pattern to all these columns and figures? But after a fruitless twenty minutes, he pushes it to one side. How the hell will he ever make sense of this? How the hell –?

He hears a rap and goes into the hall to collect his curry. But when he pulls open the front door, he finds Amy standing, huddled into her coat.

'Forgot my key, didn't I. You going to keep me out here all night?' She pushes past, bringing with her a smell of perfume and alcohol.

'Had a good time?'

She nods.

Has she really been with a girlfriend? Or is she so fed up with him that she's been on the hunt for someone else?

He follows her into the kitchen, watching her drape her dripping coat over a chair.

'I've ordered a curry. Hope you're hungry.'

'Starving.'

He reaches into the fridge. 'Let's have a drink while we're waiting.'

In the front room, he clicks on the gas fire – to hell with the bills! – and sweeps the pile of folders to one side.

'You've been busy for once.'

He decides to ignore the sarcastic tone. 'Jack's asked me to follow a lead. A really promising one. Should be some money in it.'

'You don't sound too thrilled.'

He's no intention of telling her about Hamish's attack on Jimmy – any reporter worth his salt wouldn't have let himself be intimidated by a pint-sized pensioner. 'It's just that I've been asked to sort through all these statistics and you know they've never been my strong point.'

There's another knock and he gets to his feet. 'That'll be the delivery man.'

'Tell you what, Babe. Why don't you dish up while I have a quick look through? If that's OK? Don't want to stick my nose in where it's not wanted.'

It's more than OK, although he's not about to tell her so. 'Help yourself.'

As they eat, she scribbles notes on the pad beside her. He clears away the plates and as he brings in the coffee, she looks up at him. 'I've begun by dividing the information into three sections: cargo manifests, payments and receipts, and a list of names.'

He nods, impressed.

'The first manifest itemises the quantity and description of the cargo – 40ft containers each holding 55 refrigerators, each with a capacity of over 25 cubic feet. This is followed by the document number and the route – Marseilles to Dover.'

'So what are we into here? Illegal immigrants?'

'We know all the stuff about Anglo-French co-operation is hot air – that dinghies are still bringing people across The Channel. But I've never heard of containers being used on the sea route. Have you?'

He shakes his head. 'So where does that leave us?'

'I'll need to do more work on it.'

He thinks for a moment. 'Drugs or arms are more likely. And if so, there's definitely a story here.'

Her eyes widen with excitement. 'It's like something out of *The Wire* or *Breaking Bad!*'

He wishes he could share her enthusiasm.

'How about that second bottle, Babe?'

He's just reaching for the wine when a ping alerts him to an incoming message. 'All right, Jack,' he sighs, 'keep your shirt on! I'm working on that lead, so for God's sake, give me some space.'

But the text isn't about the investigation. *Wish to inform you that you are being placed on a two-day week, with immediate effect. Jack.*

Ollie stares in disbelief. This must be because of his reluctance to pursue the Rosser investigation. But why couldn't his bastard editor have had the guts to tell him to his face? And how can he possibly break this news to Amy?

EIGHT

H E FEELS TOO DEPRESSED TO GET AN EARLY NIGHT and it's after midnight when he slides into bed, curling his body around the sleeping Amy. He stares at the ceiling, trying not to think what the hell he's getting himself into. Obviously, it's too late to pull out. He's read those files and even if he and Amy can as yet make little sense of them, he's as good as signed a contract. To say nothing of the risk of getting on the wrong side of Jack, who is perfectly capable of sacking him on the spot. And of one other thing Ollie is certain – Hamish Rosser is not a man to cross. Just the thought of that blue-eyed stare leaves him with a fear deep in his marrow.

Eventually he falls into a light doze, drifting in and out of a dream in which he's running down an endless street. The kerb is piled with plastic folders and at a crossroads a thin, old lady waves him across. 'Kindly perform the introductions,' she says, as an army truck, headlights on full beam and horn blaring, comes careering towards him.

He wakes, the sound of the horn translating itself into an incoming call. Beside him, Amy gives a groan before sinking back to sleep. It's just after six and for a moment he's tempted to curl up beside her. But what if this is Jack with a change of heart about putting him on shorter hours? Or announcing that he's being fired?

Ollie peers at the screen and then sits up with a jerk, pressing his mobile to his ear.

'Make a note of these train times, laddie,' the Scottish voice is saying.

He's off the bed in an instant, moving down the stairs and into the front room, where he scrabbles frantically for pen and paper.

'I'll pick you up outside Salisbury station at eleven sharp.'

He scribbles the information down.

'You can fill me in on the progress you've made with those documents. Got all that?'

Ollie responds with a muttered: 'yes.'

'Good. And no be late.'

He clicks off his phone. At a rough guess, the journey's going to take over four hours but at least there's time for a quick shower – he'll pick up some breakfast on the way.

Back in the bedroom Amy sleeps on, the bedclothes in a rumpled heap around her, dark hair spread over the pillow that is smeared with orange lipstick, bra and panties tossed into the corner. He leaves her a quick note – *Off to meet Rosser, Babe. See you this evening* – fighting the urge to ignore the man and his bloody assignment and crawl into bed beside her.

Outside Salisbury station, the rain falls in a light drizzle, and Ollie peers about him for a sighting of the Scotsman's car. He's pictured a beaten-up Ford or Fiat – something that would fit with Hamish's appearance – but instead a dark green Mercedes flashes its lights before moving forward and coming to a stop beside him.

From behind the wheel Hamish gives an impatient wave of his hand. Ollie pulls open the door and eases himself into the passenger seat.

Hamish gives a nod. 'Let's get on our way.'

'OK – but you haven't yet told me where. And what exactly it is that you want me to do?'

'All in good time, laddie,' and Ollie feels a knot form in his stomach.

They drive through a series of narrow streets, where a scattering of pedestrians walk, heads bent under hoods or umbrellas. The car smells of leather and polish and Ollie registers the Scotsman's small hands, encased in tan leather gloves, gripping the wheel.

It's only as they turn into a wide, tree-lined road that Hamish breaks the silence. 'You're asking what I want you to do, laddie, and it's this. We're dropping in on some people and you're to be my eyes and ears. I'm no telling you too much in advance. I need your first impressions.'

'All right.' Ollie tries to keep the doubt from his voice.

They pull into a cul-de-sac and park in front of a row of modern, detached houses, their large windows fronting onto gardens filled with neatly clipped shrubs. Amy would give her eye teeth for one of these places, Ollie thinks.

A net curtain twitches at a window. 'Won't they be expecting us to go in?'

Hamish shakes his head. 'We still have twenty minutes, so first I want you to tell me what sense you're making of those phone details – and the documents.'

Ollie clears his throat, aware of the Scotsman's blue eyes fastened on him. 'Well,' he begins, recalling Amy's final comments before she tidied the files away for the night, 'it seems from some of the manifests that not all the cargo is accounted for.'

'You're sure?'

'Several of the containers appear to have been empty.'

'Or carrying unlisted items?'

'Could well be. Also,' he continues with growing confidence, 'some of the initials on the documents appear to tally with that list of names.' He pauses. 'I'll need to do more work to be certain.'

'Good. Very good.'

He's swept with a huge sense of relief – must remember to tell Amy how well she's done. 'But what does it mean?'

'It means that we're definitely on to something.' He stares through the windscreen, muttering something that Ollie can't quite catch. 'What did you say?'

The lips split into a thin smile. 'A dish best served cold.'

'I don't understand.'

'Revenge, laddie. Calls for a cool brain. But never mind that. What I want now is for you to keep an open mind.'

'Of course.' But open to *what*?

'Now,' Hamish turns to him again. 'I'll be introducing you as my personal assistant, so it'll be fine for you to take notes. You've brought a notebook and pen?'

'My iPad,' he says, thinking that the man really needs to move with the times. He looks up to find the blue eyes narrowed on him.

'You listen to me, laddie, and listen good.' Hamish taps a gloved finger on the steering wheel. 'Nothing you see or hear when you're with me is to be recorded on-line. Not on your fuckin' iPad, not on your fuckin' phone and not any fuckin' laptop you may have. Do I make myself clear?'

He feels such a fool. 'Sorry – I should have thought.' He rummages in his rucksack for his notepad.

'Let's make a move.'

Ollie waits for the Scotsman to get out of the car but instead he switches on the engine, and next moment is executing a neat three-point turn and driving back down the close. They swing into the deserted main road. The drizzle has turned into a downpour, the rain lashing the windscreen, the wipers batting backwards and forwards.

After a few minutes the built-up area gives way to an endless straight stretch, with woodland and deserted fields on either side. What the hell do people do with themselves, stuck all day in the middle of nowhere? Perhaps his dream of a house in the country isn't such a good idea.

After a few miles they come to a bend in the road, driving in through a pair of wrought iron gates and into parkland, where huge chestnuts and hornbeams seem beaten down by the rain. In the distance a row of lighted windows come into view and he lets out a gasp. Christ! Where *was* this?

The building that looms through the mist is several storeys high, with turrets on either end, and a series of chimneys piercing the grey sky. They continue along a broad track and as they draw close, he sees the building is built of dark red brick, smothered in ivy, and inset with tall windows.

'Here we are then,' Hamish remarks, pulling up outside the main entrance.

Ollie follows him out of the car, staring about him at the acres of land, a herd of deer grazing in the distance and a glint of water, presumably from a lake.

They go up a shallow flight of steps, flanked at the bottom by stone unicorns. Hamish pulls on a bell-rope and after a long pause the studded door in front of them swings open.

'I dinna take kindly to be kept standing about in the wet,' Hamish says to the uniformed figure in front of them.

'Apologies, sur,' the man says. 'You're here for your noon appointment so if you'll just step inside, I'll take your coats.'

They follow him across an echoing flag-stoned hall with portraits of men in military uniform, staring down at them from the walls. At the foot of a wide, curved staircase, a sculptured head is set on the top of a marble plinth, the sightless eyes tracking them as the man opens one of the doors and leads them into a room where a log fire burns in the grate. 'Have a seat. I'll tell His Lordshup you're here.'

His Lordship? Ollie turns to Hamish for explanation, but he's settled by the fire, short legs stretched to the warmth.

'He won't keep you long,' the man says, giving the logs a poke that sends flames shooting into the air.

As he goes out, Ollie makes a mental note: Man in his late forties, strongly built, muscular, dark hair and eyes. Ulster Irish.

Ollie lowers himself into a chair and gazes around him. He's never been in a properly posh house before, but if he's to be Hamish's eyes and ears, he must try and take it all in. His eyes move to the green and brown tapestry of a hunting scene on the far wall, to a pair of chairs with legs like matchsticks – surely those seats can't be safe to sit on? To a side table with glasses and decanters. To the blackened hearth, to the round table in the centre of the room containing a bowl of blowsy pink flowers. The carpet – that doesn't reach to the edges of the room – is patterned in dull blues and browns and his overall impression is of how *faded* everything is. Maybe like the aristocracy itself which he thinks of as some endangered species. But of one thing he's certain – if he had this amount of money, he wouldn't give any of this old tat house room. He glances at Hamish, who is gazing into the fire. If only the man would stop being so vague – would give him more to go on.

The door at the far end opens and the Northern Ireland butler or however he terms himself, appears. 'His Lordshup,' he announces, as a squat figure comes walking towards them, hand outstretched.

'Apologies for having kept you.'

'Nae bother, Arnold.' Hamish gets to his feet, pointing at the fire. 'I always say there's nothing to beat a good blaze.' He pauses. 'I don't think you've met my assistant, Oliver Moorhouse. Oliver – allow me to introduce Lord Arnold Leebury.'

'Delighted,' the man says, giving Ollie's hand a firm squeeze. 'Now – let me get you something to drink. There's tea and coffee but also' – here he smiles across at Hamish– 'how about a glass of Macallan to keep out the wet?'

'Well, I wouldn't say no to a wee dram.'

'Excellent.' He turns, but the Irish butler is already at the side table, pouring drinks into three glasses. Ollie has always been a wine and beer man, but to his surprise finds himself relishing the smoky taste and the warm sting of it in his gut.

The butler retreats, and as the conversation between the two men continues, Ollie realises to his relief that he's not expected to participate. Ample opportunity then for observation.

He is still recovering from his surprise that Arnold Leebury is not the bearded, tweedy figure of his imagination, but a round-bellied man, with pink cheeks, thinning hair and a good-natured face. You'd never in a million years have taken him for a lord.

And the conversation seems pretty run-of-the-mill too. The initial niceties over, it quickly becomes clear that Hamish is here to offer Lord Leebury a sizeable donation to one of His Lordship's pet projects for the homeless with a smaller amount to the Salisbury branch of the Samaritans. Hamish will get his legal chappie to draw up the relevant documentation and the money should be in His Lordship's charity account by the end of the month.

'Excellent,' His Lordship concludes. 'And I have to say how very grateful I am to you, Hamish, on the other matter.' He hesitates. 'You really believe it's going through?'

'In the bag, Arnold.'

'Well, if ever I can –'

Hamish cuts him off with a smile. 'My pleasure. The government needs all the good men it can get.'

'I've still to discuss it with my wife, but I'm sure she'll be as thrilled as I am.'

'Ah – Magdalena.' Hamish pauses. 'How is she doing?'

'Very well, thanks.'

He gives another smile. 'I was just wondering if she'd be gracing us with her presence?'

'I could tell from the other evening that you were a fan. And I'm sure she'll be only too delighted to see you again.' He gets up and gives a sharp pull on a tapestried bell rope. In an instant the butler is in the room. He must have been waiting just outside, Ollie realises.

'Ah, Seamus,' Arnold Leebury says, 'please send word to Her Ladyship that she has a visitor.'

'Of course, sur.'

A few minutes later, the door opens again and a woman appears – the sight of her literally making Ollie draw in his breath. She's of medium height, slimly built, with waves of auburn hair reaching to her shoulders. She's dressed in black satin trousers and a silky blouse that affords a tantalising glimpse of her breasts. As she comes gliding towards them, he takes in her full lips and luminous eyes.

He may have come across some lookers, but this woman beats them all. The fact she's obviously not a young girl, is neither here nor there. Whatever her age, she is quite simply ravishing.

And remaining just inside the door is a small, doll-like figure in a white apron and cap – obviously the maid.

'You wanted me, darlink?' the gorgeous apparition says.

'Our guest here is longing for the chance of another word. You remember we met Hamish at the House of Lords dinner last week?'

She takes a step back. 'Of course. A pleasure to see you again.'

Hamish is on his feet. 'The pleasure is all mine.' He pauses. 'And I have something to admit.'

'Oh?' She fixes him with large grey eyes.

'I've done quite a bit of thinking about you since we last met.'

She gives an uncertain laugh. 'You have?'

'Yes, indeed.'

Arnold wags a finger. 'Now, Hamish, do try and behave!'

He smiles. 'Can't make any promises.' He turns back to Magdalena. 'I imagine you're involved in this project of Arnold's? Or at least taking a close interest in it?'

Two faint lines wrinkle the cream of her forehead. 'The government post he would like?'

'That – and also his charity for the homeless.'

'Yes?' She looks towards Arnold as if being asked to solve a difficult question.

'I don't usually bother Magdalena with these sorts of things.'

'That's a pity,' Hamish says. 'I'd have thought help for the struggling poor would have been right up her street.'

'Arnie is right. I leave all that to him.' Her voice is hesitant, nervous even. Or is that Ollie's imagination?

Hamish stares over the rim of his glass at the silver-framed photo on the table beside him.

'My brother, Rupert,' Lord Leebury says, following Hamish's gaze. 'Still find it hard to believe he's no longer with us. I take it the two of you never met?'

'Oh, I doubt our paths would have crossed. We'd have moved in very different circles.'

'Rupert was the dynamic, good-looking one– a real charmer. For him to have been killed like that feels all wrong, especially as he was such a competent skier.' Arnold Leebury sighs. 'I sometimes think it should have been me who was taken.'

'Now, Arnie,' Magdalena Leebury looks across at him, her eyes soft. 'Why these gloomy thoughts?'

'You're right. Ever been skiing, Hamish?'

But Hamish, abruptly, is on his feet. 'Never – can't stand all that snow.' He gestures across to Ollie. 'We'd best be on our way.'

'I'm so grateful again your help on that other matter.' His Lordship walks over to the door. 'Let me see you out.'

Hamish seems about to follow, but then suddenly swings round. 'Delightful to meet you again, Magdalena.' He moves closer, lowering his voice to a whisper that Ollie only just catches. 'Or should that be "Sorina?"'

She clasps her hands, staring at him mutely with those incredible eyes.

And with that, Hamish moves to the door. Ollie follows, passing the muscular frame of the Northern Ireland butler and the small figure of the maid, who stares at him, her round eyes expressionless.

In the hall, a middle-aged cleaning woman, swollen ankles bulging over her shoes, flicks a feather duster over the marble head. She holds out a piece of paper. 'You dropped this earlier, sur.'

With a nod, Hamish pockets it and with a 'thanks again for your hospitality, Arnold,' moves out into the rain, Ollie at his heels.

As they drive back through the parkland, Hamish gives him a sideways glance. 'So, laddie –what did you make of all that?'

'I'm not sure.'

'You must have *some* thoughts, surely?' There's a worrying edge to his voice.

Ollie hesitates. Suppose he gives the wrong answer? 'This new charity sounds interesting. But it does all seem above-board.'

Hamish sighs. 'I wasna referring to that.'

'Arnold Leebury's brother, Rupert,' Ollie tries. 'They said he was killed? Do we know how?'

Hamish gives an impatient wave of a gloved hand. 'Why do you always pick up on the wrong bluidy things? What I want to know is what you made of His Lordship – and Her Ladyship.'

'Oh.' He stares ahead. 'Well, they weren't at all what I

expected. I mean he's very approachable and pleasant – for a Lord.' He's never met one before but hopes the answer will satisfy.

Hamish nods. 'Bit of a nonentity, wouldn't you say? But what about *her*?'

She's the most beautiful creature I've ever seen, Ollie thinks. Aloud he says: 'A real stunner.'

Hamish nods.

The Leeburys themselves seemed all right, Ollie thinks. It was the silent presence of the Northern Irish butler and that odd little maid with the staring eyes that's left him with an unease which he finds difficult to articulate.

Another thought occurs. 'I thought Lady Leebury's name was Magdalena?'

'So it is, laddie.'

He hesitates. 'But you called her by something else.' He pictures that momentary hesitation when she first set eyes on Hamish. 'I thought she came across as rather anxious.' He pauses, thinking that was too mild a term. 'Afraid even,'

Hamish gives a vigorous nod. 'Good. Very good.'

A response that not only leaves Ollie more puzzled than ever, but also makes him wonder why on earth Hamish would want Magdalena Leebury to be frightened in the first place.

NINE

MARYA WATCHES THE GREEN MOTOR DISAPPEAR into the distance. That sleek car was the last thing she expected the shabby Scottish man to be driving. And the younger fellow with him was equally unprepossessing: of middling height and build, with cheap shoes and a shirt badly in need of an iron. His gaze was timid, uncertain – until Magdalena appeared. Then his calf eyes were all for her. Marya has seen that look many times and it always gives her a fellow feeling, even with someone who is so obviously a caddisfly. But the Scottish man, she thinks now, was something different. As he walked out of the room, he fastened intense blue eyes on her, and although it was only for a brief moment she was left with an uncomfortable sense that he was taking in everything about her – how she ended up in this household, the reason for her standing pressed against the wall – could even read in her face her devotion to her mistress. Marya has come across only a handful of such men, but she knows that, however unassuming they may appear, they are the ones with the real power. But here in this rainswept English countryside, the question is: the power to do what?

But of one thing Marya is certain – his presence here has upset Magdalena. From the moment the chauffeur came up to her bedroom to announce that: 'a Lord Hamish Rossur is downstairs, Your Ladyshup, and is asking to see you,' she has been irritable and tense and now, having seen off her guests, has retreated to the front room.

Arnold Leebury, with that lump of an Irishman at his heels, has headed for the library. The way the man brushed past her – as if she was so much kak under his shoes – leaves her with a simmering sense of anger. He may act as butler, as well as chauffeur, but she's the one who has her mistress's ear. And, anyway, what was he doing earlier coming up to the part of the house where he had no business to be when he would normally have texted the message?

She should go into the front room to see if there's anything Magdalena needs, but she feels strangely paralysed. She leans against a plinth with the bust of some dead Roman perched on the top, staring into the sculptured face as if in search of an answer to an as yet unformulated question. The clouded eyes gaze out, impassive, and other than the creak of a radiator, all remains quiet.

A door opens and Magdalena, her face drained of colour, emerges from the front room. At the sight, Marya is swept with a sense of foreboding.

'I have rotten head and will lie down for a while.'

Yet once in the bedroom, Magdalena doesn't rest, pacing backwards and forwards, the heels of her Balenciaga shoes making small dents in the Aubusson carpet. Marya busies herself smoothing the bed covers while trying to gauge her mistress's mood.

Magdalena looks across at her. 'What am I to do?'

The appeal in the grey eyes makes Marya want to rush over and clasp her in her arms. 'What about?'

'The Scottish man – he was at that dinner last week.'

'The one you wore your red dress to?' For a moment Marya is swept by a fantasy of running her tongue along the silken skin of that cleavage and across those full breasts.

'He was – how do you say? Nasty – unpleasant. I wish never to set eyes on him again.'

'Not allow him back to the Hall, you mean?'

'Have you got a fucking cloth in your ear, or what?' She pulls down the corners of her mouth. 'Sorry, darlink. Didn't mean to snap.'

It's at this point that Marya feels her anxiety levels rise. Not because of her mistress's obvious dislike of this man – he wouldn't be the first not to have lived up to her exacting standards – but because Marya can't recall a time when Magdalena has apologised to her. And her face is still so pale. 'Shall I bring you a cold drink or a coffee?'

She shakes her head. 'I need to put thinking cap on.' Suddenly she turns. 'Better to face the music– no? So, I must speak to Arnie. Tell him this Hamish man makes me unhappy and that he must stop seeing him. Surely he will agree?'

'Of course. He always does what you say.'

Magdalena moves to the dressing-table, running a comb through her hair and spritzing Chanel No. 5 on her wrists. 'Come with me and stay by the door. No one will take notice.'

Marya prides herself on her ability to blend into the background but as she follows Magdalena down the wide staircase, she still puzzles over what this Hamish person has done to upset her mistress. Their encounter seemed to consist of meaningless chatter – until that moment when he turned and whispered something that Marya couldn't quite catch, but which caused Magdalena to clasp her hands in distress.

They find Lord Leebury in the library – a long, dimly-lit room with books lined from floor to ceiling. They always give Marya the feeling they might at any time topple over. She can feel their weight, like miniature tombstones – can imagine being buried beneath them, fighting until the last breath is squeezed out of her.

Now she positions herself inside the door, alert to any signal from her mistress.

His Lordship is at his desk and when he sees Magdalena, he gets up from his chair and moves over to her. 'I thought that meeting went off pretty well,' he says, giving her a kiss. 'Hamish is going to put in a word for me at the highest level.'

She nods, but without enthusiasm.

'Something wrong, Sweetheart?'

'Arnie.' She looks at him with those large eyes. 'I have small favour to ask.'

81

'Anything at all, my love.'

She draws in her breath. 'I want you to have nothing more to do with the Scottish man.'

'Why, what on earth's he done?' He breaks off. 'Of course! He couldn't take his eyes off you! But you always handle that sort of thing so well, Lena.'

'It's not that. It's just –'

There's a knock and Seamus comes striding into the room – as if he owns the fucking place, Marya thinks.

'Excuse me, sur, but you're wanted on the house phone.'

'Tell whoever it is to call back. I'm busy.'

'It's Downing Street.'

'Downing Street? You're sure?' He turns to Magdalena. 'Hamish said he'd pull strings for me, so do you think this could possibly…?'

A flicker, like a lightbulb about to blow, crosses her face. Arnold, the fat fool, doesn't notice, although Marya certainly does.

'Sorry, my sweet. I need to take this.' He walks over to a side table and picks up the receiver. 'Arnold Leebury here. Who is this? Oh. Of course.' He listens for several moments. 'This afternoon? I can manage that. Yes. No problem. I'll see you then.'

He swings round, his usually bland expression replaced by a broad grin. 'I do believe Hamish has fixed it, Lena. You don't get a call like this unless there's a definite post on offer.'

'Excellent news, Arnie.' Her voice is flat. 'But I must –'

'Not now, Magdalena, there's a good girl. I need to change into a decent suit and allow time to get up to

Westminster.' He turns to where the Irishman waits, arms folded over his chest. 'Bring the Bentley round, would you, Seamus?'

Lord Leebury walks over to Magdalena. 'Whatever it is that's worrying you, my darling, we will sort when I'm back.' He plants another kiss on her forehead. 'I shouldn't be late and then I'll be able to give you all the time in the world.'

He moves out of the room, the sound of his humming carrying along the passage.

Magdalena sinks into a chair and puts her head in her hands. Obviously, whatever has happened is not just bad – it is catastrophic.

And, Marya thinks, it can only mean one thing. The Scottish man knows something. But what? And how much? She tries never to revisit the past but as she pours Magdalena a glass of water, she forces her mind back – over twenty years ago now – to where it all began.

The day started the same way as all the others. Out of her bunk at first light, reheating the dregs of coffee on the one-ring burner, a quick drag on a cigarette before pulling on trousers and the long-sleeved shirt that she rinsed out the night before. She pushed her feet into her shoes and, tucking her hair into a cap, set off along the deserted streets to the main gate of the docks. The guards looked up from their game of cards and waved her through, their tedious shouts following after her: 'Are you up for it, Marya? Give us a look at that arse!' She shrugged off their comments, just as she shrugged off all approaches that were made to her. She'd been working at the port for eight years now and was lucky to have this job. Her schooling, such as it was, left her with good numeracy skills but with no family support, her options would have been limited: prostitution or drug running.

The days merged into one another, filled with the clash of metal, its hot tang filling the air, the men's oaths as they pulled at the chains that hoisted the huge oblong containers onto the carriers, smoke from the cabins rising into the cloudless sky. It was a life of a sort, made more bearable the previous year when that husband of hers had the good sense to get himself knocked on the head by an iron derrick and plummeted head-first onto the deck of the cargo ship. When she recalled his hairy body pressed against hers, his blunt fingers poking inside her, the reek of sweat and beer, she felt a wonderful sense of release. But it was one that did not last long. Without the protection of a husband she was all too vulnerable and the manager, Jacques – even hairier than her late husband – wouldn't give her a moment's peace.

Marya ducked under a girder and climbed a flight of rickety stairs to the office. It was constructed out of an old shipping container, its walls made of rusty iron in which openings had been cut for a door and a window. She spent most of her day here, checking invoices and paperwork, knowing which to give the green light to and which to pass to Jacques for a final decision.

Today, that pig of a man was ahead of her, his bulk settled behind his desk. He looked up and gave a smile that turned her insides sour. It was like all those moments, when they were alone and he would lift her off her feet and press her into a corner, feeling for the zip of his trousers and groping between her legs. Although so far she had fended him off, she knew it was only a matter of time. But if it wasn't him, it would be some other pig. And she needed this job until she could work out how, by some means or other, she could escape from the port and start a new life – somewhere, anywhere.

Thankfully, part of her day was spent out of the airless container and on the dockside, ticking off the list of cargoes. Jacques was beside her now, his breath hot on her neck, but there were too many people around for him to try anything.

They stood together watching as a black van drew up and a woman emerged. Marya had seen her several times before. She was very thin, wearing flat shoes, her grey skirt and top seeming to hang off her, her hair covered by a beige scarf.

She made her way over to them and stood, shoulders hunched, eyes expressionless.

'Everything ready?' Jacques asked.

She nodded.

'Christ! Your face would be enough to curdle milk,' Jacques said, reaching down and giving Marya's rump a squeeze.

'Still can't keep your hands to yourself, can you?'

Jacques stepped towards her. 'Want them to show you what's what?'

'No.' She started to tremble. 'The cargo's all ready for shipment.'

'It had better be!' he called after her, as she began walking back towards the van. 'If she knows what's good for her,' he added.

Marya, having twisted free of his grasp, filed the incident away as part of another tedious day in which nothing of importance happened.

Only much later would she look back and realise that she couldn't have been more wrong.

TEN

MAGDALENA SITS AT ONE END OF THE DINING-table, picking at a prawn and mango salad.

The room is only used for entertaining and its unlived atmosphere suits her mood. She needs somewhere to give her a sense of space – help untangle the thoughts cluttering her brain.

She stares across at the walnut sideboard. Positioned on the top is an eighteenth century blue and white vase from the Kangxi period that Arnie has informed her is worth a small fortune. Above it, an oil painting of a man, thin lipped, in top hat and old-fashioned coat stares across at the portrait on the opposite wall – a woman dressed in dark grey, her lips turned down as if in disapproval of the foreign intruder seated at the table.

'Why all these dreary ancestors?' Magdalena protested. 'Let's have a Hockney or a Warhol to brighten the place up.' But on this Arnie has remained stubborn. 'I know they were bought at auction, but it still seems a shame to stuff them away in some cupboard. If you really insist, then of course...' As his voice tailed away, she knew he would never agree, any more than he'd remove that photo of his brother which must only act as a reminder of how different the two of them were – Rupert, handsome and charismatic, in contrast to unassuming Arnie, who plods his way through life. What he fails to understand is that, however charming his brother may have been, she would never have trusted, let alone liked, someone who never managed to put down roots – who lived a careless life, surrounding himself with a string of young women, their beauty matched only by their stupidity.

Outside, the rain falls in a steady stream and Magdalena feels the weight of the afternoon pressing down on her. She reaches for her phone. *Turn around, Arnie, and come home,* she wants to text. *We don't need any Government appointment – we are perfectly happy as we are.* But then, as she recalls his delight on receiving that message from Downing Street, she catches herself thinking that, as strong as the wish for power is the wish to belong. And perhaps that has been more important to her husband than she's realised.

They'd been going out for several months when he told her how contented he was 'to just bumble along,' living in his small London flat and working as an administrator in a solicitor's office – he flunked his law finals, he admitted. His inheritance, following the sudden death of Rupert, came as a huge shock, and on taking her to Athelford

Hall for the first time, he seemed apologetic, as if he had no right to be there – a feeling that she recognised.

'Rupert and I were never close,' Arnie told her. 'He took no interest in the Hall – spent all his time in ski resorts and Las Vegas, where he became something of an expert.'

'He was a gambler?'

'Yes – and no surprise there. Even when we were children, he would cheat at any games we played – just the way he was, I suppose. But when he was killed and I inherited this place, I found it a huge burden. All I wanted was for life to continue as normal, linking up with friends for an after-work drink, going to the odd concert and for walks in Hyde Park. I'm sure it must seem pretty dull to you. But then I'm a pretty dull sort of chap.' He broke off, looking embarrassed. 'But maybe...?'

Magdalena squeezed his hand. 'Maybe?' she prompted.

'Maybe with someone at my side, I might feel very different.'

Through Magdalena's efforts, the Hall was transformed: the roof re-tiled, crumbling stonework renovated and rotting window frames replaced. Indoors, disused rooms were opened and aired, moth-eaten curtains and hangings mended, and walls repainted in as near a match with the originals as possible. She found it satisfying to rescue these objects from their state of decay – as if in doing so she were restoring broken parts of herself.

Galvanised by her energy, Arnie took charge of the grounds, overseeing the removal of dead trees, replanting the borders and clearing ditches and, at Magdalena's suggestion, buying a pair of Indian blue peacocks from a farm in the Midlands. And now, just when she's all set to begin their carefree life together, *this* had to happen. 'This' being the appearance of that nasty Scottish man, who somehow has managed to get hold of information she'd assumed long buried. So, whatever it takes, she must persuade Arnie to turn down this government post.

She pushes away her uneaten food and, returning upstairs, despatches Marya to the kitchen, where she informs the cook that a special meal must be prepared for the Leeburys, who will be eating at eight. Mrs. Acheson listens in a glowering silence and deprived of her evening off, stomps around the kitchen, clattering pans and swearing at the radio.

Magdalena spends the rest of the long afternoon in the downstairs room. Outside the wind gets up, driving fistfuls of rain down the chimney and onto the hearth, where the wood splutters in protest.

When the ormolu clock in the corner strikes seven, she sends him a text – her fourth of the afternoon – but there is still no response. With Marya's help she changes into her low-cut black dress – chosen because it is both sexy and sombre – and waits, trying to damp down her anxiety. Arnie and she have never been apart for more than a few hours and even then they've exchanged frequent messages. For him to be out of touch like this, is totally out of character. Suppose there's been some accident?

At just after nine, headlights sweep up the drive and a few minutes' later, Arnold is in the room. She puts down the copy of *Harper's Bazaar* she's been pretending to read.

'You're back – at last!'

'Sorry to be a bit late, but you'll never guess!'

'Am longing to hear all about it, darlink. But first – we must eat.'

'I got something at my club. Hamish took me there to celebrate. He's as excited as I am.'

She raises a perfect eyebrow. 'Oh?'

'Such news, Lena! They've given me a ministerial post. Only a junior one, with responsibility for trade and culture.' He draws himself up to his full height – a movement that makes his paunch even more pronounced. 'Marvellous, isn't it?'

'Truly wonderful,' she says, wondering what knowledge he has of either trade or culture.

He plants a wet kiss on her mouth. 'Champagne is the order of the day!' He walks over and gives a sharp tug on the bell pull that makes him lose his balance.

It is then she realises that he is in fact quite drunk. But this is no bad thing. Fortunately, he is not one of those men, of whom she has plenty of knowledge, who turn aggressive when they have alcohol inside them. No – Arnie will simply become endearingly amorous, planting her with more of his sloppy kisses, muttering loving phrases into her ear before finally falling asleep in the nearest chair. So now is the time to act. To strike, in that curious English expression, while the iron is hot.

'Darlink. I know you have eaten at your club, but I have organised a special meal to celebrate this special occasion.' She flutters eyelashes at him. 'You wouldn't want to disappoint your Lena, would you?'

He eyes her unsteadily. 'Course not. Just a mouthful or two, and then I'll fill you in.'

Over Lobster Thermador he proceeds to do so. 'I saw the P.M. for just a couple of minutes. A truly impressive man, Lena. Of course, I've chatted with him a few times, but this was different. Not just a social event. You understand?'

Magdalena nods, letting Arnie's words drift over her as he ploughs his way through Stilton and Tarte Tatin. Instinct tells her not to leave this until the morning when he will have sobered up. So the important thing is to get enough food inside him to mop up the alcohol. When she gauges he is balanced between relative coherence and somnolence, she steers him back to the drawing-room, where they sit together on the sofa.

She watches him gulp down coffee that under her instructions Marya has made extra strong. 'Now, darlink,' she says. 'We need to talk.'

'Course. Talk away.' He nuzzles her ear. 'And how about a spot of the other?'

'Later,' she whispers. 'It's just that I have a favour to ask, Arnie. A *big* favour.'

He stares at her with watery eyes. 'Anything at all, sweetheart.'

She hesitates. 'You won't think your Lena is being foolish?'

'Course not.'

She strokes his cheek. 'It's truly wonderful, Arnie, that you've been given this job. You really deserve it.'

'All due to Hamish, of course. He's what we Brits call

a king-maker. He was even instrumental in getting Boris elected.'

'I know you owe Hamish a lot, but' – she draws in her breath – 'as I told you before, I don't want you to have anything more to do with him.'

His face clouds. 'He hasn't –?'

She shakes her head. 'He's not one of *those*, darlink. No – it's because he is not a trustworthy type.'

'But you've only just met him. What makes you think this?'

'I knew it the moment I saw him.'

'Women's intuition, eh?'

She nods.

'But he's done me such a huge favour.'

'I know, Arnie. But just for me. *Please*.'

'Well, if you feel that strongly.' He pauses. 'May be a bit awkward but I suppose it could be managed.'

'Oh, *thank* you!' She rubs her hand along the front of his trousers. 'I can't tell you how happy this makes me.'

He groans with pleasure. 'Me too.'

ELEVEN

MAGDALENA HAS ALWAYS APPRECIATED HER husband's ability to recover from a bout of heavy drinking – that he is not one of those men who appear the following morning, the foul mood matching the equally foul breath.

'What a day that was!' he exclaims, piling butter onto his toast. 'The best of my life.' He smiles across at her. 'Well – *almost* the best.' He pauses. 'Although I'm afraid, Lena, it'll mean I will be away from the Hall more often. But there'll still be plenty of times when we can be together, especially at those formal do's you enjoy so much.'

'That will be fine, Arnie. I have Marya for company and you know how much I enjoy ordering things for the house and seeing that the staff do their stuff. It is all so wonderful. I am very proud of you.'

'Thank you, my darling. I couldn't be a happier man.

Just to think that before I met you, I was this sad old bachelor in a dead-end job and now, thanks to Hamish, I have a position that will give me standing in the world.' He pauses. 'As well as having a wonderful wife, of course.'

'I know how grateful you are to the Scottish man, Arnie, so thank you again for agreeing'.

He gives a blank stare. 'Agreeing?"

'To have nothing more to do with him.' She sips her coffee. 'As you promised.'

'Now wait a minute.' He puts down his cup. 'When did I do that?'

'Last night. Surely you remember?'

'Bit the worse for wear, I'm afraid. But if I did, then I'm very sorry, Lena. Because I can't possibly drop him now.'

She bites back her disappointment – her fear. 'Why ever not?'

'Because, my sweet, Hamish Rosser knows all the right people. A junior post today – in the future, goodness knows...' He reaches over and squeezes her hand. 'My donations to the party have brought me a certain amount of kudos, but I can't tell you what it means to be wanted, not just for my cash, but for what I personally have to offer. Surely you can see that?'

She feels a sinking sensation inside her. 'But you could refuse the post?'

He leans over. 'I know how you struggle with our British ways, but one simply doesn't turn down this kind of offer.' He shakes his head in disbelief. 'This is a once in a lifetime chance.'

'But I, your wife, am asking you to do it.'

His face has gone very red and there's a new look of determination in his eyes. 'And I am telling you – *no!*'

She bites her lip, willing the tears to come.

He stares in dismay. 'I didn't mean to shout. But surely Hamish can't be as bad as you think?'

'But he is,' she sobs. 'Oh, why can't you understand?'

He sighs. 'Very well. Give me one good reason.'

She wipes her eyes. 'I thought you and I were going to spend our time together.'

'There'll still be plenty of opportunity for that.'

'But it won't be the same.' She pauses again. 'And isn't it enough that your wife, whom you say you love most in the world, is asking you this?'

He gets up, pushing back his chair. 'No, Magdalena. It is not.' He stares down at her. 'I thought you would be one hundred per cent behind me on this. At least try to understand what a huge favour Hamish is doing for me – for us.'

Fear makes her strike out. 'Oh, fuck Hamish's favour, Arnie!'

He doesn't reply, moving out of the room and slamming the door behind him.

For the rest of the day they ignore one another and when they get into bed that night, he turns on his side and is immediately sleeping the sleep of the innocent.

Magdalena, her innocence long gone, lies awake in the darkness, listening to the spatter of rain against the window and thinking that it sounds for all the world like distant rifle fire.

The first bomb fell just after dawn, shattering the quiet that brooded over everything in these night hours. Somehow the family were managing to cling onto their flat in the high-rise block. Half of it had been blown away and the remaining walls were fragile, an easy target for the enemy. 'Who is the enemy, Papa?' she recalled her young brother asking. 'Why such foolish questions, boy?' Her father waved an arm. 'Last year it was this group. Today it is that one. Tomorrow – who knows?'

But if we don't know, the girl thought, how can we tell our friend from our enemy? Before she could voice the question, her father beckoned her over. 'See to Mami and then bring me a cup of water.'

They were all crowded into this one room. Her father, immobile since caught in an explosion two weeks earlier, sat with his wounded leg stretched in front of him, the blood dried to a crust. Her mother lay groaning on her mattress – one of the few items they managed to salvage. It was days since she'd had the strength to sit up and the room stank of urine and faeces. At least the baby was sleeping, and the girl's two younger brothers were playing some game in the corner with pebbles and string. But the quiet would not be with them for long – not just on account of the bombs that fell out of the sky like so many rocks, but because their rations were long gone and soon the baby would start to bawl from hunger, its shrieks as piercing as a siren. When the girl last ventured out to the nearest stall it was to find only carrots and blackened potatoes on sale, but at a price that made most people, herself included, turn away.

A month earlier, her baby sister died from starvation and now six-year-old Ali wailed: 'Want something to eat, Papa.'

'Here,' her father said. 'Have a turn on this.' It was the sole of a shoe. Ali seized it, sucking on the leather, saliva running down his chin as he fought off his young brother who tried to grab it from him.

Her father took the cup of water from the girl and slurped noisily. Then he did a surprising thing – he leaned over and stroked her hair. She nestled against him, grateful to feel his solid warmth against her. After a few moments, he tipped up her chin and gazed into her eyes. 'I'm afraid there is only one thing to be done. Believe me if there was another way I would take it.' He handed the cup back to her. 'You are to go and live with some people.'

'Go?' She whispered. 'But where? And what people?'

'A family in our neighbourhood.'

'But I want to stay here with you – and with Mami. I'm good at looking after you both, aren't I?'

'You are, darling.' His face was sad. 'But at nine you are old enough to manage without us, and it won't be for long.'

'How long?' she demanded.

He didn't answer and, hearing a movement behind her, she turned.

A large man, heavily bearded, in stained tee shirt and jeans, blackened toes thrust into sandals, stood in the gaping doorway.

She shrank back.

'*Ahlan Wa Sahlan,*' the newcomer said.

'*Ahlan bik.*'

'Ready?' the man said.

Her father nodded.

The man pointed towards her. 'This is the one?'

Another nod.

'And she will give no trouble?'

She looked at her father, feeling the panic rising inside her. She wanted to shout a protest but the words seemed to have become stuck somewhere inside her.

'Go with him, girl. It'll just be for a little while.'

The man stepped forward and threw a canvas bag that landed at the foot of the mattress with a thump. 'These supplies should keep you going.' He jabbed a thumb towards the girl's mother, who lay with closed eyes. 'The medicine is also there.'

'Take her then.'

The man seized her arm and pulled her to the door. She tried to struggle free, but his grip tightened. 'Papa! Papa!' she shrieked.

Her two young brothers were crouched at the foot of their mother's mattress, their faces impassive.

'Stop this carry on,' her father ordered. 'You will be back here before you know it. So you are to behave yourself and do what this man says.'

She bit her lip, trying to stem her tears. 'He is our friend, Papa?'

'Our good friend.' He closed his eyes. 'I promise.'

Magdalena jerks upright, sweat trickling down her spine. Beside her, Arnie sleeps on. She longs for him to gather her in his arms as he did when they were first together and her memories threatened to overwhelm her. She made it clear she didn't want to talk about them – how could she have done without giving too much away? But she was always grateful that he never pressed her. 'Darling Lena, you have transformed my life and I will always be here for you,' he would say.

As she looks down at him now, she knows how fortunate she is to be married to a kind and tolerant man, safe in the world he has provided for her.

But the fact that Arnie is so good-hearted is also the problem. It would not occur to him for a moment that someone like Hamish Rosser is not to be trusted. Or perhaps, like so many English people, he chooses not to know?

She lies down once more, pulling the covers over her, her father's words echoing in her ears. 'He is our good friend. I promise.'

TWELVE

'SO TELL ME ABOUT THESE DREAMS, GREG.'
It was early December and he was in a small office attached to the hall where the meetings were held. The place, also used as a gym, smelled of dust and stale bodies. A plastic Santa squatted, Buddha-like, on top of a bookcase and the far wall was draped in tired-looking paper decorations.

June was in her sixties, a large woman with tousled grey hair and deep circles etched under the eyes. How much sleep did *she* get?

'It's obvious from your sessions here' – she waved a hand towards the hall – 'that your drinking was brought on by the loss of your wife. But you're forging ahead with this new project as well as your other interests.' She leaned over and patted his knee. 'I appreciate how very tough it must still be, but it does seem that you've turned a corner.'

He wished he could believe her. 'It's just that every time I drop off – and I know I'll sound like a blithering idiot...'

Her eyes were soulful. 'You can tell me anything, Greg. It's what I'm here for.'

He tried again. 'I get caught up in imagining what it must be like for her.'

'For Anne?'

He stared around at the battered filing cabinets and boxes of china used for those endless tea breaks the AA went in for. 'Trapped in a wooden box with all those tons of earth pressed on top of her.'

June stared. 'But she can't feel anything, Greg. She's at peace.'

He experienced an uprush of anger. 'She wasn't at peace at the end though. Was she?' And don't let anyone try to fool you into thinking that death was an easy affair, he thought, remembering the desperate gasps for breath as the pain took a stronger hold. 'How can I forget how terrified she was?'

'You must stop torturing yourself, Greg.' June gave his knee another pat. 'How about trying some of those CBT exercises?'

Now Christmas has come round once again and, as he lies sleepless, Greg tries to convince himself that there is every reason to feel cheerful.

The previous afternoon, the tree that he ordered – a six-foot Norwegian spruce – was set up in the hall. The three young ones were given the task of decorating it and he and Mrs. Mehta exchanged smiles as they watched them mock-fighting over which baubles to hang where. Greg was relieved that Jason joined in the fun – after their earlier spat, he's also settling in well. And when Frances turned to Greg and exclaimed: 'I can't tell you what this means to me – my first Christmas in a proper home!' he felt a glow of satisfaction. But still he can't shake off his despondency. If only –

A shrill noise pierces the dark. He jerks upright, reaching across for Anne, only to realise that of course her side of the bed is flat. He clicks on the Anglepoise. It's just after 2am. All he wants is to pull the covers over his head but that high-pitched cry comes again.

He pulls on his dressing-gown and crosses the landing to Mrs. Mehta's room. Outside her door, he hesitates, not wanting to disturb her. She already does so much to help the household run smoothly. So he turns, mounting the next flight of stairs and pausing at the top as the noise comes again. This is where he longs for Anne, who would have known what to do.

He hears steps and, thank God, Mrs. Mehta, in a red quilted dressing-gown, is coming up beside him. And now they catch the sound of muffled sobs coming from Poppy's room. Mrs. Mehta taps on the door and tiptoes inside while he hovers in the doorway, wishing he didn't feel so useless.

The light is on, illuminating a shelf with a row of soft toys arranged along it. He's always made it clear that the bedrooms were for the three young people to decorate as they chose, with Mrs. Mehta to give whatever help was needed. Poppy has used her earnings from the salon to buy a picture of a pink unicorn surrounded by purple and blue flowers, and the plain curtains have been replaced by ones with a pattern of woodland animals. On the side table, a plastic mermaid lies amongst bottles of nail varnish and makeup. It strikes him that this could be the room of a much younger girl.

Then he recalls her file and how little chance of a proper childhood she's had.

Poppy May Smith. Born: Mother and Baby Unit, Bronzefield Prison, Kent. Mother serving twelve-years for drug dealing. At 18 months, child placed in foster care, transferred later to an unregulated children's home. Aged 14, ran away and discovered sleeping rough…

Now, all that's visible of the girl is a tangle of blonde hair and a form shaken with sobs. The sound tugs at him.

Mrs. Mehta lowers herself onto the bed. 'Whatever's wrong, Poppy?'

She struggles onto an elbow. Even with her face blotched with tears, the golden hair and blue eyes make you realise what a pretty child she is. *Girl*, he corrects himself.

'I was having such a terrible dream,' she whispers. Then she looks across and spots him in the doorway. 'And you're here also, Greg. This is awful. I've woken you both.' And she starts crying again.

'How about a hot drink?' Mrs. Mehta says. 'It'll help you sleep.'

Poppy nods and as Mrs. Mehta goes out, the girl whispers: 'I'm sorry, Greg. I can't seem to get rid of them.'

'The bad dreams? I can arrange for you to talk things over with someone– if you'd like?'

She shakes her head. 'I had enough of that in the last place. I need to focus on the future.'

He can understand that and, anyway, who is he to give advice about nightmares?

'Talking of the future,' he says, relieved to be moving off a difficult conversation, 'you're doing really well at the salon, Poppy.' He pauses. 'Mrs. Mehta and I are very proud.'

It seems that's the worst thing he could have said, because she starts to sob even more loudly and it's a relief when Mrs. Mehta appears, placing a mug of hot chocolate on the bedside table.

As Poppy continues to cry, Mrs. Mehta and he exchange a look. But what else can they do?

'Hope you don't mind – I heard voices.' Frances is in the doorway. She's wearing navy pyjamas and those slippers that look like boots and brings with her a welcome air of calm. She moves to the bed. 'Bad dream?'

Poppy nods.

'Would you like me get in beside you for a bit?'

Another nod.

As Greg closes the door, he looks across at the young women. Poppy's crying has stopped, her blonde head resting against Frances's dark hair.

Back in his bed, he listens to the quiet of the house and, in one of the rare times since Anne's death, sinks into a deep sleep.

THIRTEEN

IT'S AFTER NINE BY THE TIME HE COMES DOWN TO breakfast and he has the room to himself. Mrs. Mehta places scrambled eggs in front of him before giving her morning update.

'Jason's left for the supermarket – on time for once. He still complains about the job, but at least he's sticking with it.' Mrs. Mehta pours coffee. 'Poppy's gone off to the salon and Frances is working a late shift, so she's still in her room.'

'But how did Poppy seem after last night?'

'She was rather pale – obviously tired.'

'As you must be, Mrs. Mehta.' He pauses. 'Do you think we should be doing more about these nightmares?'

'They've only been here a few weeks. Why don't we see how things go?' She smiles. 'But thank goodness for Frances. That girl really has a way about her.'

He nods agreement.

When he's finished eating, he carries his coffee through to the den, where he settles at the desk and opens his laptop.

Most of his meetings are scheduled for later in the week so his diary is relatively empty. Suddenly he pictures Anne come rushing in. *All quiet on the home front, Greg. Grab your coat and let's get some air!* He closes his eyes, pierced by a stab of longing.

A cough makes him jump and he looks up. Jason is in the doorway.

'Having a quick forty winks, Greg?'

He mustn't let the lad get under his skin. 'Shouldn't you be at work?' Please God don't let there be any trouble with drugs, he thinks.

'The thing is' – Jason's voice is hesitant – 'I've got something to tell you.'

'Yes?'

'I've, like, given in my notice.'

'You've *what?*'

Jason takes a step back. 'It's not what you think.' He folds arms across his chest. 'I've been spotted, like.'

'How do you mean, "spotted?"'

The boy comes over and perches on the edge of the desk. 'I was walking along, minding my own business, see, when I got this tap on the shoulder. And it was from this guy, Gary, who runs an agency, like, for actors and models.'

Greg tugs at his ear. 'What sort of acting and modelling?'

'Magazines, posters, TV.'

'It sounds pretty dubious.'

'Yeah – but hear me out. I've signed a contract and it's totally legit. I'm doing some modelling for a washing-powder ad and there's more, like, bookings lined up. It's paying more than I earn in a week at the store.'

'But you *promised* not to make any changes without discussing them with me first.'

'You'd only have tried to stop me.'

How true, Greg thinks.

'The guy in charge says I have one of the most arresting faces he's ever seen.' Jason grins. 'Arresting – didn't think I'd ever be pleased to hear *that* word applied to me! He's guaranteed me work for the next few months.' He pauses. 'Don't think I'm not grateful, Greg. Without your help, this wouldn't have happened.' He stoops to his rucksack. 'It's why I wanted to let you know as soon as possible.'

Before the store manager phones asking me where the hell his new employee has got to, Greg thinks.

Jason shoves a sheaf of photographs across the desk. 'I thought you'd want to, like, have a look at these.'

At least the boy is taking him into his confidence.

The photos show Jason posed against various backdrops: a metal park bench, a shopfront with a display of trainers and tracksuits, a red sportscar. And whoever is in charge is right – the boy *is* striking. Those chiselled features and sharp eyes, the relaxed yet confident way he drapes himself across the frame, make one want to look twice – and to keep looking.

Jason eases himself off the desk. 'I'd best get back to the store. They've agreed to let me finish at the end of the week. OK?'

Greg sighs. 'I guess it will have to be.'

'Well, cheers for now. I'll keep you posted.'

At least there's one positive in all this, Greg thinks, as the door bangs shut. The boy no longer carries with him the lingering reek of pot. And maybe this stint at modelling will give Jason a chance to do something he enjoys before he settles to a worthwhile job.

But the thought of the lad settling down – which is after all, one of the main aims of this project – is a reminder that Poppy's nightmares will have given Frances a disturbed night. How like her to come to the rescue. Mrs. Mehta is right: the girl has a definite way with her.

He moves to the filing cabinet and takes out her details, which don't make for easy reading: *Frances Matei. Born London August 14th, 2008. Abandoned as a newborn. Early years in a care home. Aged 12, forced by foster family to work as cleaner and child minder. Aged 15, sent to a second care home.*

At least Frances was treated well there, Greg thought – excelling at her schoolwork and forming good relationships with those around her. *An exceptionally intelligent, well-motivated girl,* the report concluded. *And –*

The study door bangs open. For God's sake! Is he never to get a moment's peace?

'I'm so sorry, Mr. Jacobs,' Mrs. Mehta is saying, 'She was told she must ring for an appointment.'

The 'she' is the mad old woman, who glares round

at the housekeeper and Frances. 'I do not possess one of those mobile telephones, and I can assure you that I do not take kindly to being manhandled!'

'Shall I send for the police, Mr. Jacobs?'

He sighs. 'No, better just send her on her way.'

Frances steps forward. 'Maybe just hear what she has to say, Greg? She's obviously desperate to talk to you.'

He feels a stab of remorse. The old woman must be well into her eighties, her brown raincoat hanging off her thin frame and her fingers protruding like claws from the ends of frayed mittens. Even from a few feet away he catches a manky smell off her – a potent mix of tomcat and stale food.

'Your name's been given to me, Mr. Jacobs,' she says, in her high, thin voice. Just a short time is all it will take. *Somebody* must be able to help.'

He ignores Mrs. Mehta's frantic shake of the head 'Five minutes only then.'

She sits on the edge of the corner chair, clutching her string bag, still crammed with shopping. He looks across at Frances. There's no knowing what this strange woman will come out with and he could do with an ally, which obviously isn't going to be Mrs. Mehta. 'Would you mind staying, Frances?'

'Of course not.'

He turns back to the old lady. 'You'd best start by giving me your name.'

'Amelia.'

'And your second name?'

She stares blankly.

'Greg is wondering what else you're known as,' Frances says.

'I heard him the first time, young woman, but it's really none of his business – or yours either.' She leans forward. 'It was Jimmy who gave me your name, Mr. Jacobs, because he said you might be able to do something.'

'And which charity is Jimmy connected with? The Samaritans? The Food Bank?'

She shakes her head. 'He's just a friend.'

'I don't know anyone of that name. And do something about *what*?'

She gets up from her seat and thrusts a crumpled piece of paper at him. He smooths it out and reads. Then looks across at her once more. 'This is a receipt from a company – Aquarius Bitcoin – for an extremely large sum of money.' He hands it back to her.

'You wouldn't think to look at me now, but I was worth a considerable amount once.' She taps her nose. 'I have the original receipt tucked away somewhere safe.'

'So, can you tell me what happened?'

'My Aunt Dorothea left me a big inheritance, and I was on the tube one day when I spotted this advertisement: *Don't keep your money in the bank. Let us make you rich.*

Greg and Frances exchange a look.

Amelia shakes her head. 'You're quite right – I should never have gone near any of it. But at the time it seemed to make a lot of sense.'

'And you wouldn't be the first person to have thought so,' Greg says.

'Anyway, I rang the number and when I said I didn't hold

with any of this computer nonsense, these two men arranged to meet me. Fund Executives they called themselves. We went to The Savoy where they insisted on buying me a slap-up tea.' She sniffs, wiping her nose on a frayed mitten. 'We had champagne and there was an orchestra playing. They were so well dressed – polished shoes, suits nicely pressed – and seemed so kind and reliable. Afterwards, we went by taxi to their office – in south London somewhere. They promised my money would earn a lot of interest – more than enough to set up the refuge.'

Greg leans forward, not sure that he's heard right. 'Refuge?'

'We need to do something to help these unfortunates, especially with the country being in the mess it is.'

Greg thinks of his three young charges. 'So who is it exactly you have in mind?'

'My cats, of course,' she says, in a tone that indicates she's speaking to a complete fool. 'So many of the poor darlings are turned onto the streets because their owners can't afford to keep them. The least I can do is give them a proper home.'

Frances comes to his rescue. 'But something went wrong with your investment? And who were these men you dealt with?'

Amelia hesitates. 'I don't know their names, but as they were leaving, I saw them talking to another person – an older fellow, who's been hanging about my place. Or someone who's the dead spit of him.'

'And have you tried asking this man for information?' Frances says.

'I have, but he says he knows nothing about it, so what else can I do? The plain truth is that my money has disappeared.' She waves a skinny arm in the air. 'Gone – like a puff of smoke. And you can't tell me that's right, can you? Money can't just vanish?'

'Bitcoin,' Greg says. 'I'm so sorry.'

A look of alarm crosses her face. 'But you'll be able to help? I've no money left for a solicitor.'

He exchanges another glance with Frances. He doesn't want to let this old woman down but, equally, he mustn't give her false hope.

Once again, Frances intervenes. 'Why don't you leave us your address, Amelia. Mr. Jacobs will make some enquiries and get back to you when he has any news.'

'That will be soon?'

'Hopefully,' Greg says, as he walks her to the front door. 'Although I can't make any promises. Now if you'll excuse me, I need to get on.'

She smiles up at him with watery eyes. 'I knew someone would be able to do something.'

But surely this is a project doomed to failure, Greg thinks.

'All I want is what is rightfully mine.' She pauses, her lips trembling. 'I told you about that man hanging around my place. He thinks I don't recognise him.' She points a clawed finger. 'But if I ever get him on his own, I swear to God I'll stick a knife into him.'

'You can't mean that?' Greg says, taken aback by the flash of hatred in the pale eyes.

'Oh, but I assure you I do, Mr. Jacobs.'

'Well that would be pretty stupid,' Frances says.

The old woman glares. 'How do you mean?'

'You're not allowed to keep cats in prison.'

The old woman jabs a finger in Frances's direction. 'She doesn't miss much, does she?' She gives a brisk nod. 'I'll see myself out.'

'But what do you think?' Greg says, as they watch the old woman walk off down the drive. 'She does come across as quite mad.'

Frances looks at him. 'But I thought there was a lot of shrewdness there. And what's happened to her would be enough to drive anyone insane.'

He'd like to forget the whole thing, but he must keep his promise. 'That Bitcoin company means nothing to me but I suppose I could start with an on-line search. See what the internet comes up with.'

And is rewarded by one of Frances's warm smiles.

FOURTEEN

THE FOLLOWING MORNING, UP TO HIS EYES IN paperwork, Greg finds to his annoyance that he can't get the old woman out of his head. That educated accent and the look of hope in the faded eyes somehow made it impossible to admit that there was precious little he could do to help.

Mrs. Mehta, as always, pulls no punches – 'Woman's off her rocker' – but Frances has a different take. 'She's been robbed, not just of her money, Greg, but of the life she thought would be hers. Any wonder she's so upset?' Comments that make Greg view the girl with fresh admiration. Here is someone who has every right to feel bitter but instead is filled with compassion for others.

But for now, he forces himself to concentrate on the day's business. First on the list is the chair of a local housing association with a request for funding that Greg has decided to grant, provided the figures add up. Next, a woman from a local food bank has an enquiry about setting up another centre. He has a disused warehouse in mind but will need to talk to the local council and check the rental cost. Then there are two separate queries about sports facilities for teenagers, and last, and most interesting, a meeting with a potential donor.

He picks up the letter. The wording is old-fashioned and formal. Whoever this chap is, Greg thinks, he's not your run-of-the-mill type. But then with a House of Lords address, what would you expect?

Dear Mr. Jacobs,

I trust you won't think me presumptuous in contacting you, but I have a proposition to put that I am confident will benefit one of the numerous charities with which you are associated.

The language may be out of the ark, Greg thinks, but at least the fellow's done his research.

I realise it is somewhat short notice, but I plan to be in your neighbourhood this week and would be delighted to visit your offices to discuss the matter, at a time convenient to you. My phone number is listed above.

I look forward to hearing from you.
Kind regards,
Hamish Rosser.

Greg has never heard of the man, whose suave confidence gets right up his nose, but on the other hand, he can't afford to turn down an offer of funding.

PS: Doubtless you receive many 'cold call' approaches, but it may reassure you to know that we have a mutual friend in Arnold Leebury.

He must make time to contact his old friend although the last time they linked up, Arnold was up to his eyes with house renovations – and was obviously still head-over-heels with that glamorous wife of his. *If you don't stop your gawking,* he can hear Anne saying, *I'll push you into the nearest fountain!*

Greg spends the next half hour trawling the internet for references to Hamish Rosser. Amongst a host of appointments, the man chairs a major charity for disadvantaged children, is director of two orphanages and a leading member of the all-party parliamentary committee for the monitoring of substance abuse. He is also a wealthy landowner with an estate in Scotland and an address in Mayfair. But for Greg, the most important fact of all is that he is a friend of Arnold's. Reassured, Greg picks up the phone and arranges for Lord Hamish Rosser to call at the house later that day.

He's more than ready for his lunch and with Jason and Poppy at work, it's just him and Frances at the table.

'Thanks again for helping out last night.' He hesitates. 'I don't want to pry, but does Poppy talk to you about what's troubling her?'

Frances shakes her head. 'Just says she gets these awful nightmares.'

'Well, I've asked Mrs. Mehta to keep an eye on her.' He clears his throat. 'Jason's modelling contract came as a bit of a bombshell.'

'He's so dead set on it, Greg, I don't see how any of us could have stopped him.'

So she shares his concerns. A thought that comforts.

'I know you'll be worrying about him,' she continues, 'but he seems much happier. And it's great he and Poppy are getting on so well.'

'But how about you, Frances?' he asks, thinking how good it feels to be able to talk like this.

'My last two weeks at the nursing-home.' She smiles. 'I'll miss it, even though most of the residents don't remember me from one day to the next.'

He suppresses a shudder, recalling Anne's devasting illness: the loss of movement that felt as brutal as if parts of her body were being hacked away piece by piece. And, even worse, that occasional look of surprise, when a part of her brain registered that what she was saying made no sense and that if she just tried hard enough, she'd find whatever was missing…

'I'm so sorry,' Frances is saying. 'I should have thought – your wife…'

Greg looks away to hide his tears. Here for the first time is someone who understands. 'Those patients of yours,' he manages to get out. 'Don't know how lucky they are.'

Frances shakes her head. 'I'm the lucky one.'

'Well, I'd best get on. I've someone calling round later. I'll be offering him tea and as it's Mrs. Mehta's afternoon off, I need to check she's left everything ready.'

'Can I help? Bring in the tray so you don't have to interrupt your meeting?'

'That would be champion. Around 4.30. If you really don't mind?'

'I'll be glad to, Greg.'

At a minute after 3.30, there's a ring on the door. He pulls it open and a short man in a brown raincoat extends his hand. 'Greg Jacobs? What a pleasure! I'm Hamish Rosser. I don't think we've met since Arnold Leebury's wedding. Quite a bash, wasn't it?'

A younger man steps forward, a strong scent of aftershave catching Greg's throat.

'I hope you've nae objections to my assistant, Oliver Moorhouse, accompanying me?'

'Of course not.'

As he leads the way to the study, Greg tries to recall seeing Hamish Rosser at the Leebury wedding. But then he'd have been only one among several hundred guests. Anne, educated at Cheltenham Ladies College, grew up with the so-called great and the good. "You can always spot Old Money,' she used to say: 'they have cold bathrooms and an atrocious dress sense.' Certainly, it would be easy to mistake Hamish Rosser's baggy trousers and crumpled coat as belonging to someone on the breadline. Only as he crosses one leg over the other and his patent leather boot catches the light, does Greg get a glimpse of something different.

But the chap proves reassuringly easy to deal with and it's clear that behind that unassuming exterior there is a shrewd brain. And, by gum, his contacts! Discreetly hinted at, rather than spelled out, but leaving Greg with a clear impression of the circle in which he moves: members of the government, bigwigs in the Civil Service, royalty – all those who, with their skills and money, are the lifeblood of charity fund-raisers.

'Happy to put some of these people your way, Greg – if that's what you'd like? Also, I thought a donation to your local food bank.' He pauses. 'And also one to the Samaritans?'

'That's more than good of you. Really champion,' he adds, as Hamish Rosser names a sizeable sum.

Greg looks at his watch. 'Time for tea, I think. Excuse me a moment.'

Frances is already in the kitchen. 'Everything's ready, Greg. You go on through and I'll bring the tray.'

As he re-enters the study, Hamish Rosser and his assistant are deep in discussion. They move apart, as if caught in some clandestine act. A daft thought, especially as Hamish says: 'It's been a pleasure spending this time with you, Greg. We must keep in touch.'

'Indeed we must.' He looks up as Frances comes in with the tray. 'Oh – and this is one of my protegees, Frances Matei.'

Hamish selects a mince pie from the plate Frances offers. 'And how are you getting on here, lassie?'

'Really great, thanks. I'm just about to start my nurse's training.' She pauses. 'I couldn't have done this without Greg.'

'Nice to find a young person appreciative of her good fortune. And I take it you're not the only one he's helping?'

'No – there's two others – Jason and Poppy. They're doing fine too.'

'It must have made quite a change coming here.' Hamish pauses. 'But you were born in London?'

She nods.

'Any family?'

'Afraid not.'

'Matei's not a name you often come across. Never tried to trace your father? I can recommend some good websites.'

But Greg feels this conversation has gone on long enough. 'I'm sure Frances has things she needs to be doing.'

'Of course. A pleasure to meet you, Frances. She seems a very *together* young woman,' Hamish adds, as the door closes behind her.

'A good way of describing her.'

'But she looks to be in her early twenties?'

'Twenty-two in August.' He pauses. 'Why the interest?'

'My apologies.' He hesitates. 'If I'm investing in an enterprise then I like to have as much background information as possible. And I must say what you're doing for these young people is very commendable, Greg.' He tucks his mobile into his pocket. 'Very commendable indeed. Well, now I have the details, I'll get that paperwork drawn up.' He turns to his assistant. 'Time to head for the hills, Oliver.'

Greg has forgotten that the younger man is in the room. He's sitting slightly back from Hamish Rosser and although he's been taking down details of the conversation, he's remained silent throughout.

Yet as Greg shows his guests out, he's left with the cheering thought that the promised funding will really help things along. Impatient to share the good news, he walks through to the kitchen to find Frances at the sink.

'Mrs. Mehta will see to all that.'

'It's no bother. How did it go?'

'Better than I could have hoped. Hamish Rosser has made an extremely generous donation.' He pauses. 'But I hope his questions didn't make you feel too hounded?'

'They did a bit. He's Scottish, isn't he?'

'No mistaking that accent!'

'It's funny, but I've got a feeling I've met him before – or have heard of him.'

'No surprise if so. You wouldn't think it to look at him, but he moves in pretty high circles. `He does a lot of work with children's charities, as well as with the Samaritans.'

'I expect that's it.'

'Well, thanks again for helping out, Frances.'

Back in the den, he's grateful that this is proving to be another of his good days – the grief eating away at him less. He scrolls through his emails, Frances's words echoing in his head: *I couldn't have done this without Greg.*

In the early hours, he's woken once more by a piercing scream. With a sigh, he pulls on his dressing gown and makes his way upstairs. The rest of the household is obviously sleeping but if he's to get any rest, he needs to check that Poppy is all right. He taps on the door and puts his head round.

The night light is on and looking across he sees the two forms in the bed. So Frances has once again come to the rescue. What a treasure that girl is!

He peers towards the bed again and realises his mistake. There is no dark-haired head on the pillow. Instead, lying fast asleep is Jason, with one arm around Poppy.

Should he wake the lad and order him back to his room? Yet these are young adults and he can imagine all too clearly the kind of response he'd get if he tried. Did the ground rules he'd spelled out at the start cover sex? Greg feared not, so how could he have been such a blithering idiot not to have foreseen this scenario?

His forte is budgets and spreadsheets – clear-cut and unambiguous. This complication is the last blooming thing he needs.

FIFTEEN

A FEW MINUTES AFTER LEAVING GREG JACOBS' house, Hamish is driving them across Richmond Bridge, the grey ribbon of the Thames toning with the overhead sky, the rush-hour traffic throwing up sprays of water from kerbside puddles. All this endless, bloody rain, Ollie thinks, trying to shake off a feeling of despondency, heightened by the garish Christmas decorations strung across the lamp posts. He's in no mood for celebration. The way things are going, he won't even be able to afford a decent present for Amy.

Hamish Rosser sits impassive behind the wheel, his hands encased in the tan gloves punched with ornamental holes. How many decades since they were in fashion? And what is it about this ridiculous little man, in his ridiculous clothes, that makes Ollie so nervous?

He waits to be bombarded with a series of questions he won't have the right answers to: what has he made of Greg Jacobs? Of his charitable work? Of the young people he's helping? But the Scotsman remains silent and Ollie finds himself increasingly irritated. These meetings that he still can't make any sense of – getting up at the crack of dawn – leaving an increasingly disgruntled Amy sleeping. It's small wonder her patience is running out. He's stood her up a couple of times now, returning home too late to take her for a promised meal or to the wine bar, and all while she continues to pore over the documents in those folders: receipts, bills of lading, lists of names, some of them handwritten, some typed. She still hasn't been able to make sense of them. And what if all this proves a wild goose chase?

He clears his throat. 'So – when are you going to let me in on the big secret?' There's an edge to his voice, but is it any bloody wonder? 'What these different people have in common,' he continues. 'If anything.'

Hamish doesn't answer and he presses on. 'Lord and Lady Leebury, this Greg fellow we've just seen, and that boy, Jimmy.' He hesitates, his mouth dry. 'Maybe if you just paid me for my work so far, we could forget the whole arrangement.' Forget we ever met, he thinks.

The gloved hands tighten on the wheel. 'That wouldn't be a wise move on your part, laddie.' The voice is so quiet that Ollie has to strain to hear. 'Not wise at all.'

Why does he allow himself to be intimidated by this old fool? Yet the menace in the voice, the cold look in the eyes, turns his stomach.

'Now,' Hamish continues, his voice suddenly brisk. 'I trust that lassie of yours – Amy, isn't it? – won't be too distressed if you're a wee bit late home?'

Ollie looks at his watch. It's after six so at this rate, he won't be back for hours. And he doesn't recall mentioning Amy's name, so how the hell has Hamish got hold of it? 'You could at least tell me where we're going.'

'Back to town,' Hamish announces, suddenly cheerful. 'And what I can say, laddie, is that I'm starting to join the dots. So perhaps you'd be kind enough to run through what you've got.'

Why can't he stand up to this man? With a resigned sigh, he flicks open his notebook. 'Greg Jacobs,' he begins. 'You told me his wife died eighteen months ago.'

Hamish nods. 'Brain cancer.'

If he already knows, Ollie thinks, then why the bloody hell is he asking me to go over it again?

But it seems that Hamish has read his thoughts. 'Important to double-check the facts. Ensure there are no wee hiccoughs further along the line.'

'Greg Jacobs is in his late fifties. A few years back he and his wife set up a charitable trust.' He pauses. 'Not sure where all the money came from.' He thinks of the manifest Amy's spent hours poring over and feels a glimmer of hope. According to her, the list of names and the contents don't always match up. 'Something iffy about the trust fund?' he asks.

Hamish shakes his head. 'Jacobs and his wife had a big lottery win. Good question though.'

He swallows his disappointment. 'You've promised to fund his food bank project.'

'True enough. What else?'

Ollie peers through the windscreen. They've come to a standstill and the brake lights of the car in front gleam like blood on the wet road. 'The household consists of a housekeeper, who was out when we called, and his three proteges. One of them' – he consults his notepad – 'Frances Matei– brought in the tea.'

'And what of her?'

'A quiet girl,' he says, thinking how she had none of Amy's alluring spark. 'She's about to start training as a nurse.' He breaks off. 'I was concentrating on all the financial stuff, Hamish, but…' his voice tails off. Why is he left feeling that he's missed something important?

Hamish eases the car forward. 'Let's leave it there, but now we've another visit to make.'

'I promised Amy I'd be home by seven!'

'It'll do her no harm to be kept waiting.' He pauses. 'This is important, or I wouldn't be asking.'

Ollie bites his lip. He can't afford to cut loose, and anyway, a part of him – the professional reporter's part, he tells himself – feels drawn to the mystery of the story. He sends a brief message to Amy promising, yet again, that he'll make it up to her.

Hamish is pulling into a carpark. 'We're just a few minutes' walk away.' He swings out of the car, clicking the lock and setting off up the ramp at speed.

As Ollie joins him at the top, he realises that they're back in The Strand, with the familiar outline of the Old Bailey in the distance. Hamish ploughs ahead, the other pedestrians parting to let him through, and after a few minutes they arrive in the alley, with the same tall buildings pressing down on them and the rain dripping off the broken guttering.

Hamish reaches the door, but instead of knocking, extracts a key from his pocket. Moments later they're in the narrow hallway with its stench of cat pee and the broken phone dangling from its socket. They climb the five flights of stairs to the top where the Scotsman gives a brisk rap on the door facing them. Without waiting for a reply, he pushes it open, clicking on the light.

The room is as Ollie remembers – the same sweet stink of drugs, the bare floorboards, the grimy window and the mess of dirty dishes in the cracked sink. As he did the last time, he stays in the doorway, trying to avoid breathing in the fetid air.

At first he thinks the place is empty but then he catches a movement under the window.

'On your feet!' Hamish orders.

The blanket stirs and Jimmy clambers off the bed. He is wearing jeans and a sleeveless vest that reveals the needle marks running up the bruised arms. 'Didn't know you were coming,' he mumbles.

'And you'd have the kettle on if you had.' Hamish turns to Ollie. 'Or more likely have done one of his runners, don't you think?'

'What are you after now?' Jimmy says. But the boy's tone is no longer defiant. Instead he stands, shoulders slumped in resignation.

'I've come to keep my side of the bargain.'

The boy steps forward, an eager look on his face.

'You've brought more?'

Hamish pats his pocket. 'In here. But before you get your dirty wee mitts on it, I need you to do one thing.' He reaches into his raincoat and, drawing out a Jiffy bag, extracts a bundle of photographs. He sifts through them before selecting one that he places on the table.

Curiosity draws Ollie forward and he steps closer, catching a brief outline of a seated figure before Hamish blocks his view.

'Tell me if this is the one,' Hamish says. 'Take your time. You need to be sure.'

Jimmy runs his tongue over cracked lips. 'It is, Hamish. I swear on my life it is.'

'Good.' Hamish tucks the picture away leaving Ollie frustrated that he didn't get a clear view of the face – a woman's perhaps, although he couldn't be certain. 'We'll be on our way, Jimmy. It wouldn't do to keep Oliver here hanging about all evening.'

The boy stares across, as if he's only just registered Ollie's presence. 'He was with you the last time.'

'He was,' Hamish agrees.

'So, what's he doing here?'

'Just keeping me company.' He tosses a small pack at the boy's feet.

'You promised double.' He looks across at Hamish with bloodshot eyes.

'That was before you caused me all that grief. If you continue to behave, and keep your mouth firmly shut, there'll be plenty more where that came from.'

They leave the boy scrabbling for the pack and as they

go down the steep stairs, Hamish calls over his shoulder: 'That went well. Let's grab ourselves something to eat.'

All Ollie wants is to put a distance between himself and this man, but he needs the money he's owed. And if he backs out now, what if he's given the same treatment as Jimmy? He despises himself for being so weak, but what else can he do?

Twenty minutes later they are seated opposite one another in a crowded pizza parlour. Hamish orders food – garlic bread, pasta, beer – and they eat in silence, Ollie forcing each mouthful down.

Hamish looks at him over his beer glass. 'Whatever you have to say, laddie – spit it out.'

'Jimmy says he's done all you want. Could you not at least treat him a little better?' He knows his voice is shaky. Ever since he saw his dad beat the shit out of his mum, he's never been able to stand violence. Motorway pile-ups, street fights, even animal cruelty – he's never had the stomach for any of it. Which is why, he realises sadly, he'll only ever be a third-rate reporter.

Hamish leans forward. 'You need to understand that sometimes only certain methods will get results. Especially when you're dealing with scum like that.'

'He's only a boy,' Ollie surprises himself by saying. 'God knows how he's come to be where he is, but he's obviously not got much going for him.' He pauses, thinking of the Mercedes and the leather gloves and boots. 'Unlike you.'

Hamish grins. 'And you imagine right. But low-life like that must be kept where it belongs – at the bottom of the food chain!'

'For God's sake!' He hasn't meant to raise his voice, but the couple at the next table look up. 'You can't really believe that!'

Hamish leans across and grips his arm. 'Oh, but I do, laddie. Believe me, I do.'

A thought strikes Ollie. 'The boy says you broke your promise. How do I know you'll keep your side of the bargain with me?'

'My side?'

'I want my money – *now*!'

Hamish stares at the people at the next table, who look away, embarrassed. 'Easy does it, laddie.' He reaches into his pocket and slides a wad of notes, secured with a rubber band, across the table.

Ollie glances around but none of the other diners are looking in his direction.

'Go ahead and check it.'

Ollie hesitates before easing off the band and starting to count.

'Five hundred for now, as a down payment,' Hamish says, when Ollie has finished. 'And there'll be more next week.'

Elated, Ollie pockets the notes. There's enough here to give Amy the Christmas she deserves.

'But first, you're to carry out another wee job.'

'What job?'

'Let's finish this out of here. And then I'll drop you off at the station.'

Back in the car, Hamish turns to him. 'Understand

that it's starting to fall into place.'

Despite himself, Ollie is once again swept by a wave of excitement. Maybe the big scoop Jack promised will come his way after all. 'Yes – but what does that –?'

Hamish gives one of the thin smiles that Ollie has come to dislike almost as much as his persistent use of the term "laddie." 'In a couple of days from now, it'll become clear.' He pauses. 'And, as agreed, there's another wad of cash coming your way. No doubt that lassie of yours will welcome it – and you – with open arms.'

Why does Hamish have to keep bringing Amy into this? *None of your fucking business,* he wants to say.

'Now listen,' Hamish says as they draw up outside the station. 'You'll have tomorrow free so you can catch up with some of your stories for that local rag. Or have some down-time with that girlfriend. But the following evening you're to be at Salisbury station 4 pm sharp.'

'But that's Saturday!' he protests, thinking of the table he's booked at Amy's favourite Japanese restaurant.

'This'll be the last spot of overtime I'll ask you to do. Be sure to dress for the weather – and wear stout shoes. Now, out you hop.'

'But where will we be going?'

'On a wee hunting trip.'

'To Athelford Hall?' he says, trying to recall if the landed gentry go shooting at night.

Hamish ignores the question, instead holding out a sheet of paper. 'A shopping list. Bring all the items with you. Do I make myself clear, laddie?'

Ollie tries to recall a time he's hated anyone as much. If

it weren't for the money and the promise of this scoop, he'd like nothing better than to shove Hamish Rosser under the nearest bus.

SIXTEEN

THE RAP COMES ON THE FRONT DOOR JUST AFTER seven. In an instant, Ollie is down the stairs, seizing the package from the courier and carrying it through to the kitchen. The fridge emits a low hum and the house has the empty, hollow feel that he has come to hate. Amy, understandably angry that he's cancelled yet another evening together, has gone back to her mum's. 'You need to shape up,' she told him over the phone, 'and for once in your life, to keep your frigging word.'

But for now, he needs to focus on the job ahead. He lays the contents of the box on the kitchen table, ticking them off on the list provided by Hamish: a flashlight, a pair of strong gloves, surgical gloves, a roll of black masking tape and disposable shoe covers. He realises Hamish's reference to hunting was not to be taken literally, but this is the kind of stuff used in a hospital or – ridiculous thought – for carrying out a kidnap. Or is it so ridiculous? he thinks, recalling Hamish's brutal treatment of Jimmy. Hamish has also instructed Ollie to bring a credit card so he hopes to God he's not going to be asked to fork out for any expenses. He's overdrawn enough as it is.

As he stows the various items into his rucksack, he's once again left infuriated. Why all this cloak-and-dagger stuff? He's half a mind to call the little Scottish shit and tell him so. But anytime he's tried to phone, a bland Englishwoman's voice informs him that the number is unavailable. And whenever he tries raising his queries: what do these various manifests mean and how, if at all, do they tie in with that letter on House of Lords notepaper, the man's response has been the same: 'You need to work this out for yourself, laddie. That way it will be *your* scoop. Which is what you want, isn't it?'

And since that is exactly what Ollie *does* want, he can hardly argue with the logic. And anyway, what option does he have? He's in too deep, although he'll draw the line at becoming involved in any kidnapping scheme.

The train out of Waterloo is crowded, the aisles jammed with rucksacks and carrier bags of shopping. He's never liked this run up to Christmas with its reminder of the half-hearted attempts his mother made when he was growing up to give him a good time. Money was tight and the celebration dinners of his childhood were always the same: melon: not quite ripe enough, chicken, with overdone sprouts, dry roast potatoes and glutinous gravy, with shop trifle to follow. They ate early, after which he slumped on the sofa downing crisps and lemonade, while his Mum fell asleep in front of the telly. She's been dead over eight years. 'But you must still miss her?' Amy says. 'My mum drives me up the walls, but I can't imagine life without her.' Ollie shakes his head. How can you miss someone if they were never really with you in the first place?

He reaches Salisbury just after five and treats himself to a baguette and an espresso, before heading out into the wet in search of Hamish's car. When he sees the flash of headlights he walks forward and moments later is sliding into the passenger seat.

With a nod of greeting, Hamish pulls into the street. He's still in his brown raincoat and battered hat, but the orange scarf tied around his neck gives him a jaunty air. And for once he is full of talk. 'You've brought the list of items?' Without waiting for a reply, he adds: 'As I've told you, we're about to pay a wee visit to the home of His Lordship and that gorgeous wife of his.'

Ollie looks down on his jeans and Doc Martens and experiences a moment's panic. 'I should have worn something decent.'

'You're just fine as you are, laddie. 'Now,' he continues, as they turn off the main road and enter a wooded stretch. 'I'm sure you're wondering why I've not filled you in sooner, but the truth is I felt the less you knew in advance, the better.'

The better for *whom?* Ollie thinks.

'So, although we're calling in at the Hall, there won't be any welcoming party to receive us.'

'No welcoming party?' Ollie echoes, as their headlights pick up a cat streaking towards an overturned wheelie bin, the contents scattered over the wet tarmac. 'Hang on a moment.' How is it that Hamish always makes him feel as if he's missed some vital piece of information? 'What's the point of visiting Athelford Hall if no one's going to be in?'

'So we'll have the place to ourselves, laddie. I'm reliably informed that they're away at some pre-Christmas bash outside Salisbury. It's held every year and the staff are also invited. So that chauffeur of theirs will be driving and they'll be taking the maid with them. So,' Hamish adds, as they turn off the road, 'all I need from you, laddie, is a cool head. Think you can manage that?'

'Yes. But ...'

'Good. Because your job is to get into the house.'

Ollie stares at Hamish's profile. The man is focussed on the road ahead, his small hands in their leather gloves gripping the wheel.

'Break in, you mean?'

'Break sounds rather violent, don't you think? Let's just say you'll ease open a door nice and quietly, pop along to the library and collect something from the safe that's in there.'

Ollie is aghast. 'For Christ's sake – I don't intend to become a burglar!'

'You want the money, don't you?'

'Of course I do. But –'

'Then you'll have earn it, laddie.'

They are driving in through the iron gateposts, the headlights picking out the endless expanse of grass, dotted with trees and shrubs. Ollie wishes to God he were back with shops and people– not trapped in this endless sweep of desolate countryside – and certainly not about to break into a stately home.

A shape looms out of the mist and the car swerves, the seat belt cutting into Ollie's chest. Then, with a kick of the heels, the form veers away. 'Roe deer,' Hamish announces, as it bounds off into the gloom. 'Park's full of them.'

How can the man stay so calm? But then he's not the one taking any risks and, at the thought, Ollie's stomach knots with fear.

'Now listen, laddie,' Hamish continues, still in the same measured tone. 'No doubt the safe will have money and valuables in it, but they don't concern us and on no account are you to touch them. All I want you to remove is a small box with "Confidential" written in red ink across the top. Got that?'

'I'm not sure …' Ollie begins.

Hamish brings the car to a halt and switches on the overhead light. 'Take a look in that front pocket.' And as Ollie hesitates, he says: 'Go on!'

Ollie reaches in, his fingers making contact with a bulky envelope.

'Give it here.'

Ollie watches Hamish slit open the flap and extract a thick wad of £50 notes.

'Five thousand.' He replaces the cash. 'Breaking in worth your while now?'

Ollie reaches for the envelope but Hamish is too quick for him, tossing it onto the back seat. He pats his breast pocket. 'The same again once you've completed the next phase of the job. '

'And that will be?'

'All in good time, laddie.'

Ollie swallows. The money – far more than he'd dreamed of – will pay off his outstanding bills, with enough left to take Amy on one of those cruises she's always going on about, or maybe a holiday to the Bahamas. Aloud he says: 'There's really no risk?'

Hamish restarts the engine. 'Stake my life on it, laddie.'

The drive to the house seems to go on for ever, but at last the outline of the building comes into view with higher up, a couple of dimly-lit windows. 'Left on for security,' Hamish says and Ollie detects satisfaction in the voice.

'But what about CCTV?'

'Arnold Leebury has always been the complacent sort, so no worries on that score.'

They turn off to the side, driving through an archway into a courtyard where a lamp-post – one of those posh Victorian affairs – illuminates a stable block. Hamish switches off the engine. 'Now, listen carefully. You have the items on the list?'

Ollie pats his rucksack.

Hamish points forward. 'That door there,' he says. 'Do you see?'

It is ordinary-looking, small and painted dark brown. Compared with the grandeur of the main entrance, it makes this whole enterprise seem far less daunting.

'Staff entrance,' Hamish explains. 'Now – when you get inside–'

'But won't it be locked? And what about burglar alarms?'

'I'm coming to that. You'll find the door easy enough to manage. You have your credit card?'

Ollie nods again.

'You'll just need to slip it down the side and press it against the Yale catch. It'll open straight away.'

How in God's name does Hamish know all this? But the man continues speaking. 'You've brought the masking tape?'

'Yes. It's here, along with the other stuff.'

'Good. You'll need to put a strip of tape over the catch to stop it clicking shut and setting off the alarm. Now' – he holds up a piece of paper – 'Shine your torch on these security codes written along the top here. The first de-activates the house alarm and the one underneath is the combination for the safe.' He pauses. 'Dinna forget to put on your shoe covers and surgical gloves. We don't want you leaving any prints. Once inside, you'll find yourself in the kitchen. You go up the stairs in front of you and into the hall. You remember it from our visit?'

Ollie nods, recalling the high domed ceiling, the brass gong in the corner and the flag-stoned floor.

'You take the first passage on your right and go along to the door at the end. Open it, and you'll find yourself in the library.' Hamish pauses. 'The safe is on the end wall, covered by a Still Life painting – fruit in a bowl. You can't miss it – it's the only picture in the room. And remember what I've told you: you're to remove only that one box.'

Ollie takes the piece of paper from him, trying to keep his hand from trembling.

Hamish restarts the engine. 'Time for you to get moving,' he says, as he restarts the engine.

Ollie stares in surprise. 'You're not going to wait here?'

'Best to keep the car out of sight. Just to be on the safe side.' He gives Ollie's arm a brisk pat. 'I'll be parked at the top of the rise, a few minutes' walk away. I'll keep the lights on to guide you. Now, let's check our watches. It's just after seven. We'll allow plenty of time: Ten minutes for you to get inside and into the library. Another ten to open the safe and then you need to get down the kitchen stairs again. So, I'll see you at the car around 7.45 or as soon as you can make it. We need to be away from here fast.'

Despite his qualms, he's impressed by the way Hamish has thought everything through. Of course it will all go smoothly and in less than an hour he'll be back in the Mercedes, job done.

He gets out of the car, looking over at the back seat where the envelope of cash nestles on a tartan rug.

'Soon be yours,' Hamish says, following his glance.

Ollie picks up his rucksack, Hamish's 'Good luck, laddie!' echoing in the damp air.

SEVENTEEN

As Ollie watches Hamish execute a neat three-point turn and drive off through the arch, he fights off a moment's panic. The cobbles glisten under the lamplight, the only sound the beat of rain on the stable block. He pauses outside the back door to pull on the gloves and the wraps for his shoes. Now comes the tricky part. He places the torch on the ground and, extracting the credit card from his pocket, turns the metal knob of the Yale lock while sliding the plastic into the narrow gap at the side. Nothing happens. He takes a deep breath and tries once more. Still nothing. A sound like the bang of a door makes him spin round, but he can detect no movement and the courtyard remains deserted. With growing desperation, he has one more attempt, letting out a sigh of relief as the lock finally gives. He pushes the door wide, wedging it open with his foot while he tears off a strip of masking tape and places it over the catch. Then he steps inside, shining his torch over the metal box on the left-hand wall. He pulls open the cover and taps in the security code, his hands shaking. An orange light blinks on and then off. Does this mean it's deactivated? He should have asked Hamish for more details. When no alarm sounds, he inches forward. His torch reveals chairs, a long wooden table and one of those up-market Agas, with above them a row of bells set into a whitewashed wall. Ahead of him are the stairs, just as Hamish told him they would be. And once again he's reassured by the meticulous planning the Scotsman has put into all this.

Ollie goes up the stairs, holding his breath as they creak under his weight. He emerges into the hall, his torch picking up the floor tiles and the curve of the staircase. Then he freezes. There, over to his right, a man is standing. Ollie clicks off the torch. Christ! The place was supposed to be empty. He could make a run for it, but suppose it's that beefy Irish butler, who would overpower him before he was halfway down those stairs? The fear in his gut has turned to terror, so he waits. Above the thrum of blood in his ears, he can hear the tick of a clock and the creak of a stair. Still the figure makes no move. And then it dawns on him. He clicks on his torch, the beam spotlighting the head perched on top of its column.

Mentally cursing his stupidity, he moves past the sculpture, its wall eyes staring blankly out, and along the passage, the carpet softening his tread. At the far end he pushes open the door and swings his torch around once more. He's in a long room with walls of books floor to ceiling and everything smelling of leather, polish and dust. His flashlight picks out the single picture at the far end and he walks towards it. Now comes another tricky part. He places the torch on the floor, taps in the code and turns the handle. To his huge relief it swings open. He stoops for the torch and shines it inside. The safe has two shelves. The bottom one contains what looks like a strongbox holding, he imagines, family jewels and documents. Resting beside it is a tall stack of banknotes. He hesitates, a quick estimation running through his head: there must be fifty, a hundred thousand here. What could he and Amy not do with that amount of cash? Then he brings himself up short. One thing to be removing an item that will lead to the cracking of this whole puzzling case. Quite another to be a common thief that everyone would hunt down. Although he realises it's not the police he would fear the most. As Ollie knows only too well, Hamish is not a man to be crossed.

Ollie shines the torch onto the top shelf. It contains several large envelopes, title deeds and there, in the corner, a brown box with "Confidential" written across it in red ink. He stuffs it into his anorak pocket, locks the safe and, replacing the picture, moves out of the room. In the hall, he pauses, listening to a sound from somewhere below. Perhaps it's just those bloody stairs creaking again? He doesn't wait to find out, rushing down the steep flight and into the kitchen.

And now he's certain he can hear someone approaching so he needs to get out of here fast. He has another moment's panic as he struggles to remember the security code, but somehow he manages to reset the alarm, pulling the door shut behind him. He pauses to rip off the covers from his hands and feet before going at a half-run across the courtyard, desperate to reach the safety of the car.

The wind has increased, driving the rain into his face and he blunders into a pothole, cursing as his ankle twists under him. He stumbles over rough ground, the beam from his torch sweeping across dead bracken and the muddy ridges of grass. His torch picks up the outline of trees at the top of the rise, where a dim shape – doubtless another bloody deer – moves in front of them.

After a few minutes, he stops, peering into the dark. By now, he should be able to spot the car but he can see no sign of it. Has he missed it in the dark? For a few long minutes he continues up the slope, panting and out of breath. Then, almost weeping with relief, he makes out the faint pinpricks of the Mercedes lights. Whatever reservations he may have about Hamish, at least the man is keeping his word.

He limps up the remainder of the track. He can't wait to tell Rosser how smoothly everything has gone. He pulls open the car door and as the inner light comes on, he realises: Hamish is not behind the wheel. Where the hell has he got to?

Ollie gets out of the car and shines his torch around. 'Hamish!' he calls. Then he gives a start of surprise for there, sitting upright under the nearest oak, as if on a warm summer's evening, is Hamish, orange scarf around his neck and hat perched on his head – although much good it will do him in this wet. 'There you are!' Ollie calls.

No reply but he's in no mood for more of the man's games. All he wants is to get away from here as fast as possible. Once Hamish has dropped him off in London, he'll treat himself to a cab home – and phone Amy to give her the wonderful news that for once in his life he has a decent amount of cash.

He moves closer to the Scotsman. 'I've got that package. Shall we get going?'

Still no response. He raises the torch, the beam picking out the blue eyes staring straight ahead. 'Hamish?' he whispers, a worm of fear twisting inside him. He steps forward and when there's still no movement from the seated figure, he puts a tentative hand under Hamish's scarf and feels for a pulse. Nothing. In a panic now, he gives the man a brisk shake. The head nods forward and next moment he slumps onto his side, hitting the ground with a thud.

'Hamish – for Christ's sake. Talk to me!' But already a part of him knows the man is beyond help.

Ollie straightens. He must stay calm – think what in Christ's name he should do. Call for a taxi? But that would alert people to his presence. Return to the house? Pointless if it's empty and if those footsteps were not just in his imagination, the last thing he wants is to alert anyone to his presence. He could try and make it out of here on foot but it's at least a mile to the main gate and then there's that long stretch of deserted road. And who in this filthy weather is likely to stop for a hitch-hiker? There seems only one option.

He stoops, putting his arms around the shoulders and dragging Hamish forward, the boots catching on the wet grass. He may be small but he's heavier than Ollie imagined. Next moment, Ollie slips, falling back with Hamish clasped to him, as if in a lover's embrace. Why the fuck couldn't the man have had a heart attack in his own home? Ollie thinks, easing himself out from under the body. He shines his torch and the eyes stare up at him, as if in surprise at finding themselves in this situation. Ollie recoils. The only other body he's seen was during his mercifully brief stint as a cub reporter covering traffic accidents. The twisted form of that motorcyclist sprawled in the central reservation, his severed head lying a few feet away, haunted his sleep for months.

He can't bring himself to close the blue eyes, but he knows he must keep moving – to get the hell out of here as fast as he can. He stoops down, feeling in the pockets of Hamish's coat. He draws out two thick envelopes, a quick flash of the torch revealing the bank notes inside. No wonder Hamish wasn't bothered about taking money from the Hall safe – he had more than enough of his own!

Ollie stows the envelopes in his anorak before straightening and limping over to the Mercedes. Even though he detested the man, it seems important to treat him with respect – not to leave him exposed to the elements and God knows what else. Only the previous week Amy regaled him with an account from one of those thrillers she watches of a corpse's eyes being pecked out by ravens.

Then he remembers something, and tugs opens the rear door. There on the back seat is the tartan blanket with the second envelope of cash resting on the top. Ollie pockets it, before lifting out the blanket, and walking across to Hamish, spreads it over him, pulling the material over the head. 'Sorry,' he mutters, though for what he's not sure.

A few seconds later, he's in the driving seat. He fastens his seat belt and moves the car forward. He's never driven such a powerful motor and as it kangaroo-jumps, he curses it under his breath. But by the time he turns onto the main road, he's more or less got the hang of it, driving as if in a dream, the evening's events seeming increasingly surreal.

Thankfully, the traffic is light and he makes good headway. When he reaches the outskirts of Salisbury, he pulls into the side, searching his phone for the train timetable. The next departure for London is in twenty minutes, so if he's quick, he should just about make it. He restarts the engine and follows the signs to the town centre. His first thought has been to leave the Mercedes in the station car park, but it's bound to have security cameras, so he drives past the entrance and along a series of side streets. The area is run-down and the Mercedes will stick out like a sore thumb, but it's a risk he'll just have to take. He pulls into a kerbside space, getting out and leaning against the car. Thanks to the rain, the few passers-by are walking with heads bent and don't even glance in his direction. His twisted ankle throbs and he can't stop shaking. For Christ's sake, get a hold! He tells himself.

He gets out of the car and hesitates. He could leave the keys in the ignition – that way the Mercedes will be viewed as just another dumped vehicle, but when Hamish is found, people would realise that someone was with him.

Ollie locks the car and, pocketing the keys, limps towards the station. He'll work out his next move once he's safely home – and has some food inside him. It's hours since he's eaten and he feels hollowed out. He boards the train and, slumps into his seat, his jacket heavy with the weight of cash and that package. Too late to wish he'd never stolen it in the first place but if it proves to be the missing piece of the puzzle, that scoop may still be his. And he has the money. He'll worry about the rest of it later.

The phone is ringing as he enters the house. When he picks up, Amy's voice says: 'Where the hell have you been this time, Ollie? I've been trying your mobile for ages.'

'Sorry. I've only just got in from an assignment.'

'Finding someone's missing cat? Reporting on the latest pothole?'

She's obviously still pissed off with him. He longs to tell her about the terrible evening he's had but some instinct holds him back. He needs to work out how much to say to her – or to anyone.

'I've got some terrific news. I've earned a bonus – a large one.' He pauses, catching a background hum of voices, followed by a burst of laughter.

'Great.' Her voice is unenthusiastic.

'When are you planning to come back?' *Make it soon,* he thinks.

'Got to go, Ollie. My mum and her new partner are celebrating.'

He waits, hoping to hear her say how much she's missing him. When she remains silent, he adds: 'OK to give you a bell in the morning?'

'Sure.' She pauses. 'A bonus, did you say?'

'Enough to go on one of those holidays to the Caribbean you've always wanted.'

'Are you telling me this is for real?'

'Yup. Fill you in when I see you.'

'If this is a joke, Ollie, I swear I'll never speak to you again.'

'It isn't. Promise.'

'I won't be back till after work tomorrow.'

'That's great. See you then.' He rings off thinking how he'd give anything to have her beside him now, her body pressed against his.

He picked up a Chinese meal on his way back and dishes out dumplings, sweet and sour pork and Kung Pao chicken. He carries his plate into the front room, taking a large slug from the wine he's poured and collapsing onto the sofa.

Weak with hunger, he starts shovelling the food down, trying to push away the thought of what he's done. Because only now it hits him: Not only has he burgled someone's home but he's taken a car that doesn't belong to him – and left a dead body out in the rain.

As long as Hamish was here, assuring him everything was going to plan, his actions never felt that foolhardy. But without Hamish, things look very different.

'Christ!' he mutters, placing the package and envelopes of money beside the cartons of congealing Chinese food. 'What the fuck do I do now?'

EIGHTEEN

A MONTH HAS GONE BY SINCE THE ROW OVER Hamish Rosser and, shaken by Arnie's reaction – the first time she has ever seen him lose his temper – Magdalena has been careful not to raise the subject again. Yet just the recollection of the Scottish man's whispered 'Sorina,' fills her with panic and, to add to her anxiety, two days ago Arnie announced his intention to invite Rosser down for a weekend. So she must act fast.

To this end, she has worked hard to keep Arnie in a good mood, listening to his tedious account of a trade deal with some obscure African country, of the latest cuts in theatre funding and, on their return last night from the party in Salisbury, treating him to several glasses of Dom Perignon, followed by a blow job, which left him murmuring assurances of his undying love.

Yet now they are seated at the breakfast table

she feels less sure of him. He eats his bacon and eggs with such dogged determination, giving no more than an occasional nod to her attempts at conversation. But maybe this is because he is hungover? Or used to breakfasting alone?

At last he glances up and, to her relief, his face wears a decidedly hang-dog look. Two thoughts occur: First, gratitude that he is so easy to read, and second, that her plan may yet succeed.

He clears his throat. 'Afraid I had rather a skinful last night. But what a great evening.' He pauses. 'Especially back here when we – when you –' He breaks off, reaching for her hand. 'God, Magdalena, you don't half know how to turn a man on!'

She strokes his plump fingers. 'My pleasure.'

'And you're OK about my new post? It is taking me up to London rather a lot.'

'As long as you're enjoying it.'

'Thank you, Lena. And we'll have plenty of time together over the Christmas weekend.'

'I'm looking forward to it too, Arnie.' She bites her lip, trying to gather her thoughts. 'But there is something I need to discuss with you.'

'Well, go ahead then. If it's about that latest bill from Liberty's, I've already settled it.'

'No – it wasn't about that.'

'What, then?'

She stares at the debris on the table: the plates smeared with crumbs and butter, the cold slices of toast in the silver rack that Arnie always insists on. The puddle of coffee on the linen cloth. Why does breakfast have to be such a messy business?

'You suggested that we invite Hamish Rosser for a weekend.'

Arnie sighs. 'Not him again.'

'Please don't be angry. I know you thought I was being a teeny bit stupid when I asked you to have nothing more to do with him. But I had my reasons.'

'So, talk to me about them.'

As she looks into his round, good-natured face, she thinks: he has absolutely no idea. Not a clue, as the British would say. For them life is all one jolly treasure hunt, where hiding is a game. 'It's just that –'

The door behind her opens and Arnie swings round. 'Good to see you, Seamus. Are you over that virus?'

He doesn't return the smile. 'Sorry, sur, but you need to come.'

'Why? Has something happened?'

'We've found your Scottish visitor, Lord Rossur.'

'He didn't tell me he was coming, but show him in.'

'Can't do that, sur.'

'Why ever not?'

'He's out there.' He waves an arm towards the rain-streaked window. 'Afraid things aren't looking too good.'

And behind him in the doorway, as if to emphasise the point, is Marya, hands twisted in agitation.

Arnie pushes back his chair. 'He's been taken ill?'

A nod. 'I've phoned for an ambulance.'

'Good man. But what in the world was Hamish doing here? Did his car break down? Or what?'

153

The chauffeur shakes his head.

Arnie turns to Magdalena. 'You hang on here, Lena, while I investigate.'

Through the window she watches the two of them striding off towards the trees. Then turns to Marya. 'Why has that Scottish man come without warning? You don't think…?' She breaks off. 'I need to see for myself. Fetch my coat, would you, darlink?'

With the maid at her heels, Magdalena walks into the wet morning, a vicious wind tugging at the branches of the trees and the grass squelching under her feet. They pass Edna, the cleaning woman, and Mrs. Acheson, the cook, huddled together in conversation. In the distance she can see Arnie, with the chauffeur standing a few paces back, as if keeping watch.

As she nears, Magdalena realises that they are bent over a blue and green rug spread under one of the big oaks.

When Arnie catches sight of her, he straightens.

'So, what's going on?' Her voice is sharper that she intended.

He points to the rug and then she sees, sticking out from the far end, the head with its closed eyes and the material tucked under his chin, for all the world as if he's just lain down for a nap.

She moves closer. 'He is unconscious?'

'Afraid he's dead, poor fellow. Seamus has also phoned the police, who are on their way.' Arnie puts a protective arm around her. 'Don't stay, my darling. It will only upset you.'

She ignores him, stooping down and giving the pale cheek a prod. When there is no reaction and no movement from the chest, she straightens, filled with a sense of satisfaction. 'He is certainly kaput.' She looks round, and aware of Seamus's silent presence, adds: 'Important to make sure he is really dead. Such a sad thing to happen.'

'But what on earth was he doing out here?' Arnie pauses. 'He must have been coming to see me, although it's odd he didn't phone first.'

Marya steps forward. 'Maybe he felt ill and only had time to stretch under the tree when the heart attack or whatever it was took him?'

Arnie nods. 'He always seemed so fit, but often it's types like that who do just drop.' He points to the blanket. 'And where did that come from? I've never seen it before, Lena. Have you?'

She shakes her head.

'He's been out here a good wee while,' Seamus says. 'Overnight, I'd say. That rug is soaked through.'

Arnie's forehead creases with concern. 'I know this is hardly the time to be thinking of this, but do you suppose he might have been on his way with an urgent message? Maybe from the PM? Hamish might have wanted to deliver the news personally – he was always so considerate.'

Seamus gives a discreet cough. 'If that were the case, sur, isn't it more likely that Downing Street would call you direct?'

A look of relief crosses Arnie's face. 'You're right, Seamus. I'm not thinking straight – must be the shock.'

But what is less likely, Magdalena thinks, is for Arnie's chauffeur to be more familiar with the workings of Westminster than her husband. Whenever the Irishman drives them about the place, she's always conscious of him listening in to their conversation. And looking at him now, she realises that here is a man who drinks in every word.

'Well, let's hope these boys can shed some light on it all,' Arnie suggests, as a police car striped in yellow and black comes up the drive, with an ambulance following behind.

Magdalena swallows. The sight of official vehicles always fills her with unease, although as long as the man in charge is not some hostile pig, she should be able to handle him.

But the two figures who come walking over the grass towards them don't reassure. In the lead is a tall, black woman and beside her a younger man in a turban.

'Det. Inspector Johnson,' she announces, showing her identity card. She looks to be in her late forties, with shrewd eyes, the two deep lines running from each corner of her mouth giving her a permanent look of disapproval at what she's seeing. 'My colleague here is D.S. Janda.'

Arnie extends his hand. 'Arnold Leebury.'

The woman policeman ignores it. 'Lord Arnold Leebury?'

He nods.

She points around her. 'And these are?'

'Let me introduce my wife, Magdalena.'

Magdalena gives a tentative smile. It's always best to come across as subservient – at least until she knows in which direction things are headed.

'And these other two,' Arnie continues, 'are the maid and our chauffeur, who made the phone call earlier.'

The policewoman's tone is brisk. 'And the body is?'

Arnold gestures to the oak tree. 'Over there.' She moves forward and as he goes to join her, she holds up an arm. 'Please stay where you are, sir. My colleague and I need to take a closer look.'

She moves forward, bending over Hamish. She and her sergeant whisper together before she turns towards them again. 'So, which of you put the blanket over him?'

'I've really no idea,' Arnie says. 'Couldn't he have done it himself?'

Seamus clears his throat. 'Edna Cox was the one who found him. She came running over to my room to tell me. I'm usually up early but I'm still getting over a bout of sickness and was having a bit of a lie-in.'

Yet he looks surprisingly healthy from someone recovering from a virus, Magdalena thinks.

'If we could have a word with the other staff members?' the inspector asks.

Arnie beckons Edna and Mrs. Acheson forward.

'So, which of you first discovered –' the policewoman gestures towards the blanket – 'him.'

Edna, cheeks blotched with tears, a frizz of grey hair plastered to her cheeks, shuffles her feet. 'I always takes a cup of tea to Pete – he's my other half – first thing.' She starts to sob, and Mrs. Acheson puts an arm around her.

'Edna does the cleaning,' Arnie explains. 'That's Pete over there – he works as a groundsman.'

'I give him his tea,' Edna continues, 'and then I thought I'd cut across the grass – and that's when I spotted him.' She points to Hamish. 'Gave me a terrible shock, I can tell you, seeing him lying out in all this rain. I pulled the blanket off him and then those eyes were staring up at me and I realised...'

The policewoman turned back to Arnie. 'And I take it the deceased is known to you?'

'Yes, indeed. Hamish Rosser is a valued colleague.' He glances towards Magdalena before adding, 'and friend.'

The policeman is writing in his notebook.

'Scottish, was he?' the inspector asks.

'That's right. How did you –?'

'The rug is Black Watch tartan. Though of course that may mean nothing on its own.'

She pauses. 'And do you know if Lord Rosser suffered from a heart condition?'

Arnie frowns. 'If he did, he never mentioned it.'

'I see. And what about his car?'

Arnie looks blank. 'Car?'

'Well, this dead man didn't get here by himself. Either he drove or someone else did – you can see the tyre tracks.'

Magdalena stares. Why hasn't she spotted them before? Two parallel lines like coiled snakes stretching across the wet turf.

Arnie turns to the chauffeur. 'I assumed you'd taken Lord Rosser's car to the garage, Seamus – to get it out of the wet.'

He shakes his head. 'Might have done if it had been here. But it wasn't.' And as the woman policeman continues to stare, he adds: 'I thought maybe Lord Rossur parked it round the back, but I've checked and there's no sign of it.'

The ambulance team are approaching – two men

carrying bags and a stretcher heading towards them across the grass.

'If you could all could return to the house.' The woman police officer's voice is brisk. 'We'll need to examine the body and then ask you a few more questions.'

'Of course,' Arnie says. 'Such a dreadful thing to have happened, although thank God it seems Hamish went peacefully.' He pauses. 'But it's still a puzzle as to what he was doing out here.' He loops his hand through Magdalena's arm before looking across at the staff who are grouped together in a huddle, Edna still sobbing into Mrs. Acheson's shoulder. 'I know this has come as a shock,' Arnie continues, 'but the best thing is for all of us to get on with our work.'

'Oh, and no one is to leave for the moment,' the policewoman says. 'That includes you, sir.'

'But I've an important meeting in London.'

'We'll be as quick as we can.'

'Very well.' Arnie turns back to Magdalena. 'We may as well make ourselves comfortable. If you could get the fire going in the front room, Seamus? And perhaps, Marya, you'd bring us some coffee?'

Once indoors, Magdalena feels like skipping about the place. The Scottish man is gone! She turns to Arnie. 'At least he got you your government post.' *Your precious post,* she thinks.

He looks sad. 'Yes, but it's quite a shock losing a business colleague so suddenly – and one who was fast becoming a friend.'

'I do understand, Arnie, and I'm truly sorry for having upset you.' She pushes her tongue into his ear in a way that usually turns him on. 'Just put it down to another of your Lena's silly moments.'

He runs his hand over her bottom – a sure sign that he has forgiven her.

Their coffee finished, he pours himself a whisky and they sit on, the silence broken only by the chime of a clock. 'Wonder how much longer they're going to keep us?' he mutters, getting up and staring through the window.

Magdalena hesitates before moving over to join him. In the distance they can make out a second police car and uniformed figures moving about in the rain.

They are standing together when there's a knock and the two police officers are ushered in by Marya.

'All done, are you?' Arnie asks.

The black D.I. meets his gaze. 'Afraid not, sir. I have to inform you that we are now treating this death as suspicious.'

Arnie stares. 'How do you mean?'

'Can't give you any details at the moment, sir, but we will need to take statements from you and your wife, as well as from the other members of your staff. Meanwhile, I must ask that you remain here.'

Arnie sighs. 'Very well. I'll ask the Ministry to reschedule my meeting.'

'It is all too tragic.' Magdalena puts a hand to her face to hide her smile of satisfaction. If the Scotsman didn't die from natural causes, someone must have given the little shit what he deserved.

Then she freezes, aware that both police officers are staring across at her.

'Will that be all?' Arnie asks.

'For the moment, sir. The forensic team are on their way and then we can get things moving. We'll see ourselves out.'

As the door closes behind them, Arnie turns to her. 'I realise you obviously detested Hamish, but you might try not to look so pleased.' He hesitates, his voice studiedly casual. 'So out of interest, Magdalena, what *was* your reason for wanting me to drop my contact with him?'

NINETEEN

OLLIE IS ON HIS HANDS AND KNEES, CHUCKING UP his stir-fry into the lavatory bowl. As he flushes away the stinking, yellow mess, he wishes he'd gone easier on last night's alcohol, instead of washing his food down with wine, followed by vodka – Amy's tipple that he doesn't usually touch.

He hauls himself to his feet. Although up to now he's succeeded in blocking out the events of the previous day, the memories now unspooling in his mind seem even more terrible: his frantic search for the Mercedes in the dark and rain, Hamish's body flopped in his arms and the blank stare in the blue eyes. It's only now he can recognise the man for what he was: a player of games – a leopard toying with its prey.

It's not quite six – too early to phone Amy – but he's desperate for advice as to what the hell he should do next.

But Christ! his head is pounding and his mouth tastes like the inside of that toilet bowl. He swallows down a couple of painkillers before brewing himself strong coffee and walking through to the lounge.

In his drunken state the previous night, he'd flung the stolen box into the corner. Now he retrieves it, weighing it in his hands. It's the size and weight of a small paperback, with that 'Confidential' written across the top in red ink. Perhaps this will provide the answer to the puzzle he's been investigating these past weeks – or it might even be another wodge of cash. He's removed several £50 notes from one of the envelopes he'd taken from Hamish and stuffed the rest into a rucksack that he's hidden in the back of the wardrobe. He'll count it all later but, even by his rough estimation, there must be at least forty thousand there.

Now he has all this cash, he no longer needs to bother with the investigation. But his curiosity is aroused. He rips off the Velcro fastening that secures the lid and pulling apart a layer of tissue paper, feels a stab of disappointment. All the box contains is four British passports. He lifts them out, staring at the lion and unicorn crests stamped into the navy covers. He flips the nearest one open. The details are of a Carolina Maryna Koval, born January 1973. The second passport is in the name of Louise Elisabeth Meyer, date of birth August 1993. The third belongs to a Theresa Logan, date of birth November 1995, and the fourth and last to a Susanna Wilma Stepanov, date of birth June 1996. He draws in his breath, removing the passport for Carolina Koval and placing the other three side by side on the table. Louise Mayer wears her medium-length hair in a fringe; Theresa Logan's hair is cropped short and swept back from her face, and Susanna Stepanov's hair falls to her shoulders. He studies them again, but there is no mistaking: they are all photographs of the same woman. It's possible of course that what he's looking at are the faces of three sisters – obviously not triplets. But no, the images are all of Lady Magdalena Leebury.

He thinks back to his first and only sighting of her at Athelford Hall. She had the effect – as the very beautiful so often do – of seeming to be possessed of some inner spotlight that dimmed her surroundings, so that Ollie found himself mesmerised by the fluid grace with which she came walking towards them, by the large eyes and the soft lips parted in a smile.

But now it comes back to him – her hesitancy as she caught sight of Hamish and the look that crossed her face – trapped, panicked even. And then there was the Scotsman's question as they drove away. 'So, what did you make of our hostess, laddie?' 'She came across as afraid,' he said and Hamish gave a nod of satisfaction.

But of course, all this now makes sense, because you'd have to be an idiot to believe that to have several passports in different names isn't a cover for something. But why had Hamish needed to steal them? Or rather, to get Ollie to do so?

He gets up to pour himself some water and as he takes the first sip he thinks: It's because Hamish wasn't just a thug, beating up that wretched boy, Jimmy. He was also a blackmailer – and on a big scale, if that cash is anything to go by. But if Ollie has any chance of holding onto the money, he needs to distance himself from Hamish and Athelford Hall.

He looks at his watch. It's gone nine, so most people should be awake, including his friend, Nick. Well, 'friend' might be putting too much of a gloss on it. A few years back, when Ollie's career was having one of its rare up-moments, they shared an office. Since then, Nick has done well for himself, promoted to sports reporter, and spending enjoyable afternoons at football and cricket matches, county tennis and gymnastics, while Ollie still pounds the streets, covering petty burglaries, lost dogs and planning applications. The two of them used to spend the occasional evening in the pub but recently they haven't exchanged more than the odd text. Partly Ollie's fault – he prefers to spend his spare time with Amy. But during his recent visit to the office Nick did agree to go for a drink when he had the time. Ollie hesitates, but who else can he turn to?

He dials Nick's number. and a sleepy voice picks up his call. 'Fuck you want, Ollie? This is Sunday.'

'I need your help, Nick. I'm in a bit of a tight spot.'

'Well, ask someone else.'

Ollie struggles to keep the desperation from his voice. 'I'm looking for someone to drive me to Salisbury to pick up a car. Today.'

'You're taking the bleeding piss! Ever heard of Hertz or Avis?'

'I'll make it worth your while.'

There's a pause at the other end of the line. 'How much worth?'

'A hundred, plus your petrol.'

Another pause. 'Two hundred. Okey-doke?'

He thinks of the £50 notes stashed in the wardrobe, and smiles. 'All right. But we need to get down there as soon as possible.'

'I'm onto it.'

'Good. And for Christ's sake, Nick, don't let me down.'

'Keep your shirt on! Let's have your address and I'll pick you up.'

Nick rings off and Ollie, heart thumping in his chest, runs up the stairs to shower and pull on some clothes.

'So, how's tricks?' Ollie manages to get out, as they turn onto the M4 an hour later. It's important, no matter how terrible he's feeling, to come across as normal as possible.

'Not bad. Though Noreen – my latest – is playing up.' Nick turns to him, his grin revealing a surprising dimple in each cheek. 'That's women for you!' He's a squat man with thinning ginger hair and a large stomach that pushes against the steering wheel of his Mazda. He lowers the window, dropping an empty crisp packet that bowls along the road in the rain. He's had numerous relationships resulting in three or four kids, who live at various addresses with their respective mothers. Mothers who wanted their children – who didn't abandon them for hours on end.

'But fill me in on this recent fuck-up, Ollie. I take it you're following a lead?'

'Sort of.'

Nick grunts. 'Got a bit plastered, did you?'

He gives a weak smile. 'Just a bit.'

'So not in any fit state to drive yourself home. But sure you're all right now, mate? If you don't mind my saying so, you look really crap.'

'Yeah – still a bit hungover. But thanks for helping out.'

'No problem. Crisps in the glove compartment if you fancy some.'

He shakes his head, listening as Nick chats on about his team's winning goal at the previous day's match, and the interview he has lined up for an opening in local radio.

He wishes he felt more alert, but of course it's not just the after-effects of alcohol that's leaving him so exhausted. He's haunted by his memories: Hamish's patent boots catching on the tufts of grass as he dragged him under that tree, the thud of the head as Ollie dropped him onto the wet ground.

'Want to stop for a coffee?' Nick asks, as they move along the A303.

Through the windscreen Ollie glimpses the blurred outline of Stonehenge and shakes his head. 'We'll be in Salisbury soon. The car's parked near the station, so we could get something there?'

'Okey-doke.'

Half-an-hour later, they're driving into the forecourt. Nick hands him the keys. 'I'm busting for a pee. See to the ticket, will you? I'll be in the buffet.'

Ollie waits for the bulky figure to disappear into the building before limping over to the machine. He pays for an hour's parking, trying to tell himself that everything is going to plan. He just needs to keep his nerve.

He finds Nick in the café, seated at a table. 'Can recommend the sausage bap and fries.'

Ollie has no appetite, but orders coffee and a sandwich.

Nick gives him a look. 'That must have been one hell of a bender!'

He nods.

'Now' – Nick pauses to squirt brown sauce on his food – 'I know we're mates and all that, but how about you give me half that money now?' He pauses. 'Not that I don't trust you, but...'

'That's fine.' Ollie takes out two £50 notes from his wallet and, as he places them beside Nick's plate, his actions take him back to the boy, Jimmy, in that grim attic room and Hamish slapping money down on the cracked table. But just an hour from now and that whole nightmare scenario will be behind him.

'So,' Nick says, pocketing the cash, 'When are you going to tell me about this assignment?'

He pushes his uneaten sandwich to one side. 'Still in the initial stages.'

'Suit yourself.'

'Shall we make a move?'

Back in the Mazda Ollie, increasingly nervous, goes over the instructions. 'You just need to follow behind me, Nick. As I told you, we're going to drive into this place, I return the vehicle and then we travel back together.' They have reached the side street and there, sandwiched between a beaten-up delivery van and an ancient Renault, is the green Mercedes, its paint gleaming in the wet.

'Christ!' Nick says, as Ollie signals for Nick to pull into

the space behind. 'You didn't tell me you were in charge of *this!*'

'Yes – and it's a bit tricky. I don't want the people living in the place to catch sight of us.'

'Won't ask who you were with, though I bet your life there's a woman in it somewhere.' Nick grins. 'Need to keep it quiet from Amy, do we?'

'Something like that.'

They set off through Salisbury and head out into the countryside that Ollie only dimly recalls from his previous journeys. But then of course he wasn't driving, so he needs to concentrate to make sure they're on the right route. He could use Satnav, but he's no idea of the postcode – do places like Athelford Hall even have one? From time to time, he glances in the mirror to check the Mazda is still following. This whole bloody enterprise will be over soon, he tells himself again, although the journey seems far longer than he recalls – just this endless winding road with the occasional car swishing past in the wet. Surely it can't be much further?

Then, up ahead, he spots a familiar tree-lined bend. Just round this corner and the entrance should be further along on the right. He slows the car and clicks the indicator on. Behind him, Nick is doing the same. And, yes, there is the wide turning, framed by a pair of wrought iron gates. But Jesus Christ! Parked in the entrance is a marked police car.

He cancels the indicator and, putting his foot on the accelerator, roars on past. When he looks in the mirror, he sees that, thankfully, Nick is following. A few hundred yards further on, Ollie pulls into a layby, winds down the window and waits for Nick to get out and join him.

'Bit of a bummer that,' Nick says, leaning in through the open window.

'Someone must have reported the car stolen.'

'So how about we dump it? Wipe the steering wheel of prints and get the hell out of here?'

They turn up a deserted-looking track that leads into woodland. Ollie parks and runs a tissue over the interior and the door handles, before slamming the door shut and tossing the key into the undergrowth.

'Cheer up,' Nick says, as Ollie climbs into the Mazda. 'They'll find the car soon enough and as long as it's not been damaged, there's no harm done.'

As they pass the wrought iron gates, a police officer turns to stare after them. Ollie fights off the urge to duck down in his seat – only a few more hours to go until he's safely back home.

TWENTY

B Y LATE AFTERNOON, MORE POLICE HAVE ARRIVED,
crawling about the place. Uniforms are a shell, Marya
thinks, and the moment the wearers put them on, all
decency and compassion become trapped inside. British
police are said to be different, but you only had to follow
the reports of those scandals in the Met to realise that
officials are the same the world over.

But however on edge she may feel on her own
account, she knows this is nothing compared with what
her mistress is going through. That earlier euphoria has
gone, to be replaced by a trapped look in the grey eyes and
a restless pacing of the front room. From time to time she
glances over at Marya, as if to say: Don't leave me! A silent
message that turns Marya's heart over. Not that others will
perceive any of this, least of all that lump of a husband,
who sits, absorbed in his newspaper.

'For heavens' sake, Magdalena, settle down,' he says, his harsh tone stopping his wife in her tracks. 'I realise all this is upsetting your routine but it won't be for long.' He sighs. 'And do try, if you can, to think of someone other than yourself. It's quite hard enough to be told that Hamish's death is suspicious without knowing that it's probably the finish of my new career.'

'I'm truly sorry, Arnie.'

'Governments don't take kindly to scandals,' he adds, his tone softer.

Magdalena moves over to join him on the sofa. 'Perhaps you'd like a hot drink? Or a whisky?'

He looks up, registering Marya's presence by the door. 'More coffee would go down well. If you could, Marya?'

He's smiling but as she goes out, she catches his whispered: 'Let's ask her to wait somewhere else. I can't think clearly with her hovering about the place.'

In the kitchen, Mrs. Acheson and Edna are seated in front of the range, Edna's swollen feet, encased in a new pair of slippers, propped on a chair. Neither bothers to move as Marya comes in – something that unsettles her because it's been hard work making them understand she is the one in charge.

'Lord Leebury would like coffee, Mrs. Acheson,' she says. 'His usual cafetiere. I'll carry the tray up when it's ready.'

'How are they both doing?'

'As well as you'd expect,' Marya says – a comment that makes Edna burst into tears once more. What on earth has the stupid woman to be so upset about? But then she won't have had as much to do with death as Marya has. 'Oh –and put out a plate of those chocolate digestives for His Lordship,' she adds.

The cook makes a great show of getting to her feet, before moving over and switching on the kettle. 'Suppose you're not going to tell us what's happening?' she asks.

'You suppose right. Lord and Lady Leebury will fill you in when they're ready.'

'Stuck up cow!' Marya hears, as she carries the tray upstairs. But the remark washes over her. More caddisflies and anyway, she's had worse said. Far worse.

The Leeburys are on the sofa, Magdalena staring into the fire and Arnold absorbed in his reading. Marya pours the coffee and as she moves to the door, Magdalena says: 'Please stay, Marya.' Her voice is strained. She turns to Arnold: 'It's useful to have her around – in case we need anything.'

He lowers his paper, glancing sideways at his wife. 'Very well.' Is it Marya's imagination, or is the look he gives his wife not just lacking affection, but one of actual dislike? Of course he's upset about his precious Government post, but surely he realises Magdalena must come first?

There's a rap on the door and the police inspector and the sergeant are in the room and with a brief nod, turn their attention to the couple on the sofa.

'We just wanted to run through recent events, Lord Leebury,' D. S. Johnson says.

'Of course.' Arnold gestures to the seating opposite. 'Have a pew. It's a terrible business, but I hope this isn't going to take long.'

'We'll be as quick as we can, sir.' She remains standing. 'Although I have to inform you that the situation is looking more serious.'

'How do you mean?'

'I'm afraid that this is now a murder enquiry.'

Arnold clutches his head. 'But that's terrible. Who on earth would want to harm poor Hamish?'

'If we could just ask you a few questions?'

He nods. Beside him, Magdalena sits tight-lipped.

'So, Lord Leebury, you said that Lord Rosser visited you recently? When would that have been exactly?'

'Let me see – a couple of weeks ago.'

'And it was for what purpose?'

He pauses. 'Well, no reason to make a secret of it. He is – was – a man with considerable influence and it's largely thanks to him that I've been appointed to a government post.'

The inspector remains deadpan. 'I see. And you were also at this meeting, Lady Leebury?'

She glances up, her startled look reminding Marya of the one of the deer in the park. 'For a short time.'

'I see. And how well did the two of you know Lord Rosser?'

'We met only recently,' Arnold says, 'but as I say, he's been more than kind – and generous – to us both.' He looks across at Magdalena, who nods agreement.

'And yesterday evening. Can you go through your movements with me?'

'Certainly. My wife and I were invited to a pre-Christmas dinner in Salisbury. We attend every year. We left here at about seven.'

'You drove yourselves?'

Arnold smiles. 'The alcohol flows pretty freely at these do's, so we ordered a cab. Normally our chauffeur, Seamus – you met him earlier – would have taken us but he was recovering from the latest virus.'

'So he'd have been alone in the house?'

'Apart from our maid, Marya.' Arnold waves a hand in her direction. 'We asked her to stay behind to make sure Seamus was all right. He's been really poorly.'

'Ah, Marya.' The policewoman turns to her. 'We noted your details earlier, but perhaps you could tell us if you saw or heard anything suspicious during the night?'

She shakes her head. 'After Lord and Lady Leebury left, I had supper in kitchen. Then I went upstairs and turned down the bed.'

'Turned down?' The policewoman looks mystified.

'Folded back the duvet and laid out the nightclothes,' she explains.

'I see. And then what?'

'I had an early night. My room is on the top floor so I heard nothing.'

'And you were alone?'

'Except for Seamus. But he was in his room over the garage.'

'And is there anything missing from the house?'

'No – everything seems in its place,' Arnold says.

'Well, I think that'll be all for the moment,' the policewoman says.

Arnold clears his throat. 'One thing I meant to mention, though it may not be important – and that is that Lord Rosser wasn't alone when he came here. He had an assistant with him.'

The policewoman leans forward. 'An assistant? Who was this exactly?'

'I didn't catch his name. Did you, Lena?'

She shakes her head.

'And can you describe him?'

'Youngish – late thirties, I'd say. Brown hair, medium height. Nothing remarkable about him, I'm afraid. And as far as I can recall, he didn't say much in the meeting.'

The *caddisfly*, Marya thinks.

'Any idea where he lives?'

''Fraid not.'

'Well, let's hope that once the story breaks he'll come forward.'

A look of alarm crosses Arnold's face. 'Will this make a very big splash?'

'A splash, sir?'

He hesitates. 'It's just the situation is rather delicate. My wife and I wouldn't want anything to get in the way of my recent appointment.'

The two police officers exchange a glance.

'Of course, we're both shocked and distressed by poor Hamish's death.'

'We'll need to question you again, sir, as well as the staff, but in the meantime you can all carry on with your lives as usual.'

Marya darts forward and pulls open the door.

'Just before you go,' Arnold says. 'Can you tell us exactly how Hamish – Lord Rosser – was killed?'

'Not able to comment on that at this stage.' She pauses, the lines by her mouth seeming to deepen. 'What do you imagine?'

'Well, I don't think the poor fellow can have been shot – there'd have been plenty of blood.'

'Knifed or strangled?' Magdalena suggests.

There's a silence.

'We'll see ourselves out,' the policewoman says.

As the door closes behind them, Arnold presses Magdalena's arm. 'Thank God that's over. And sorry to be a bit off with you earlier, sweetheart. It's been a trying time.'

'No worries, Arnie.'

'At least Seamus is back on his feet, so if it's OK with you, I'm going to head up to town.'

She gives him an anguished look. 'How can you even think of leaving me, when there's someone roaming around killing people?'

'You need to stay calm, Lena. No doubt this is the work of some homeless junkie– Salisbury is crawling with them – and they'll soon catch whoever it is.' He points through the window. 'Anyway, the place is filled with police so you'll be safe enough.' He gestures towards Marya. 'And it's not as if you're being left on your own.'

'It's just I thought we might have…' Magdalena's voice tails away.

'I'll have dinner at the club, so don't bother keeping anything for me.' He gives her a brisk kiss on the cheek, and then he's out of the room, whistling as he crosses the hall.

Marya looks at her mistress and sees with a pang how drawn her face is. And maybe with reason. Because those two police officers didn't miss a thing. They not only clocked up that Arnold's main concern was this stupid government post, they also spotted Magdalena's hand move to her face when she heard Hamish Rosser had been killed. And it was not a gesture of horror, but one that was trying, unsuccessfully, to hide her smile.

At times of stress or when she needs space to think, Marya seeks the comfort of her bedroom, and this is where she now heads. She stands in the window looking out to where the rain beats down on the flattened winter grass.

For the first time in her life, she has found a refuge. But now, with some sixth sense, she can feel a change in the air – and one that is not for the good.

A movement catches her eye and she peers down. The Bentley has drawn up and Seamus, seemingly oblivious to the wet, is holding open the door for Arnold Leebury, who settles into the back seat. As the Irishman slides in behind the wheel, she wonders what it is about the man that leaves her so uneasy.

But for now there are more urgent things to think about. With a shake of her head, she returns downstairs to offer what support she can to her mistress.

TWENTY-ONE

A S NICK DRIVES THEM BACK ALONG THE A303, Ollie's thoughts bat backwards and forwards, as if keeping time with the sweep of the windscreen wipers. Has he really just dumped a stolen car and has a wardrobe stuffed full of cash, obtained by God knows what means? Knowing Hamish as he does, perhaps it's counterfeit.

'Must have a pee,' Nick says, pulling into a roadside café. Ollie follows him in a daze and he must have eaten something because back in the Mazda, he burps up pickle and cheese. He just needs space to think things through, he tells himself, leaning back and closing his eyes.

'Don't mind a spot of music, do you?' Nick says. A moment later Justin Bieber's "Stay" blares out: *I'll be fucked up if you can't be right here…*

A wave of fury hits Ollie like a punch to the gut. No one stays – not his mum, not Amy and certainly not Hamish, who should bloody well be here, sitting at the wheel in those ridiculous gloves with the holes in them. Ollie knows his anger is also at his own stupidity for having got himself caught up in this mess and because, underneath it all, he can feel the panic waiting to surface.

'Sure you're OK?' Nick taps his fingers on the wheel in time to the music. *I need you to stay, need you to stay, hey...* 'Always best to give the rozzers a wide berth. But why the fuss over one missing car?' He turns his head so that Ollie catches a waft of bacon breath. 'Suppose that's what you get for living in a big house. I take it there *is* one behind those gates?'

'What? – Oh, yes.'

'Something you're not telling me?'

He shakes his head.

'Know what your problem is, mate – you worry too much. In our line of work, you need a thick skin.' Nick overtakes a caravan before swerving back into the inner lane. 'That Merc will be picked up and returned to the owner. So mission accomplished.' He pauses. 'And you'll soon be back home with Amy.' He gives Ollie a sideways glance. 'How are things on that front?'

'Fine.' But oh God! – he hasn't phoned her when he swore blind he would. He struggles to remember their last conversation. Since finding Hamish's body, his mind has had no room for anything else. Will she still be at her mum's? But he'll text her from home when he's had time to think up a convincing reason for once again having broken his word.

A couple of hours later, they're pulling up outside the house. Ollie can't wait to be safely inside, downing his first glass of wine. He turns to Nick. 'Thanks again. Couldn't have done this without you.'

'You're welcome, sunshine.'

Ollie opens the car door.

'Aren't you forgetting something?'

His mind blanks.

Nick extends a hand, rubbing fingers and thumb together. 'The rest of the dosh?'

'Of course.' He feels a fool, fumbling for his wallet and extracting another two banknotes.

'Okey-doke.' Nick pauses. 'But how about a bit more – to make up for the additional aggro?'

It's not you who's had any, Ollie wants to say, as he hands over another hundred. Anything to get this man off his back.

'Thanks, mate.' Nick stuffs the money into the glove compartment. 'Good someone is flush. And just be grateful you don't have any exes going on at you all the time – they're a bottomless pit, especially around Christmas. Well, see you around.'

Ollie climbs out, shutting the door with a slam and turning with relief to his front entrance. A cardboard container and scraps of paper blown in by the wind lie in a sodden heap by the door. He'll deal with them later. He enters the house, feeling the emptiness of the place wash over him.

He lifts a bottle out of the fridge and, sinking onto the sofa, dials Amy's number. She picks up at once – a positive sign. 'Babe!' he says. 'Truly sorry not to have been in touch. I've been caught up in this latest assignment.'

'Another missing poodle?' Her voice is shrill. 'Or a row over building regs?'

'Nothing like that.' He hesitates. Better not to say more over the phone. 'Do you know when you're coming home?'

'Since when is living with you home, Ollie?"

'You're right. But I promise you from now on things are going to be different.'

'And how many times have I heard that?'

'I've been paid for this latest job so I'll be getting someone in to replace the boiler. I'll foot the bill, of course.'

Silence.

'Amy?'

'I'm not in the mood to be messed with, Ollie.'

'Listen – I've got cash – a lot of it.'

'You're joking me. What did you have to do to earn it?'

He's tempted to tell her about Hamish's death and the hidden banknotes, but then she mightn't want to have anything to do with the money – or with him. And he couldn't blame her.

'I'll explain when we meet.' He pauses. 'We could have a weekend away – maybe to that spa place you've talked about?' When she doesn't answer, he adds, 'This is for real, Babe.'

'You promise?'

'Promise.'

'That would be great. And I'll be happy to keep working on those stats.' She lowers her voice. 'Missed me?'

'Of *course*.' He daren't ask if it's the same for her.

'See you in the morning.'

Relieved, he takes another swig of wine before

switching on the TV news. There's no reason why there should be anything on Hamish Rosser. After all, thousands die of heart attacks every week. But for his own peace of mind he needs to make sure.

The reporter, a well-groomed middle-aged man, whom Ollie detests and envies on sight, is reporting on the latest nuclear threat. This is followed by an analysis of the further cuts to the NHS and coverage of the various wars. And then an announcement comes that makes him sit bolt upright in his seat: "Wiltshire police are investigating the murder of an eighty-five-year-old peer. The body of Lord Hamish Rosser was discovered early yesterday morning. And now – over to our reporter, Jenny Williams."

A young, bespectacled woman appears on screen, short hair slicked back by the rain, and behind her a pair of iron gates that look all too familiar. "Half a mile from where I'm now standing, a member of the House of Lords, Hamish Rosser, was found dead. The shocking event occurred two days ago, and I am reliably informed that he was stabbed. There is no information yet as to who might have carried out this terrible crime or, indeed, what the motive may have been, but we will keep you updated with further developments. Meanwhile, anyone with information that might assist the police with their enquiries is asked to contact –"

Ollie switches off the set and slumps back on the sofa. Hamish murdered? But the man looked so peaceful, sitting there under the trees, and with no hint of fear in those blue eyes. And a lord? Surely not or he'd have informed him? He tops up his glass, struggling to make sense of it all.

Hamish must have been killed when Ollie was inside the Hall. He runs through his mind the opening of the side door, the disabling of the alarm and then his slow progress through the empty house. That moment of panic when he thought the marble bust was an actual person, before he entered the library and, heart hammering in his chest, opened the safe and retreated through the house with that package. At some point he thought he heard steps, so might they have been the murderer's? And was Hamish the intended victim? Or might he, Ollie, also have been a target? And if so, for what reason? Suddenly, nowhere feels safe.

He reaches for his mobile. He needs to call the police and explain that Hamish was already dead by the time he got back to the car. But – wait a moment! He'll then have to explain his presence at the Hall and suppose they find out about the burglary? It would carry a prison sentence and there again, would he be believed? If he has broken into the house, the logical thinking will be that he has also committed this murder. And no doubt he'd also be pressurised into giving up the money. He places his glass on the table, feeling the sweat pooling in his back.

He needs to get advice. But from whom? Then it comes to him – there's only one person who may be motivated to help. For a price. But thank God money is now no object. *For Christ's sake, be there!* He urges, punching the number into his phone. It rings on and just as he's gearing himself up to leave a message, a voice says: 'Wasn't expecting to hear from you so soon, sunshine.'

Ollie draws in his breath, willing himself to speak slowly and calmly. 'Something terrible's happened, Nick.'

'Pinched any more cars? Got pissed out of your brain again?'

'I mean *really* terrible.' He pauses. 'The thing is, that Merc belonged to a Lord Rosser and –'

'Not the Hamish Rosser on the news just now? The one who's gone and got himself stabbed?'

'That's right. He and I were working on a lead and he asked me to get some documents for him.' Ollie pauses. How much is Nick to be trusted? But there again, who else can he turn to and now he's started he needs to keep going before Nick tells him what a bloody fool he's been and hangs up. 'So he drove me down to this place, Athelford Hall,' Ollie continues. 'Showed me how to get into the house and waited in his car while I went ahead and took what he was looking for from the safe.'

He can sense Nick's ears pricking up on the other end of the line.

'From the *safe?*'

Too late to take back the words. 'But when I returned to the car,' he continued, 'Hamish was sitting under a tree – dead. I thought he'd just had a heart attack, so I laid him on the ground and drove off. Well, what else could I have done? No point calling for an ambulance. The man was obviously a goner.' He pauses again. 'I really need your advice, Nick.'

A long sigh comes down the phone. 'Let me get this straight. You're saying that Lord Rosser asked you to break into a stately pile and steal from a safe? I won't ask how you got into the house or circumvented any burglar alarms there may have been. But then you get back to his car and find him dead. So you leave him there, drive away and phone *me* to help get you out of this mess?'

'I'm sorry, Nick. I should have given you the full story earlier. I just didn't think there'd be the need – didn't want to drag you into any of it.'

'Well, you listen to me, sunshine, and listen good. I want nothing more to do with it. Do you hear? The radio job I've landed is a fucking good break for me. So keep me out of this. I never burgled anyone's home. Never drove the bloody Merc. Have no knowledge of this stabbing.'

'*Please,* Nick. There's no one else I can ask.'

'Let me spell this out loud and clear. If you drag my name into it and the police come asking questions, I'll deny ever being with you. *Comprenez?*'

Ollie does, clicking off the phone with a feeling of despair. He gets up and starts pacing the small room. But wait a moment. Maybe – just maybe – he's in the clear after all. Because how would the police find out that he was at the Hall with Hamish? Nick is right. When the Merc is found, as it surely soon will be, there'll be nothing to link him to it.

He hears the sound of a key and turns, his heart lifting as Amy comes into the room. She's dressed in trainers and one of the short skirts that have become all the rage again. She's carrying her overnight bag so, after the usual cooling off period at her Mum's, she's obviously forgiven him.

He gets up. 'Am I glad to see you!'

'Wasn't sure you'd be here, Babe.'

'Well, here I am and – tell you what – how about you and me making a night of it? My treat.'

'You're having me on!'

He places a wad of notes on the table. 'Told you I'm pretty flush!' He hesitates. 'It's for my work over the past year, plus a bonus. And you've earned it too with all the hours you've put in over those documents.'

'Christ! Ollie. It's amazing. *You're* amazing.'

'Earned fair and square. Promise. And you can forget doing any more work on those files.'

'Great!' Her smile widens. 'Just give me time to get changed.'

As he listens to her moving about overhead, he realises that the only person who knows what's happened is Nick and he's not going to tell anyone. And now Amy is back, suddenly, wonderfully, everything is right with his world.

All he needs do is keep his head down and wait for this whole mess to blow over.

TWENTY-TWO

G REG STANDS IN THE HALL, BREATHING IN THE smell of lavender polish. It's the second week of January and stripped of Christmas decorations, the space feels cleansed and airy. He listens to the sounds of the morning – the tick of the clock, the clatter of pans from the kitchen. Christmas has gone better than he dared hope, helped by the fact that, after the long, dreary weeks of rain, there was a let up in the weather, a warm sun making it feel more like spring than winter. His various projects are going well and he's just received an invitation to take part in a programme on Radio 4 – information that Mrs. Mehta, Frances and Poppy greeted with cries of congratulation but which caused Jason to raise a studded eyebrow and mutter: 'Whatevs.'

His phone buzzes. He clicks it on and a familiar voice says: 'Greg! How are you?'

'Fine, thanks, Arnie. But what about things your end?'

It's the first time they've spoken since the murder – nearly three weeks ago now.

'Sorry not to have been in touch, Greg. This business with Hamish has been quite a shock.'

'And the police still haven't made an arrest?'

'Afraid not. Apparently a strike at the government lab is delaying things. My theory is that some homeless person or perhaps an illegal immigrant is the culprit. But I do wish the police would get on with it.' He pauses. 'I realise we've not been in touch lately, but it would be very good to see you. I know it's quite an ask,' he continues, 'but any chance of your making it down here this week? I could really do with some advice – on a related matter.' He pauses. 'There's few people I can trust.'

How great it feels to be wanted, Greg thinks, as he checks his diary. 'Friday seems pretty clear.'

'Excellent.' Arnold sounds relieved. 'Come and have a spot of lunch. And I meant to ask: how are your protégés doing?'

'Well, thanks.'

'Why not bring them with you? It would do Magdalena good to see some young faces.'

'Two of them will be at work, but I could ask the older girl.'

'Splendid! See you both then.' And he rings off before Greg has a chance to say that Frances may have other plans for Friday.

She does her studying in the front room. The glow from the wood burner forms a welcome contrast to the dark curtain of drizzle that falls steadily outside. She sits in an armchair, feet tucked under her, her head deep in a book. He gives a cough, and as she looks up he notices how her grey sweater matches the colour of her eyes. 'Am I disturbing you?'

'It's fine. I was about to take a break anyway.'

'I've had an invitation from a friend, who lives outside Salisbury. He and I shared a flat back in the day. He's got one or two things he'd like to discuss and I wondered whether you'd care to come along? It would be this Friday.'

She gives one of her wide smiles. 'Sounds cool.'

'Arnold and his wife live in quite a stately pile so it might make an interesting outing. And they'll provide a very decent lunch.' He hesitates. A visit to where a brutal killing has taken place might not seem so desirable. 'You remember Hamish Rosser – the Scotsman who was murdered?'

'The one I served tea to and who asked all those questions?'

'I realise you're not on social media so you may not know that his body was found in the grounds of Arnold's home.'

'Your poor friend. What a thing to happen!'

'Yes, it's been a bit of an upset.' He pauses once more. 'And I'll quite understand if you'd prefer not to come.'

'Good of you to say so, Greg, but it'll be great to have a break from my books.'

She gives another smile that leaves him with the ridiculous thought that if he were twenty years younger, he would be dancing around the room.

He's only been to Athelford Hall half-a-dozen times – the last for Arnold's wedding, when the day was a scorcher. But how different the place looks in the rain. As Greg drives through the parkland and the house comes into view, he wonders how on earth anyone could enjoy living in a place like this. But then he's never gone in for all this fancy stuff. There are still times he yearns for the run-down Yorkshire farmhouse.

The building facing him now is built of grey stone, with mullioned windows and chimneys like twists of barley sugar piercing the dark sky. He glances at Frances, who is staring, wide-eyed. 'Although the house looks sixteenth century,' he explains, 'in fact it was built in the 1930s by Arnold's grandfather, who used his fortune in the cotton trade to track down original materials – bricks, stonework, oak – and create an Elizabethan manor house.'

'It's truly amazing!'

He nods. 'But don't let the grandeur put you off. Arnold is one of the most unassuming people you could hope to meet. Especially as he wasn't expected to inherit.'

'Oh?'

'I probably shouldn't be telling you this, but he and his older brother didn't get on. Rupert was everything Arnold was not. Handsome, charming, a product of Eton and Cambridge – a playboy, as well as a gambler.'

'So, what happened?'

'He was killed on a skiing holiday in Switzerland. Both parents had died a few years earlier so Arnold moved from a small London flat to the Hall. Poor chap– I think he found it quite overwhelming.'

'And he's a member of the House of Lords?'

'A reward for cash donations. But don't get me wrong – there's absolutely no side to him. Arnold will take you as he finds you. He married late and my wife always said she'd never met anyone as beautiful as Magdalena.' For a moment he's taken back to the Leebury wedding – a Mozart concerto filling the air, Anne's arm linked through his. 'It'll be interesting to see what you make of it all.'

He pulls up outside the main entrance and as he and Frances get out, a figure comes striding towards them through the rain. 'I'll just park your motor round the back, sur. Turrible day. Best get yourselves out of the wet.'

They hurry across the gravel and up a flight of stone steps. Immediately the front door is opened by a short, elderly woman with straight black hair and round, expressionless eyes. And then Arnold is coming forward, hand outstretched. 'Good of you to come, Greg. Give your coats to Marya here and let's go on through. Our cook says she doesn't want the food to spoil so we'll eat straight away, if that's all right?'

Frances is introduced and they are ushered across the vast hall and into a dining-room where four places are laid at a long table. The gleaming furniture, the bowl of perfect cream roses and the fire burning in the hearth, are like an illustration from some magazine. A place like this needs children, Greg thinks. They're what fill a house – fill life, for that matter. Strange to think that Billy Boy would be in his twenties now – the same age as Frances.

'And here's Magdalena!' Arnold is saying.

As she comes into the room, Greg is struck again by the sheer magnetism of the woman. She's dressed in dark clothing, broken only by the gleam of pearls in her ears and at her throat. Beauty like hers, he thinks, is not a mere arrangement of features. As they settle at the table, he's reminded of Poppy – such a sweet-natured, pretty girl, but without that mysterious force that Magdalena brings with her. Not many women would warm to her, he decides, although she and Frances seem to be getting off to a good start– Frances answering questions about her training and Magdalena giving nods of approval.

'This murder,' Arnold murmurs, as the maid who answered the door serves them Beef Wellington – 'such a terrible thing to have happened.'

'It's quite a coincidence,' Greg says, 'but I saw Hamish only a couple of days before he was killed.'

'Really?'

'He came to the house to offer funding for a couple of my projects.'

'That would have been just like him. He was such a generous chap. What possible reason could anyone have had to go sticking a knife into him?'

'Well, I suppose a person of his influence is bound to pick up enemies along the way, and –'

'Must we keep going over all this again?' Magdalena interrupts. 'It's quite bad enough to have the police with their stupeed questions. Why can't they leave us alone?'

'They're just doing their job, Lena,' Arnold says.

Frances, who has been sitting quietly, looks across at Magdalena. 'I'm sure I'd feel the same in your shoes.'

She pulls down the corners of her mouth. 'Just looking at official uniforms fills me with guilt. Silly, isn't it?'

Greg has never heard her talk like this. Of course, he thinks now, she will have had plenty of dealings with the authorities and probably not positive ones. As he recalls the details on her file – her abandonment as a baby and the abuse she received from that foster family – he resists the urge to reach out and take her hand.

Magdalena gives a tight smile. 'The important thing to remember, darlink, is never to let them see you rattled.'

They finish their main course and the maid serves them Tarte Tatin with raspberries, followed by a cheeseboard. But the excellent food doesn't make up for the strained atmosphere and, despite all Greg and Frances's efforts, the conversation remaining desultory.

'Well,' Arnold says, 'if everyone has had their fill, you girls might like to take your coffee in the front room. I thought we'd go through to the library, Greg. Give us the chance for a quiet chat.'

Magdalena pushes back her chair. 'Excuse us a moment, Greg,' she says, with an unmistakable flash of anger. 'It's just that Arnie is such a hard man to pin down – doesn't have time these days for his wife. Won't even tell me what he's done with it.'

'Done with what?' Frances asks.

'Please, Magdalena!' Arnold says. 'We'll talk about it later.'

'More fucking hot air!' Magdalena declares, and Frances looks away, embarrassed.

'Sorry about this,' Arnold mutters. 'We're all under a

bit of strain. Let's leave the girls to it.'

In the library, they settle into two chairs. Greg glances around at the shelves of books. There must be well over a thousand of them and surely Arnold, who in his days as a solicitor's clerk struggled with even basic legal documents, won't have read more than a handful? For all its priceless artefacts, Greg thinks, Athelford Hall is more a museum than a home.

'I must apologise again for Lena,' Arnold is saying. 'Once she gets an idea into her head, there's simply no arguing with her. I keep telling her to stop being paranoid.'

'What's she so worried about? I don't understand.'

Arnold hands him his coffee. 'She says that a bible of her mother's has gone missing from the safe. Of course I understand why she's upset. It obviously means a great deal to her.'

Greg stares. 'From the safe? You don't think this might be connected to the murder?'

'I doubt that. I did suggest she mention it to the police but she said it wasn't worth bothering them. And she's probably right.' He sighs. 'And then of course she was dead set against my taking up this ministerial post.'

'Ministerial? You're a dark horse, Arnold! Are congratulations in order?'

'I didn't say anything over lunch because Magdalena really got herself worked up about it. But to be honest, I was chuffed to bits when I heard.'

'But she'll come round, won't she?'

Arnold leans forward. 'This is where I'd value your advice. It was Hamish who put my name forward and the

PM's office have assured me his death won't affect anything. But you've seen how Magdalena is – losing her temper over the smallest thing.' He puts down his cup. 'And the truth is, Greg, I do feel guilty. I've always assured her that our lives would be centred around our home and social activities. And of course this job may well put paid to all that.'

Who would have imagined, Greg thinks, that staid, unambitious Arnold, should end up, not just with a beautiful wife and a landed estate, but also with a government post? Not that he envies him any of it.

'I honestly don't know what to do,' Arnold continues. 'Maybe I should just resign the post?'

'I'd like to be able to help, but as you know, there's not an ounce of the politician in me.'

'I realise that, and it's one of the reasons I'm asking. Magdalena seems willing to go along with it, but she's still so stressed.'

Greg sips his coffee, struggling to find the words that might help. 'Goodness knows, Anne and I had our ups and downs. What marriage doesn't? But we weathered them, so given time no doubt this whole thing will blow over. Especially as you say that Magdalena is now willing to support you.'

Arnold takes another sip of his coffee. 'You're right.'

'So I don't understand what the problem is.'

Arnold frowns. 'Although Magdalena only met Hamish a couple of times, she really took against him.' He pauses. 'She's not merely relieved that he's no longer around. She seems triumphant about it – if that doesn't sound too strange?'

'But just because the two of them got off on the wrong foot, doesn't mean she'd be *pleased* that Hamish Rosser is dead. If that's what you're suggesting?'

'Of course not,' Arnold's voice is clipped. 'Let's just leave it there.'

But looking at the lines etched across his friend's forehead and the strained look in his eyes, Greg is left wondering what it is that Arnold's not telling him.

TWENTY-THREE

MAGDALENA WATCHES THE TWO MEN WALK OFF towards the library, Arnie nodding over his shoulder at something Greg is telling him. She can see why they get on so well. They are both reliable, conscientious, and very – she gropes for the English word – "solid." And already, as she ushers the young girl, Frances, into the front room, she regrets having lost her temper with Arnie. But why couldn't he admit that he must have lifted out the package by mistake and will have a proper search for it?

Of course she knew the risk in keeping the passports but always at the back of her mind was the thought that one day she might need to make a quick get-away. And now, even with Hamish Rosser gone, she has lost that safety net.

As she watches Marya slip silently out of the room, she realises there is fresh cause for worry. What is it that her husband needs to discuss with Greg Jacobs that can't be said in front of her? She's always been careful not to give Arnie reason to doubt her, but suppose…?

'Goodness!' Frances is staring around her. 'Is that suit of armour real?'

'Fraid so, darlink. Now – you must tell me more about your plans when you qualify.' Why, given the state of the British health service, anyone would want to be a nurse is beyond her, but she likes hearing this girl talk. Likes the way there seems no side to her.

She thinks of the wives of Arnie's friends, who don't bother to conceal their envy of her looks and lifestyle. 'Spoilt bitch,' she overheard one of them whisper. 'Why he doesn't he see through her is beyond me.' Although she tried to dismiss the comments, the truth was that they cut. These women couldn't imagine what it's taken to get where she is – and to understand that when she and Arnie met, she had no idea of his wealth.

After working her way up in an exclusive London restaurant, she finally landed a job as Front of House Manager. As she was checking through the day's menu, her attention was caught by a man sitting by himself at a corner table. He seemed unremarkable – middle-aged, plump and balding – yet something made her walk over to him. 'I hope everything's to your satisfaction, sir?' she smiled.

He looked up, his face wearing a decidedly moonstruck look. 'Thank you – yes.' He paused. 'Name's Arnold. I came in here with a friend last week.' A flush spread over his neck and cheeks. 'I hoped I'd spot you again.'

'I work most evenings,' she replied, topping up his wine glass. 'To fund my studies.'

He invited her for a late-night drink and listened, eyes filled with sympathy, as she told him of how much she missed her parents, whose hard-earned savings had enabled her to leave their country; of how, once she had enough put by, she planned to return to study economics or accountancy.

From there, how quickly things had moved on.

She was used to a different breed of man: one who treated women like possessions or conquests, and from the start she was touched, not just by his generous gifts, but also by his tentative suggestions that they have dinner together or take in a show. And if his early attempts at lovemaking were clumsy, this was more than compensated for by the enjoyment she took in teaching him how to give and receive pleasure.

A few months after their first date, he took her down to Athelford Hall. 'I never expected to inherit, but then my older brother, Rupert, was killed.' He waved a plump hand towards the damp patches on the ceiling, the rotting floorboards and the paper hanging in skin-like strips off the walls. 'My parents would have hated to see how Rupert let the place go, but I'm afraid I'm not much good at sorting it either.'

Magdalena smiled. 'It needs life breathing into it, darlink.'

'Into me,' he said, putting a plump arm around her.

Of course, she's enjoyed renovating the Hall and choosing the finest of everything – silk fabrics, Egyptian cotton sheets, her pick of glass and porcelain. But money is precious, she realises, not because of what it buys, but because of what it can conceal. So now, whenever she wears the latest designer frock or twists a strand of Hatton Garden pearls around her neck, it feels as if she is putting on an impermeable layer that will act as a protection against the thinly-veiled hostility of the world…

She comes to with a start to find Frances sitting silently beside her, sipping her coffee.

'I've been miles away,' she apologises.

'No worries. I'm enjoying the quiet too. And –'

Marya is in the doorway. 'Those two police officers are here again, Madam. They've been talking with Lord Leebury and are asking to see you.'

'How tedious,' Magdalena murmurs. 'You'd better show them in.' She turns to Frances. 'Sorry about this, darlink. Hopefully they won't take up much of our time.'

Frances looks thoughtful. 'It's funny how in a film or book a murder can seem exciting – fun almost – but in real life it's such a truly horrible thing.'

Magdalena wonders what this girl would think if she knew the pleasure she'd taken at the sight of Hamish Rosser's body stretched out on the wet grass. If she knew –

Arnie and Greg are in the room, with Inspector Johnson and D. S. Janda behind them. Magdalena can't decide which of the two officers she mistrusts the most – the tall, black woman with her mouth downturned in a permanent look of disapproval, or her lean, turbaned assistant, whose eyes don't seem to miss a trick. 'Afternoon, Lady Leebury,' he says. 'OK if we ask you a few more questions?'

People like this never wait for permission, Magdalena thinks, signalling to Marya to remain inside the door.

'We're still trying to piece together Hamish Rosser's last moves,' Inspector Johnson says, 'and wanted to check if there's anything more you can add.'

Magdalena is now on full alert. The murder was nearly three weeks ago, so what are they after *this* time. And although the missing package has nothing to do with the killing, the last thing she wants is for Arnie to draw attention to it. 'I would like to help, but I've already told you all I know.' She lowers her eyes. The important thing to remember is always to give away as little as possible.

'I've just been telling the officers that Hamish Rosser visited me a couple of days before he was killed,' Greg Jacobs is saying.

'Quite a coincidence,' D. S. Janda says. 'You said you discussed your charity work, Mr. Jacobs?'

'As I've explained, he offered funding for a new food bank as well as the local branch of the Samaritans. The chap was only in the house a couple of hours. Frances saw him, of course.'

'That's right,' she says.' I brought in the tea and he and Greg – Mr. Jacobs – were just talking together.'

'So, Frances – anything about this man, Hamish Rosser, strike you? Did he seem particularly anxious or agitated for instance?'

She shakes her head. 'I don't think so. And I don't

remember his assistant saying anything – he just sat there taking notes.'

The policewoman looks across at Arnie and Greg. 'You've both mentioned this man. Do you remember his name?'

'I think Hamish Rosser called him Oliver,' Greg says.

'None of you can recall anything else about him? His surname, for instance?'

A general shaking of heads.

'That's a pity. We're very keen to trace him. As he was also at the meeting here, he may be a significant witness.'

'Well,' Arnie says, in the voice Magdalena recognises as his it's-time-to-wrap-this-up voice, 'if there's nothing more…?'

The policewoman treats him to a cool stare. 'For the moment – no. But obviously if you think of anything else, please let us know. Lord and Lady Leebury – we'll need you to come to the Salisbury station to make full statements. And we will also be questioning the other members of the household.' She consults her pocketbook. 'If you could just verify their names again?'

'Of course. There's our chauffeur, Seamus Doyle, who also acts as butler. Mrs. Acheson, our cook. Edna, who does the cleaning and her husband, Peter Cox, who's our head groundsman. Oh, and my wife's maid, Marya Bondar.'

'Quite a houseful,' D. S. Janda remarks. 'And can you confirm that you and your wife weren't at Athelford Hall on the night Hamish Rosser was killed?'

'As I've already explained, we were out all evening at a

pre-Christmas party.' Arnie hesitates. 'When did you say the killing took place?'

'The post-mortem and DNA results are still not through,' Inspector Johnson's disapproving gaze sweeps the room. 'Which of course complicates matters.'

'Good God!' Arnie exclaims. 'You surely don't think that anyone here …?'

'Let's just leave it there for the moment, sir.'

Magdalena follows the police officers into the hall where, with that unnerving knack of being able to anticipate their every move, Seamus waits by the front door. 'Anuther turrible day,' he remarks as he pulls it open. The patter of rain on the steps carries towards them and, above that, a crash that makes the police officers swing round.

Edna is by the Roman bust, the bucket she has dropped pooling water over her pink slippers. Really the woman has no idea how to behave. And what's she doing out here when she should be cleaning the upstairs?

'Sorry – it just slipped,' she mutters.

'Easily mopped up,' Arnie smiles. 'As long as you're all right, Edna?'

But the response sets off another of her tiresome crying fits.

D. S. Janda looks across at her. 'You've told us you didn't know the deceased personally, Mrs. Cox?'

'That's right,' she sniffs. 'But it still gave me a turn finding him lying out like that in all the cold and rain.'

'Why don't you get yourself a cup of tea, Edna?' Arnie suggests.

She shuffles off, wiping her eyes on her sleeve and, to Magdalena's relief, the police officers move past and head to their car.

Greg extends a hand. 'Frances and I must be on our way too, Arnie. Always great to see you. And you too of course, Magdalena,' he says, blushing in a way that she finds endearing. 'And thanks for the delicious meal.'

The girl steps forward. 'And I'm really grateful to you for including me.'

'You must visit us again,' Magdalena finds herself saying, 'so we can continue our talk.'

'I'd love that.' She leans forward and kisses Magdalena's cheek.

'What a delightful girl,' Arnie says, as Seamus closes the door on them.

'And he's obviously *extremely* taken with her.'

'Not in that way, surely? Anne's only been dead a couple of years!'

Arnie hasn't a clue! she thinks. Aloud she says: 'Well, he was certainly giving her some very fond looks.' She pauses. 'And we know that age is no barrier to a good marriage.'

They exchange a smile.

Encouraged, she says: 'Perhaps, darlink, we could sit together?'

'Afraid I do need to get on, Lena.' His tone is brisk. 'I owe it to Hamish to make a success of this new appointment.'

'Please don't be angry, Arnie, but my mother's bible and icon are very precious. I just want to make sure you've not seen them.' She hesitates. 'We change the combination each month and you're the only other person who knows it.'

'So I would hope!' His voice rises. 'It is *my* safe, in *my* house.' He glances away, biting his lip. 'I hope you're not accusing me of theft?'

'Maybe you've removed them in an absent-minded moment. If so, I'd quite understand.'

'I may be older than you, Magdalena, but I'm not yet senile! Now for God's sake, give me some peace!'

She turns from him, running up the broad stairs to her room. Once there, she flings herself on the bed, beating her fists into the pillow and crying tears of frustration.

After a few moments, she feels Marya's hand on her shoulder.

'Tell me what's making you so upset. You've been like this for days.' She holds out a handkerchief and Magdalena sits up, wiping her eyes. 'Oh, Marya – the passports are gone.'

'From the safe?' Marya puts her hand to her throat. 'How can that be?'

'Nothing else was taken and –' she pauses – 'only Arnie and I have the code.' She stares up at her. 'He's always so open and honest, but I know he's hiding something. And if the information gets into the wrong hands...' her voice tails off.

'...It will be the finish of us,' Marya murmurs.

TWENTY-FOUR

Amy's breath is on his cheek and with the warm curve of her bottom pressed against him, Ollie is filled with a sense of well-being. He's bought her the gold bracelet she spotted in a jeweller's window and treated them both to an eye-wateringly expensive Thai meal – things that only two days earlier would have been beyond his wildest fantasy. As is her praise which, understandably, has been effusive. 'You're incredible, Ollie – simply the best.'

Now, however, his fragile sense of contentment evaporates. He's not told her about the rucksack stuffed with cash or about his involvement in Hamish's death. When she finds out, how could she possibly view him as other than a liar and a thief? And once again he's haunted by a picture of the Scotsman sitting upright under that oak, the blue eyes staring straight at him, as if in accusation. And no wonder.

The man wasn't dead from some heart attack or stroke – he was murdered. Perhaps there was something that he, Ollie, could and should have done to prevent it?

The headlights of early traffic sweep like searchlights across the ceiling. He cups one of Amy's plump breasts and as she turns towards him, nuzzling his shoulder, he thinks how perfect life would be if only the Scottish man hadn't gone and got himself killed.

He disentangles himself from Amy and eases himself off the bed, trying to control his panic. Presumably the Mercedes has now been found and if the police do come knocking on his door, he can deny being at Atherton Hall on the night of the murder.

Once downstairs, he makes himself a coffee and peers through the window at the wet morning. He switches on the gas fire – at least he can now afford the bill – registering the fact that Amy has hoovered and dusted. He must remember to thank her. A pile of stock-taking forms is stacked on the coffee table and beside them the passports and folders. He flips the top one open to reveal a sheet of paper filled with Amy's looped writing. She's been spending an increasing amount of time on the project and as he scans the lists she's made – dozens of shipments with their specifications and departure and arrival times from Felixstowe, Marseilles, Rotterdam and Portsmouth – it still makes little sense. So the best thing would be for him to bin the whole bloody lot. Whatever information Hamish had has gone with him to his grave, but still Ollie's left frustrated. What the hell was the man up to?

Amy is moving about overhead, so time to join her

in the shower. As they soap one another down, he can't remember the last time he's felt as loved, or as wanted.

'Let's go out to lunch,' she says, after they've made love, 'Maybe to that pub with the jazz band?'

'Perfect!'

He's upstairs shaving, humming a Louis Armstrong number, when there's a ring on the doorbell. Seconds later, he hears voices and Amy yells up the stairs: 'It's the police, Ollie. They need to talk to you.'

For a second he stands frozen, before drying off his face and forcing his lips into a tight smile. He just needs to sweat this out.

The front room, small at the best of times, seems dwarfed by the two police officers – Inspector Johnson, a middle-aged black woman, and a turbaned man – who flash their identity cards, then stand looking about them. Following their gaze, Ollie sees with dismay that the files are still spread over the coffee table. 'Excuse me a sec,' he says, brushing past and gathering up the folders, together with the passports.

'You look as if you've been busy, sir.'

'Working on a story.'

'You're a journalist?'

He nods, shoving the passports into his pocket and bundling up the files and carrying them through to the kitchen. When he returns, the woman inspector takes out her pocketbook. 'OK if we have a seat?'

He nods, watching as they settle on the sofa.

'We're here to ask you a few questions about the murder of Hamish Rosser. No doubt you've seen the reports?'

He hesitates. 'There was something on the news. Terrible, isn't it?'

'Murder?' Amy says from the doorway. She's wearing a short leather skirt with calf length boots and a denim jacket. She tosses her hair back from her face. 'You never told me you were working on anything like that, Ollie?'

'I wasn't.' Maybe he's said that a little too quickly?

'And you are?' Inspector Johnson asks.

'Amy Phillips. Ollie's girlfriend.'

'And you live here, Ms Phillips?'

'Part of the week.'

'So were you here on Saturday night?'

She shakes her head. 'I'd have been at my mum's.'

'All night?'

'Yup.'

'And have you met this Hamish Rosser?'

'Who?'

'The man who was murdered.'

'Can't say that I have.'

'And do you recall Oliver here ever talking about him?'

'Nope. This is all news to me.'

'I think then, Ms Phillips, if my colleague here could just take your contact details, we won't need to keep you any longer.'

'Oh, but –'

'You go on ahead, Amy,' Ollie says, anxious for her to leave before she started asking awkward questions about the murder or, even worse, told them she was the one working on the files. 'I'll see you in the pub,' he adds.

'Great,' Amy says, blowing him a kiss and with a wave of acknowledgement to the two police officers is gone.

'Now,' Inspector Johnson says, 'we just need to go over some points with you.'

He swallows. 'Of course.' He wishes they didn't look quite so at home, leaning back on the sofa and crossing their legs. He's the one on the edge of his seat. Stay calm, he orders himself.

His name and details jotted down by the male officer, the questioning begins.

'You knew Hamish Rosser?'

There's no point denying it. 'I did.'

'For how long, sir?'

'Just a short time – a couple of months or so.'

'And the nature of your relationship?'

'Purely business. I was carrying out some enquiries for him.'

'About?'

He hesitates. 'Some consignments of cargo.'

The officers exchange a look. 'What sort of cargo?'

'Mainly white goods – fridges and washing machines.'

'And Hamish Rosser was paying you for this work?'

'That's right. But not all that much,' he adds quickly.

'So he owed you money?'

'A bit.'

'And would the documents we saw you remove just now be in any way connected with this job?'

He fends off a wave of panic. 'Not really.'

A silence, during which a vein starts throbbing in his temple.

'Could you tell us where you were last Saturday night – the 14th?'

'I was here – at home.'

'With Amy?'

'No – as Amy said, she was with her family.'

'Anyone else vouch for you?'

'Afraid not.' He tries a smile. 'I ordered a takeaway, watched something on my laptop and then to be honest just got a bit plastered and crashed out.'

The smile is not returned.

'I wonder, Mr. Moorhouse?' Inspector Johnson says.

'Yes?'

'Might we take a look at some of those documents you've just cleared away.'

'Now, wait a moment. You can't do that!'

'We believe any documents in your possession may be pertinent to our enquiries – this *is* a murder investigation. If you're objecting, then we can finish our discussion at the station while I sort out a warrant.'

He doesn't need the reminder from the countless police procedures Amy loves to watch, that this is the moment when he should be asking: 'Do I need to call my lawyer?' But wouldn't that make him look even more guilty?

He goes into the kitchen and, extracting Amy's notes and pushing them into a drawer, hands the folders over in silence.

'Thank you,' Inspector Johnson says. 'My colleague here will write you a receipt.'

The passports seem to burn a hole in his pocket but to his relief, both officers are on their feet. 'We'll need you to come along to the station to make a full statement, Mr. Moorhouse. Before the end of the week, please.'

He trails after them to the door, where they pause, looking back at him.

'I really don't know anything about this murder,' he says. 'Straight up.'

'We'll see you later, Mr. Moorhouse.'

He closes the door, filled with a shameful sense of his own inadequacy. His incompetence. It crosses his mind briefly that Nick wouldn't have let himself be browbeaten like this. But then, he thinks – not for the first time – Nick would never have landed himself in this situation in the first place.

He returns to the front room and switches on his laptop. At least the police haven't asked for that and even if they do, thanks to Hamish, there will be no digital record. But suppose the police discover he was at Athelford Hall on the night of Hamish's murder? After all, he's admitted working for the man. And then it comes to him. Of course – he must talk to Jack, who can advise as to whether Ollie needs to get a solicitor on board. And after all, the editor is part-way responsible – he's the one who put him in touch with Rosser in the first place. But once Ollie fills him in on what's been happening, surely the paper will stand by him?

The buzz of his phone makes him jump. 'Are you going to be much longer, Babe? I'm starving.'

'Sorry. The police have only just left. Be with you by half-past.'

'Great! I've texted Chloe and Esme who are super excited.'

'About what?'

'This murder, of course. Can't wait to hear all about it.'

To her it's just a game, he thinks, and as he clicks off his mobile, suddenly he feels very alone.

TWENTY-FIVE

'LIKE OLD TIMES – ALL OF US SITTING DOWN together.' Greg tries to sound enthusiastic. It's just that over the past weeks he has become used to it being just him and Frances at the table. Since their visit to the Leeburys, he has felt the friendship between them growing – purely paternal, of course. He loves the way her eyes widen in excitement as she talks of her lectures, her fellow students and the simulated wards where they practice on virtual patients. At least he's altered one person's life for the better. If only he could say the same for the two other young people at the table. Jason has decided to put in one of his rare appearances. Whatever was the lad thinking to ditch a secure job in order to go chasing after some dream? And in a recession? He says he's still getting modelling work and certainly he's in and out of the house at all hours. But where does he get to in between all these photo shoots and auditions? And although her nightmares have stopped, Poppy remains pale and anxious. Maybe he should be doing more to find her the right sort of help? 'She's still settling in,' Mrs. Mehta declares. 'Best leave her be.'

The boy is concentrating on his food – one of Mrs. Mehta's excellent chicken curries. He's wearing a shapeless grey jumper, a leather necklace round his throat and a metal stud in one ear. He obviously hasn't shaved, but that designer stubble suits him and with his sharp cheekbones and tousled hair he is, Greg realises, not merely eye-catching, but handsome as a Greek god. And then he's ambushed by a familiar thought: Jason is the same age as Billy would have been. And maybe he's so impatient with this lad because he's had the chance of life his own child never had?

'So – how are things going, Jason?' he asks.

'Fine, ta,' the boy replies, shoving a forkful of curry into his mouth.

'Any more modelling work lined up this week?'

The boy chews and swallows. 'Some. But a lot of this is about, like, waiting around.'

Perhaps the waiting takes place in some pub, Greg thinks, recalling his university days in Leeds – the beer drinking competitions, the all-night partying, the hangovers. Jason is young and doing what the young do the world over. And yet still Greg can't help worrying.

He's suddenly aware of the silence and looks around the table.

'Anything the matter?'

No one replies.

'Well, *something* obviously is. So one of you please spit it out!'

'It's just that Jason…' Frances begins.

The boy glares at her.

'Nothing,' she finishes.

Greg tugs at his ear. Suppose the boy has started using again? Or has got involved in some underhand activity? 'Whatever the trouble, Jason, I'm sure that between us we'll be able to sort it.'

'Trouble?' Jason narrows his eyes at him. 'Why do you have to treat me as if I'm some stupid kid?'

'Well, is it any wonder?' Greg feels his voice rising. 'Coming in and out of this house at all hours. Leaving Poppy and Frances to clear up after you. Chucking in a perfectly good job to go chasing after God knows what. Spending your day God knows where –' He breaks off.

The two girls remain silent, staring down at the table.

'What the fuck has it to do with you?' Jason demands.

'Oh, I think it has everything to do with me! Have you forgotten that you're only here because I arranged it?'

'So you can go round telling everyone what a big deal you are? Greg Jacobs – the great I am?'

'For God's sake, Jason. If you're unhappy here, then you don't have to stay.'

'You're turning me out? Is that it?'

Greg gives a sigh. 'Of course not. I've always made clear it's your life – your decisions. I'm sorry I spoke like that.'

Jason puts down his fork. 'And so you fucking should be!'

He pushes back his chair, struggling to control his

anger. 'Well, I've plenty to be getting on with.'

'But you haven't finished your curry!' Frances says.

He hates to see her look of distress and the way Poppy is biting her lip.

'Take no notice,' he manages to get out. 'I know I can put my foot in it at times.' He attempts a smile. 'See you all later.'

As he reaches the door, it swings open.

'Ready for your dessert?' Mrs. Mehta's smile fades as she catches his expression. 'Everything all right, Mr. Jacobs?'

He gives a brisk nod, ignoring her raised eyebrows. She'll learn about this spat soon enough. Aloud he says: 'Anyone want to join me for tea later, I'll be in the front room as usual.'

'Not us,' Jason says, pushing past, with Poppy at his heels. 'We're off out.'

'How about you, Frances?'

'You'll have to excuse me, Greg. I've a bit of a headache coming on.'

And no wonder, poor girl, he thinks. Jason's rudeness has obviously upset her too. 'Is there anything you want?'

'That's kind but I'll be fine once I've had a lie down.'

'She studies too hard,' Mrs. Mehta says, when Frances has gone out. 'Pity that young fellow isn't more like her.'

Once at his desk, Greg starts going through the latest accounts, thankful for the space to calm down. He's obviously blown it with Jason and after this recent argument he can't imagine the lad will hang around long. What a failure his handling of the lad has been. He'd pictured all three of his charges settled into steady jobs, eventually moving out to set up homes of their own. And always showing him their gratitude. *You're such a dinosaur!* He can hear Anne saying – and of course she's right. He's been far too naïve about this whole project.

Mrs. Mehta is in the doorway. 'Sorry to interrupt, Mr. Jacobs, but there's a call for you on the landline.'

'Who is it?'

'An Oliver Moorhouse.'

'Moorhouse? Never heard of him!'

'Well, he's asking for you.'

'Oh, very well. Put him through.'

The voice at the other end is hesitant. 'Greg Jacobs? I'm not sure you'll remember me?'

'Afraid not. Could you make this brief? I am rather busy.'

'I came to see you a while back – with Hamish Rosser.'

Greg sits bolt upright in his seat. With all that's been happening, he's pushed the murder to the back of his mind, but now it comes to him. The little Scotsman sitting opposite him in this very room, smiling and chatting away, and making that very generous promise of funding, which won't be happening now the poor chap is dead. And in the chair that Jason usually slumps into, a younger man who barely spoke but just sat there taking notes. Greg struggles and fails to remember his face. Aloud he says: 'Of course. What can I do for you?'

'I wondered if I could come and see you?'

'What about?'

A long pause on the line. 'To be honest, I've got myself

into a bit of a mess.'

Greg sighs. 'Is it money you're after?'

'No – I'm fine for cash, thanks.'

'So?'

'I need your advice. The thing is, Mr. Jacobs, the police are asking me a lot of questions.'

'About this murder?'

'Yes. And I don't know what to say to them.'

'I'd have thought it was perfectly straightforward. Just tell them what you know.'

'It isn't as simple as that.'

'But why come to me?'

'I've nowhere else to turn.'

'Well, I don't –'

'*Please,* Mr. Jacobs. Hamish told me you help a lot of people with your charitable work.'

Greg thinks for a moment. He's still smarting over his argument with Jason. It would be good to be of use to someone – and someone who worked with and valued Hamish Rosser.

'I could come sometime this week?' Oliver Moorhouse is saying.

Greg suppresses a sigh. 'Friday at five o'clock, then. But I can only give you half an hour.'

'That would be great.' The relief in the voice is obvious. 'See you then.'

TWENTY-SIX

MARYA STARES OUT OF THE OPEN DOOR, FACE turned up to the rain. It has been years since life has felt so precarious. Now, like some animal using its sixth sense, she sniffs the air for an approaching, though as yet unseen, danger.

The track beyond the archway is deserted and in the courtyard a lone pigeon pecks at the crumbs Mrs. Acheson threw out earlier. Several more birds are perched on top of the Victorian lamp post waiting their chance to swoop.

From behind Marya comes the rattle of plates and cutlery, sounding louder than usual because there's no getting away from the fact that the household remains deeply shaken by this murder. First of all, there is Edna, still prone to fits of uncontrollable crying – although if anyone bothered to ask, Marya could tell the police a thing or two about why the woman should be so upset by the death of a man she hardly knew. And what about that new Ford Fiesta that Edna is now driving, when previously she turned up in Pete's battered van?

Then there is Mrs. Acheson, who no longer seems capable of producing a decent meal. In the past week, Arnold has sent back soggy vegetables, overcooked beef and chicken oozing blood. And as for Magdalena – her decision to breakfast with her husband in the dining-room, rather than having her usual tray upstairs, is yet another sign of things being out of kilter.

Marya is about to retreat inside when she spots the chauffeur, Seamus, striding across the yard, a basket of logs balanced on his shoulder. He's wearing a short-sleeved shirt so that even from this distance she can see the pattern of tattoos snaking up his arms. He seems oblivious to the rain, whistling a piercing tune that sends the pigeon flapping into the air.

When he's a few feet away, he smiles across at her, revealing two rows of strong, white teeth. 'Morning, Marya' – he pronounces it "Mah-ree-ah," which adds to her irritation. 'Anuther soft day!'

Since the death of that nasty Scottish man, he seems more pleased with himself than ever. Too pleased by half, Marya thinks, wondering why he always leaves her with the feeling of knowing something she doesn't.

Although she leaves him room to pass, he knocks against her and she resists the temptation to give him a sharp kick. He's a man who wouldn't think twice about taking his revenge – in private, of course.

'How are you doing, ladies?' he calls to Edna and

Mrs. Acheson, before disappearing into the side room to change his boots.

'Breakfasts are ready?' Marya asks.

The cook nods.

The two trays are on the table and as Marya's eyes alight on a jug of cream, she gives a tch of annoyance. 'Lord Leebury says he is watching fat in his blood. Have you wood between your ears?'

'Oh, take a running jump,' Mrs. Acheson declares, stomping over and removing the offending jug.

Marya ignores this, picking up the first tray and heading up the stairs. 'Foreign bitch!' Mrs. Acheson mutters and Edna, following behind with the tray of coffee and hot milk, lets out a snort.

Normally you couldn't put a slip of paper between the Leeburys but today they sit at a distance from one another. Arnold, his bald patch visible above the copy of *The Times,* gives a nod of thanks as she and Edna unload the trays. Magdalena stares ahead, a faint smile on her lips. Edna shuffles out of the room, but Marya remains behind, straightening cutlery, shifting the bowl of roses to the centre of the table and arranging the preserves and spreads in a row. With her mistress so unsettled – that smile and carefully-applied makeup doesn't fool Marya for a moment – it seems important to make each detail perfect – to show that at least some things are under control.

'That'll be all, thanks, Marya,' Arnold Leebury says, his tone dismissive, but Magdalena waves a hand at the space behind him. She moves over, pressing herself against the wall.

The couple eat in silence, the only sound the rustle of

Arnold's newspaper and the scrape of Magdalena's knife as she butters her toast.

After a few minutes, she clears her throat. 'I am very sorry, darlink,' – her voice is hesitant – 'to have bothered you about my missing package – especially when you are so busy.'

He lowers his paper. 'What's that?'

'The package, Arnie.'

'Oh, yes.' He frowns. 'I expect you'll get it back soon.'

'Back?' Her voice rises. 'From where?'

'I've got more important things to think about than this, Lena. So for God's sake, stop your nagging. It's not good for either of us.'

She reaches across the space for Arnold's arm and he puts down his knife and fork. 'Didn't mean to snap. I've a lot on.' He sighs. 'So, what are you planning to do with yourself today?'

She gives a small laugh. 'There is always plenty to see to, but I thought I would try and source that red and gold House of Lords wallpaper we both liked so much, and then –' she hesitates – 'we have dinner booked at Quaglino's.'

'Afraid I've had to cancel. Too much work.'

'But I was looking forward to it so very much!'

'There'll be plenty of other times.' He pauses. 'I've been asked to help organise the memorial service for Hamish. The funeral's still to come, of course– once the police have released the body. Don't imagine you'll want to be at either service though.'

'Why ever not?'

'Really, Magdalena, you don't have to pretend with me!'

'I know I didn't warm to him.'

'*Warm?*' Arnold shakes his head. 'That's one way of putting it!'

'How do you mean?'

'Well, it was pretty obvious that you couldn't stand the sight of the man.' He stares across at her. 'And where were *you* in the early hours of …?'

Magdalena's voice rises. 'You think I had something to do with his death, don't you?'

'No need to be so hysterical.'

'But you can't think that I was involved? We were both at that Christmas party.'

Arnie folds his newspaper and looks across at her. 'And got back well before midnight.'

'And went straight to bed.'

'Except the police suggested–' he breaks off. 'Now is not the time for this conversation. And if it's OK with you, I thought I'd stay in town. My club will put me up.'

'But we've never had a night apart!'

Her look of appeal tugs at Marya's heart – although obviously not at Arnold Leebury's. 'Try not to fuss, there's a good girl.' He pushes back his chair. 'Now, I must press on.'

She gives a tight smile. 'Whatever you wish.'

He pauses behind her chair, a plump, unremarkable man with thinning hair. Yet despite his unprepossessing appearance, it seems to Marya that there's a new air of authority about him. He stoops and, giving his wife a quick kiss on the cheek, is out of the room.

Marya can tell from the rigid set of the shoulders that

Magdalena is holding herself together with difficulty. She swings round. 'Whatever am I to do?'

'He is just busy with this important new job.' Marya has only a vague idea of what it might be. 'This trouble will pass,' she adds.

'Oh, darlink, but suppose it doesn't?' Magdalena looks up at her. 'I don't know what I've done to make Arnie so suspicious of me, but I'm certain he knows something about those passports – may even have taken them.'

'Why would you think that?'

'The house hasn't been broken into and Arnie and I are the only ones who know the code for the safe.' She pauses, her mouth trembling.

Marya fights the urge to lay her head on Magdalena's breast, to kiss those rose painted lips. Instead, she says in as bright a voice as she can manage: 'There'll be some explanation. For now you need Arnold to see that you are perfectly happy over his new post.' She strokes Magdalena's arm. 'So let's plan what you will wear. Maybe the blue-green Balenciaga?'

'I was saving it for Quaglino's, but why not? I cannot sit around mopping. Or is it "moping?"'

'Let me help you dress and then I will bring fresh coffee.'

Yet an hour later, as Marya carries the tray into the front room, she finds her mistress sitting motionless, staring out at the rain.

Will she spend all day here, waiting? As Marya follows her gaze, she catches a splash of colour. One of the peacocks is roosting in the nearest oak – no doubt

226

to escape the waterlogged ground. Marya glances back at Magdalena, hunched in her blue-green dress, and is struck by the resemblance between the two. It's as if both her mistress and the bird have been reduced from proud and confident splendour to a miserable huddle. The sight makes Marya want to weep.

'Can I get you something?' she whispers, because to speak in normal tones seems out of keeping with this atmosphere of mourning. For deep in her bones, Marya knows that Arnold Leebury is turning his back on his wife. Yet if he's distancing himself because he believes she had something to do with the murder of that nasty Rosser man, it will surely only be a matter of time before he concludes that however frightened and provoked Magdalena might be, she would never actually kill? Although there again, were he to dig into her past, as Magdalena is convinced he has started to do, he might learn something very different – a thought that causes Marya's insides to twist in alarm.

She excuses herself before making her slow way up the stairs to supervise Edna, who uses her swollen ankles as an excuse for skimping on cleaning. She finds the woman, one hand flicking a duster over a military portrait and the other snivelling into her handkerchief. 'For God's sake!' Marya says. 'Tell the police what you know.'

'Nothing to tell, is there?'

Marya bites back her further comments and continues up the stairs.

In contrast to the rest of the house, her room is plainly furnished, containing a single bed, a wooden chest-of-drawers, a wardrobe and a chair. The walls are bare, apart from a picture of a donkey, its ears sticking through the straw of a Mexican sombrero – the one reminder of childhood that can bring a smile to her face. She still recalls what it was like to beg for her next meal and to search for a disused outhouse or alleyway in which she could spend the night.

She lowers herself onto the bed, her feet dangling above the cord carpet, and gives herself over to thought. She's always trusted her instincts – it's how she has survived. So, despite the reassurances she's just given her mistress, she also fears that this distancing on Arnold's part is not temporary – that he may well have taken those passports. 'And where were *you* in the early hours?' he asked. So perhaps it is not just that he suspects his wife of this murder – perhaps he has started to dig into her past.

Marya's eyes narrow. She and Magdalena never speak of their experiences – there has been no need. But now the nightmare is returning to haunt them, just as it did all those years ago.

TWENTY-SEVEN

Already Greg regrets having agreed to see that assistant of Hamish Rosser's but he'll just have to hear the man out and then get rid of him as soon as he decently can.

He is so taken up with his thoughts that, as he crosses the hall, he almost walks headlong into Poppy. She still looks so pale, giving a muttered, 'morning,' before turning away. He hasn't set eyes on Jason since their argument three days ago– something that fills him with guilty relief. He should have handled the lad better – been less judgemental.

He'd like to talk the whole tricky subject through with Frances, whom he knows would be sympathetic, but she's still keeping to her room. 'Migraine, poor girl,' Mrs. Mehta declares. 'Or maybe a bug going the rounds.'

Or perhaps she is just fed up with his company? A

thought that leaves him realising how much, in quite a short space of time, he has come to rely on her. You don't often gel with people in the way he has with her. Not that he's thinking of her in a romantic way. He's not that daft.

He eats a solitary lunch of soup, bread and cheese before retreating to the study to run his eye over the household accounts that Mrs. Mehta draws up each month. As usual, she's done an excellent job – he must think about giving her a pay rise.

He's so absorbed in his task that when she puts her head round the door and announces, 'Your visitor, Mr. Jacobs,' he looks up in surprise.

The man who steps forward appears to be in his thirties, with mid-brown hair and anxious eyes that glance about in a way that doesn't inspire confidence. In a way that implies guilt, Greg thinks. But for what?

'Thanks again for seeing me.' He moves forward, extending a hand. Greg shakes it, feeling the palm sweaty in his. 'Oh yes. You're Oliver –?'

'Moorhouse. Ollie Moorhouse.'

Of course – Greg remembers him now. He sat in that chair by the door taking notes, but otherwise didn't participate in the meeting with Hamish Rosser.

'Can I get you a coffee or tea?'

'No, I'm good, thanks.'

'Well, have a seat and tell me what I can do for you.'

Oliver gives a smile as insincere as his gaze. He comes across as decidedly shifty – something that makes Greg even more determined to keep this encounter as short as possible.

'You said the police have questioned you about Hamish Rosser's death?' he prompts. 'They can come over a bit strong at times, but no doubt they were just doing their job.'

'Yes, but–' Oliver breaks off, trembling.

Greg would like nothing better than to see him to the door, but what if he's come here to confess to the murder? If so, Greg has a duty to see justice done for poor Hamish Rosser, who after all was a friend of Arnold's. Perhaps he can get this man to open up?

Aloud he says: 'You look to me, Oliver, as if you could do with something a bit stronger than tea. How about a whisky?'

'Thanks. You're not having one yourself?' he asks as Greg hands him his drink.

'Trying to keep off the stuff. But you go ahead.'

Oliver gulps the liquid, his hands shaking. 'Sorry.' He wipes the spill away with his sleeve.

'No worries.' Greg leans forward. 'So what exactly is it you wanted to tell me? I only met Hamish Rosser once, when you both came here. Though I imagine you must have known him pretty well?'

Oliver is on the edge of his chair, his lower lip trembling. 'I was put in touch with him through the editor of my paper.'

'You're a reporter?'

'For my local rag. I'd just had my hours cut, so when Hamish invited me to investigate a story – a big scoop, he said – you can imagine how pleased I was. And he was offering good money.'

Greg gives what he hopes is an encouraging nod.

'We were looking into various angles. There's this boy, Jimmy, who had all these papers about illegal shipments.' He pauses. 'Hamish was supplying him with drugs.'

Greg does a double-take. 'I find that hard to believe.'

'That's just it, Mr. Jacobs. No one else is going to either. But now Hamish is dead, I must speak out.' He takes another gulp of his drink. 'We visited Athelford Hall twice. He took me down to meet the Leeburys and then he asked me to steal something from their safe.'

'Wait a moment.' Greg struggles to follow this. 'You're saying you broke into the Leebury's home?'

'Yes – well, no. Hamish gave me the security code for the door. He knew this was an evening when the house would be empty. So he drove us down there and I got the package he asked for.' The words were coming out in a rush. 'He was to wait for me in his car but when I got back to it, I found him sitting under a tree – dead.' He stares past Greg. 'I thought his heart had given out, but obviously I couldn't hang around. I mean, what explanation could I have given?' He drains his glass. 'So I left Hamish there – I do feel bad about that – and got the hell out of the place. Later I dumped his car and thought that would be the end of it. But it wasn't, Mr. Jacobs, was it?'

Either this man is mad, or a crook, or maybe a mixture of the two, Greg thinks. 'Obviously not,' he manages to get out.

'I only learned later that Hamish had been stabbed. It honestly wasn't me, Mr. Jacobs. Just the thought of blood makes me sick. It's why I've never got any further in my reporting career – all those motorway smashes, and cases of domestic violence.' He leans over the desk. 'But you see, Mr. Jacobs. I'm terrified the police won't believe me.'

And is it any wonder? Greg thinks. Hamish Rosser, a respected member of the House of Lords – a man known for his philanthropic work, chair of God knows how many charities and parliamentary committees – to be labelled a drug dealer and an accessory to burglary? Greg has never heard such a cock-and-bull story and wants nothing more to do with it. It's quite enough having to cope with what's going on in his own household without getting caught up in whatever nightmare this young man has got himself embroiled in. But there again, suppose he's about to confess to the murder?

As if reading his thoughts, Oliver says: 'And what possible reason could I have had for killing Hamish?' His shoulders start to shake. 'I didn't do it, Mr. Jacobs!'

Greg leans forward. 'Do you have a partner or someone to advise you?'

Oliver blows his nose. 'I haven't wanted to worry my girlfriend with the full story. I've a couple of work colleagues, but everyone is busy with their own lives...'

'Look, I'm sorry you're obviously in a tight spot,' Greg says, relieved that Oliver seems to be calming. 'And my advice to you is to make a clean breast of it – tell the police all you've told me. It really is the only way.'

'What if I just keep quiet?'

Greg shakes his head. 'With forensics the way they are, it's only a matter of time before they establish you were at the murder scene.'

'Murder scene?' he repeats, running a hand through his hair. 'Oh, God!'

But Greg has heard quite enough. 'I'm sorry – I really do have to press on.' He pushes back his chair and opening the study door ushers the young man into the hall.

Oliver turns towards him. 'I think I will take your advice, Mr. Jacobs.'

'Excellent – remember that truth will out!' But, dear God, he thinks, according to the saying, so will murder. He wonders if Oliver's having the same thought but he's staring about him, biting his lip, and seeming in no fit state to go anywhere. 'Know what I'd do if I were in your shoes, Oliver? I'd go to my nearest police station – now. Always better to face up to things.'

'Well, thanks for listening.' And with a nod, the younger man is off down the drive. Greg closes the door on him with relief. Then turns, to see Mrs. Mehta emerge from the kitchen.

She blinks back tears. 'Oh, Mr. Jacobs!'

'What on earth's wrong?'

'It's Frances. She's running a high fever and seems in a really bad way.'

He feels dread seeping into the pit of his stomach. 'Well why in God's name didn't you tell me earlier?'

'I'm sorry, Mr. Jacobs. I didn't like to interrupt your meeting.'

'Never mind that now. Let's take a look at her.'

'Shall I get you a mask?'

'A bit late for that, isn't it? We've all been at close quarters.'

He takes the stairs two at a time, pausing at the top to

allow Mrs. Mehta to catch up. 'When did you last check on her?' he whispered.

'About half-an-hour ago.'

The bedside light casts splashes of sickly yellow across the pillow where the girl lies, eyes closed, dark hair sticking to her cheeks.

'How are you feeling, Frances?' Mrs. Mehta whispers.

Greg moves beside her, staring down at the flushed face. She makes no move to open her eyes. Then, suddenly her whole body is convulsed by a bout of violent coughing. Mrs. Mehta props her up, offering her a sip of water, but she shakes her head, sinking onto the pillow again, the sound of her laboured breathing filling the room.

'We must get the GP out,' he says.

'I doubt anyone from the practice will come. And you know what the guidelines are. Better to ring for an ambulance.'

He nods, hearing her words as if from a great distance.

Another sound comes from the bed, and it takes him a moment to realise that Frances is speaking, her voice hoarse. 'I had a text earlier. A student on my course has gone down with this latest virus, which I'm afraid is what I've got.'

Mrs. Mehta stoops over her. 'We need to get you to the hospital.'

Greg nods. 'Best take no chances.' He tries not to think that, despite the latest round of boosters, a few unlucky people don't pull through. Pray God Frances won't be one of them.

She raises herself onto an elbow, her chest heaving, her

face filled with panic. She clutches Mrs. Mehta's sleeve. 'I – can't – breathe.'

Suddenly, Greg is galvanised into action. 'Stay with her,' he orders Mrs. Mehta. Then he is down the stairs, seizing his mobile from his desk and dialling the emergency number. As he paces the hall, waiting for the ambulance, he tries not to think of Frances's desperate struggle to breathe – all too reminiscent of Anne's last hours.

Mrs. Mehta reappears. 'We should get in touch with Jason and Poppy.'

'Do you know when they're due back?'

She shakes her head. 'That's another worry, Mr. Jacobs. Those two haven't bothered with vaccines and of course Poppy needs to be especially careful...'

'Poppy is at risk from this virus? She never said.' But then, he thinks sadly, neither she nor Jason tell him anything.

Mrs. Mehta sighs. 'You may as well know. Poppy is pregnant.'

He stares. 'You're not serious?'

'They wanted to tell you but were afraid that you might turn them out of the house.'

'*Them?* Jason is the father?'

She nods.

So maybe the lad's obstreperous behaviour was nothing to do with drugs or crime. He feels a surge of indignation. 'To think of the pair of them carrying on under this roof.'

'Well, what did you expect?' Mrs. Mehta's look makes him feel like a not very bright child. But he can't think about any of this now. Not with Frances, lying so ill.

An hour later the paramedics arrive, running up the stairs with their equipment. Greg stands to one side as Frances is stretchered down, lying motionless, her face covered by an oxygen mask. He steps forward. 'She will be all right?'

They don't answer.

'I must go with her!'

'Sorry, sir. With the virus levels so high, even next-of-kin aren't being allowed into the hospital. 'Best to give a ring in the morning.'

He and Mrs. Mehta watch in silence as the stretcher is loaded onto the ambulance, and moments later is pulling out of the drive.

Mrs. Mehta touches his arm. 'She's in good hands, Mr. Jacobs.'

He's too caught up in his own thoughts to reply.

Don't leave us, Frances. For God's sake, don't leave me.

TWENTY-EIGHT

'**Y**OU'VE GOT TO BELIEVE ME,' OLLIE CAN'T STOP HIS voice shaking. 'I honestly had nothing to do with it.'

He stares into the milky scum of the tea that has been placed in front of him. The tabletop is ringed with the imprints of other drinks – ghostly traces of those who have sat in this same chair. Were they found innocent? Or guilty?

This is his second visit to the police station. The previous time he just had to confirm his identity but now he's been summoned for a formal interview.

At least the two policewomen facing him are not openly hostile, which would have added to his growing panic. His story may seem far-fetched, but surely once they hear all the facts, they'll realise he's nothing to gain from spinning such a tale?

The black officer, D. I. Clarke – the one who called at

his house – clicks on the recording machine. Her gaze is shrewd and assessing – not someone to get on the wrong side of. She has the same dark hair and eyes as Amy, but she must be several inches taller, long, thin arms folded over her chest. Beside her D.S. Mullan, younger, with a narrow face and ginger hair swept into a ponytail, clears her throat. 'You've been read your rights, Oliver, so suppose you give us your version of events.' The tone is casual – chatty almost – but no doubt they're just out to trap him.

Beside him, the duty solicitor, Jonathan Elliot, a man well into his fifties, with round, pink cheeks and greying hair, remains impassive. In their preliminary discussion, he didn't seem much on the ball but has promised to intervene if Ollie says the wrong thing. Although he has a horrible sense that no words of his will come out right.

He tries to cling to Greg Jacob's comment: 'Truth will out.' The man is obviously a thoroughly decent sort – a million miles from someone like Hamish Rosser. What the hell made him get mixed up with someone like that? But of course he needed the money to make Amy stay with him, and now he's got more than he dreamed possible, he must extricate himself from this mess so they can get on with their lives. The alternative doesn't bear thinking about.

'When you say you had nothing to do with it, Oliver,' D. I. Clarke is saying, 'what exactly do you mean?'

'That I know nothing about the murder – who did it, I mean.'

'But what we're here to establish'– a rustle of paper as she studies the folder in front of her – 'is what exactly you *do* know. You'll appreciate that the murder of a member of the House of Lords makes this a high-profile case.' She stares across at him. 'And of course we'll be doing everything in our power to find the killer.'

He looks around the interview room – the plastic chairs, scuffed lino and smeared windows an unwelcome reminder of his secondary school. Even the smell is similar: damp raincoats and stale bodies. His splitting head is making it hard to think clearly. Why didn't he prepare himself better instead of spending the evening in the pub drinking himself into oblivion?

'Oliver?' the ginger-haired policewoman prompts.

It's an effort to meet her gaze. 'OK – I admit I should have come to you before, but I was scared. Bloody terrified if you want the truth of it.'

'Scared of what, Oliver?'

'That you wouldn't believe me.' Fear gives an edge to his voice and D. S. Mullan nods, as if Ollie's response confirms her thoughts. 'But I've come here voluntarily because I am innocent.'

'O.K, Oliver. So let's go over the details once again. When my colleagues called at your house, you assured them you were at home the night Hamish Rosser was murdered.'

'That's not right.' He swallows. 'I *was* at Athelford Hall that night.'

The policewoman sighs. 'So perhaps you'd tell us what your story is now.'

If only his head would stop pounding so that he can get his thoughts into some sort of coherent order. For now is the time to explain everything – to tell these police officers of that young addict, Jimmy; of the manifests Amy's spent hours poring over; of the visits paid to the Leeburys and Greg Jacobs, and finally of the evening when Hamish drove them down to Athelford Hall and someone – certainly not Ollie – came out of the dark and killed him.

He's opening his mouth to speak when Jonathan Elliot leans over and whispers in his ear.

'You're sure?' Ollie asks, hoping to God this man knows what he's doing.

The solicitor nods.

'No comment,' Ollie says.

D. I. Clarke taps her fingers on the table. 'And then there's also this, Oliver. You've recently had a big pay cut but your bank account shows a substantial deposit was made recently. Could you tell us about that?'

'Five hundred. It was from Hamish.' What would they think if they knew of the thousands stashed in the bottom of his wardrobe?

'From Lord Rosser?'

'It was for the project we were working on together.' He pauses. 'You can check with my editor. He's the one who suggested I meet with Hamish.'

'Ah, yes. Jack Coslett. He tells us he's never actually met Lord Rosser. A contact of Mr. Coslett's suggested the lead and, knowing you were only working part-time, Mr. Coslett passed it on to you as a way of helping you out.'

A silence in which Ollie struggles to recall when Jack ever helped anyone if it wasn't in his own interests to do so.

'And so,' D. S. Mullan takes over, 'you're agreeing that Lord Rosser was paying you for this work. Did he owe you money?'

'Only in the early stages, but then he ended up giving me most of it.'

'It doesn't sound a very satisfactory arrangement. You were happy about it? About the delay?'

'Not at first, but as I said, we managed to sort it.'

'All quite amicable, was it?'

'Of course.'

D. I. Mullan purses thin lips. 'You see, Oliver, we have witnesses who saw you and Lord Rosser arguing.'

'That's simply not true!' I was far too scared of him, he thinks.

'You were seen together at' – she looks down at her file – 'Luigi's Pizza Parlour in The Strand on – let me see. Ah yes, December 17th last.'

It must have been after that second visit to Jimmy. The memory of the boy's terror and the attic room, stinking of drugs, still sickens. 'Well, yes, Hamish and I *were* having a disagreement.'

'So you admit you were arguing?'

'Yes, but –'

'The witness also says he heard you demanding money from Lord Rosser, who then handed over what appeared to be a very substantial sum.'

'It was what he owed me for my work on the project – to say nothing of my train fares and other expenses.'

'If you look at this from our point of view, Oliver,' D. I. Mullan continues, 'none of what you're saying really adds up, does it? You've admitted that you visited Athelford Hall but have given no clear explanation as to what you were actually doing there. You found Lord Rosser dead, although you deny stabbing him. However, instead of reporting this, you drove off in his car, which you later dumped.' D. I. Clarke pauses. 'It really is in your best interests to give us the full story.'

He hesitates, longing to comply – to make them believe him.

Jonathan Elliot once again shakes his head. Ollie supposes he'd better trust the man. After all, what option does he have? He looks across the table, trying unsuccessfully to meet the eyes of the two policewomen. 'No comment.'

They exchange a nod before gathering up their papers.

Ollie pushes back his chair.

'If you could just wait here a moment, Oliver,' D. I. Clarke smiles.

As they go out, he lets out a sigh of relief, watching through the glass panel at the top of the door as they stand conferring together.

He turns to the solicitor. 'Thank God that's over!'

'Let's just take things one step at a time, Oliver.'

What in Christ's name did he mean by that? But before he can ask, the police are back, lowering themselves into their seats once more.

'Oliver Moorhouse,' D. I. Clarke begins, 'we are arresting you on suspicion of the murder of Hamish Rosser. You do not –'

'I knew you wouldn't believe me,' he blurts. 'The word

of an Essex boy against that of a peer. I never stood a chance!'

'Please do not interrupt! You do not have to say anything,' she continues, 'but anything...'

He blocks out the words just as she has blocked out his, but he can't control the terrifying thoughts swirling in his head. If convicted of premeditated murder, he'd be looking at fifteen to twenty years. By the time he comes out he'll be in his fifties – not far off retirement and the best of his life gone. Along with Amy, of course. 'Why can't you understand?' he yells, burying his head in his hands to control the sobs that are tearing through him. 'I didn't do this!'

The solicitor leans towards him. 'Try not to panic. For a start it's unusual, but not impossible, to get bail.'

He looks up at him through tear-filled eyes. 'You mean I mightn't be going to prison?'

'With any luck just an overnighter in the cells. Your case will come before the magistrates in the morning. It's obvious you don't pose a threat to the public, so I'll be pressing strongly for bail.' He pauses. 'Hopefully, by this time tomorrow you should be out of here.'

'Th-thanks,' he stutters, feeling he's misread him. That he's not just a disinterested lawyer going through the motions for whatever money he can get.

Jonathan Elliot gives his arm another pat. 'Try not to worry.'

As Ollie is led away, he carries that touch on his arm. But it doesn't console. Instead, he feels disempowered, as if in treating him like a defenceless child, the solicitor has turned him into one.

TWENTY-NINE

ONE MOMENT GREG IS AT HIS DESK SCROLLING through emails – with no memory of how he got there – and the next he's at the window, gazing out at the water-logged garden and the willow fronds hanging like wet strands of hair over the lawn. Then he's wandering across the hall and pushing open the door of the sitting-room. He knows it's illogical but a part of him still expects to see Frances curled in a chair, turning towards him with that look of warmth in the grey eyes.

He walks through to the kitchen in search of Mrs. Mehta – the one stable influence in the household.

'Just doing the week's shopping list, Mr. Jacobs,' she says, looking up from the table. 'I thought I'd make another korma for later– maybe use up that bit of lamb – and perhaps just an omelette for your lunch?'

'Oh yes.' He searches his memory. 'Poppy said she and

Jason wouldn't be back until late.' He pauses. "Have you any idea where they were going?'

Mrs. Mehta shakes her head. 'With that young man, who knows?'

At least the pregnancy is now out in the open, but to his deep disappointment, Poppy has also given up her work and although he's pressed her on how on earth she's going to manage, she refuses his offer of any more support. Another failure to lay at his door, Greg thinks. Aloud he says: 'I just hope to God Jason's looking after her.'

'She seems OK – a bit peaky perhaps, but at least she's avoided Covid.' She pauses. 'I expect she's missing Frances.'

'As we all are.'

Mrs. Mehta gives him one of her looks. 'You said the hospital were sounding more positive?'

'Yes, thank God. Apparently she's still pretty weak but she's off the ventilator and has been moved to a general ward.' He sighs. 'This wretched virus. Although it's never the illness itself, is it? It's how it leaves people.'

'The main thing is she's pulled through,' Mrs. Mehta says, getting up to check the store cupboard.

He thinks of his nights of broken sleep when he was convinced she wouldn't make it. No one understands the after-effects of a close death, he thinks, until they experience it for themselves. That way it has of sinking its teeth into one and refusing to let go. It's only in recent months that he's been able to come to terms with the devastating loss of Anne, and he realises it will still take all his courage to visit Frances: fearful that the sight of her in a hospital bed may bring back memories of his wife's last terrible days.

246

'So, you're planning to visit Frances soon?' Mrs. Mehta is asking.

'I phoned earlier and they said it would be fine.' He tries to keep his voice casual. 'In fact I thought I might look in on her later. I think she'll appreciate the visit, even for a short while.'

'I'm sure she will.' She pauses. 'It's my afternoon off, so would it be all right if I came with you, Mr. Jacobs?'

He'd been hoping for time alone with Frances – to fill her in on how things have been going in her absence and to tell her how much he's looking forward to her return. But he can hardly refuse Mrs. Mehta's request. Aloud he says: 'Of course. Let's leave as soon as we've eaten.'

They make their way to the station under a steady drizzle, a blanket of cloud hanging over the houses and shops. Although it's early afternoon, traffic headlights are switched on, sweeping across the puddles and the wet surface of the road. Like so many others, he finds the endless rain depressing, yet as their train arrives at Waterloo, he walks along the platform with a spring in his step, pausing at the ticket barrier to allow Mrs. Mehta to catch up.

Once in the hospital, they put on the masks provided before navigating their way along corridors and into a lift that opens onto a reception area. The nurse behind the desk points them to the women's ward: a large airy room with bright yellow walls and a dozen beds. Greg pauses, scanning the room. Some patients sit upright, staring at TV screens or chatting to their visitors. Others are shapeless forms under the sheets.

'There she is!' Mrs. Mehta says, moving past him towards the far corner.

Greg follows. As he stands by Frances's bed, she looks up, giving a weak smile, and he feels his heart lift.

'Good to see you looking brighter, my girl,' Mrs. Mehta declares, straightening Frances's covers.

Although in truth, Greg thinks, Frances is much failed, with sunken cheeks and deep circles etched under her eyes. It's never mattered to him that she's not good-looking, but now with her drawn face and pasty skin she seems to have aged years. She will need careful looking after and once she's home he'll make sure that is what she gets.

Mrs. Mehta settles into a chair just as a nurse appears. 'We're allowing Frances two visitors at a time, but a few minutes only with her, please.'

'It's so kind of you both to come,' Frances whispers. 'And I am feeling stronger.'

'Poor girl,' Mrs. Mehta says. 'You've really been through it. We must take good care of you.'

Since this is precisely what Greg has been planning to say, he fights off his irritation. 'We must indeed,' he says, thinking that he needs to check with the nurse that flowers are allowed so he can bring some on his next visit. Cream and blue, he decides.

Anne's favourite colour was yellow – a thought he pushes away.

Frances is asking after Poppy and Jason. 'I've become so fond of them,' she murmurs. She gives another weak smile before adding: 'And I've really missed you both.' A comment that leaves him with a warm glow inside.

'I expect they'll be in to see you soon,' Mrs. Mehta says. 'Poppy's pregnancy is going well?'

'We don't see much of them,' Greg says, 'but they seem happy enough.' No point worrying Frances at this stage by telling her he has no idea how they spend their days, or how they are managing financially.

'I can't wait to get back to my course,' Frances says, closing her eyes once more.

Mrs. Mehta turns to Greg. 'Perhaps we should let her rest.'

He nods before stooping over the bed. 'See you soon,' he whispers, pressing Frances's hand. And is rewarded with a gentle pressure on his. As he moves away, two more nurses appear: a plump young woman with a round, cheerful face, and a slightly older man, with soulful eyes and a thick beard. The girl throws a beaming smile towards the bed. 'We thought by now you'd be out clubbing, Frances!'

'She's certainly better than she was,' Greg says, trying to hide his disapproval at the casual tone.

'Great!' The nurse seems not at all put out. 'She's given us quite a scare. We're training together,' she adds, turning back to Greg. 'I'm Carys and this is Ahmed, who's in his final year.'

'Oh,' Greg says, feeling deflated. 'Good to meet some of Frances's friends.'

In the manner of a conjuror producing a rabbit from a hat, Ahmed raises an arm and holds up a small bunch of orange roses. Even from where he's standing, Greg can see the flowers are poor quality, the edges of the petals browning and the flower heads starting to wilt.

As he and Mrs. Mehta make their way out of the hospital, he decides that on his next visit he will bring Frances those flowers – a large bunch of blue hyacinths and perfect cream roses.

An hour later, he's back at his desk, looking through the proposal for the new food bank. Maybe, even without that funding from Hamish Rosser, it will still be possible to go ahead.

There's a tap on the door and Mrs. Mehta puts her head round. 'Sorry to bother you, Mr. Jacobs, but the police are here again.'

'This must be to do with the murder.' He lets out a sigh. 'Very well. You'd best show them in.'

The two who enter are very different from the previous pair. These are youngish women, looking to be in their forties. Both are dressed in dark suits. One of the women has short blonde curls while the other seems to be Far Eastern with straight black hair cut in a fringe.

They show their identity cards and the blonde says: 'We're from the Serious Fraud Office, Mr. Jacobs. My name is Lauren Stubbs and my colleague here is Lilian Chan. We're investigating a number of crimes.'

Greg braces himself. Jason? But surely not? He swallows. 'Of course. Anything I can do to help. Although I can assure you that all the charitable enterprises I run are totally above-board.'

She gives a smile. 'We're not here to enquire into your affairs, Mr. Jacobs. But we would be grateful for any help you can give us on another matter.'

'Oh?'

'We understand that a Miss Fitzpatrick has been to see you.'

'Fitzpatrick?' He shakes his head. 'Doesn't ring any bells, I'm afraid.'

'A Miss Amelia Fitzpatrick? An elderly lady. She says that she's visited you on several occasions to ask your advice.'

'Oh, yes,' he says, picturing the strange old woman with her watery eyes, clutching her string bag. And Frances, in Anne's raincoat, chasing after her down the drive. He's meant to make more enquiries on her behalf, but since Frances's illness hasn't had much energy, especially for what is undoubtedly a doomed cause. Aloud he says: 'I've told her I'll give what help I can, but I'm afraid I've not been able to find out anything so far.'

'Help with what exactly, sir?'

'A Bitcoin investment. The whole thing is most unfortunate. Tragic even. The poor woman was persuaded to part with the very substantial sum she inherited from an aunt. I've consulted a couple of my lawyer friends, but they're not hopeful she'll see her investment again.'

'Quite so.' Lilian Chan leans forward. 'And has she described any of the people with whom she's had dealings?'

Greg thinks for a moment. 'She tells me that she's fairly sure one of the men involved has visited her block of flats. Somewhere in central London I think.'

'Did she give any description of the man?'

'I'm afraid not.'

'And you're due to see her again?'

Greg sighs. 'I will be in touch, though it will only be to

tell her that we have absolutely nothing to go on.'

'No paper trail or internet information,' Lilian Chan adds.

'Yes – and it seems truly terrible that an old woman can be defrauded like that.'

'Indeed.' The two women get to their feet. 'Thanks for your time, Mr. Jacobs.' In the doorway Lilian Chan turns. 'We understand that you also had dealings with a Lord Hamish Rosser?'

Where do they get their information? He wonders. 'That's right. A thoroughly decent chap. He promised a very generous donation to a couple of the charities I'm involved with.' He pauses. 'Unfortunately, his murder has put paid to that. It came as a huge shock. But I expect you know all about it?'

She remains deadpan.

'I don't suppose you can tell me what this is about?'

'Our enquiries are still at a preliminary stage. Well, thank you again, Mr. Jacobs.'

As he closes the front door on them, he's left both irritated and discomfited. People are happy enough to come to him for help and advice but are not prepared to share whatever information they have. And that last question about Hamish Rosser. Up to now Greg has viewed him as a generous and upright philanthropist. But were those two policewomen implying that the man may have been involved in this Bitcoin scam? If so, then perhaps Oliver Moorhouse's story wasn't as mad as it sounded.

Greg shakes his head, feeling more in the dark than ever.

THIRTY

OLLIE STEPS OVER THE RUBBISH THAT HAS accumulated under the doorstep and draws in deep breaths of the damp air. It's Sunday morning, the quiet broken by a burst of music from an upstairs window.

Oh the relief of being out of that overnight cell! Thank God his solicitor was proved right and the magistrates have granted bail, on the condition that Ollie lives at home and reports once a week to the local police station. Now he can't wait to get under the shower and wash off the smell of metal and stale urine. He wishes there was something he could have said to convince the police of his innocence. But even worse than facing this murder charge is knowing that once Amy has the full story – and he can't put off telling her any longer – she won't want anything to do with him. Well, why would she? Why would anyone?

The front door opens and there she is, standing in front of him. She's wearing a short red skirt and a top that shows the deep vee of her breasts. She gives a broad smile. 'Let's have your jacket, then.' She hooks it over the peg before turning and wrapping her arms around him. 'Welcome back!'

He'd been so sure he would be returning to an empty house. He can't believe his luck. 'Sorry – I must smell terrible.'

'Yes – you stink. Get into that bathroom and I'll see to the food. Eggs and bacon OK?'

'Fine. But why –?'

She squeezes his arm. 'That murder's all over the media, and then they go and arrest you.'

He's expected her voice to be high with excitement – no doubt this resembles a plot from one of the thriller series she loves – but instead she sounds concerned.

'I didn't murder anyone,' he says.

'I know that, you pillock!' She presses herself against him. 'And we need to think what we're going to do.' She gives him a push. 'Now, get your arse into that bathroom!'

He stands for ages under the shower, scrubbing away at his skin as if to wipe out the humiliation of his arrest and court appearance. After breakfast, they sit together on the sofa and, for the first time in weeks he feels his tension drain away. He pulls her towards him and she lifts her top over her head and presses her hand against the front of his trousers. He feels himself harden and rolls her off the sofa onto the rug, pushing her skirt up around her waist. As they undress one another, he relishes her wonderful smell and the feel of her skin against his. They find each other's mouth and start moving in rhythm. And as she cries out in pleasure and he climaxes inside her, he thinks: as long as there is this, nothing else matters.

'So,' she whispers, as they pull on their clothes, 'when are you going to tell me what's been going on?'

He sits up, propping her against him and thinking what a relief it will be to confide in someone who has his back. So he spills it all out. His first meeting with Hamish in the wine bar; their visits to Jimmy, to Arnold and Magdalena Leebury, and to Greg Jacobs; the encounter with the mad old woman, Amelia; the passports stolen from the safe at Athelford Hall and of course, Hamish's murder.

She strokes his cheek. 'Quite a story, isn't it?'

'How do you mean?'

She gets to her feet and stands looking down on him. 'Don't you see, Babe? Since your arrest you've taken your eye off the original investigation. But just because this Hamish person is dead, doesn't mean you should give up. Those shipping manifests must mean something – if I can just work out what.'

He shakes his head. 'I'm really grateful for the time you've spent on them, but we're still no nearer to solving what Hamish was up to. But –' He breaks off. 'Why the hell didn't I think of it before? There's one person who can back me up. I did mention it to the police, but they took not a blind bit of notice.'

'You know what the Met are like. They'll try to frame their own grandma if it suits them.'

He's on his feet. 'Sorry about this, when I'm only just back, but I need to follow up a lead.'

'To do with Rosser's murder?'

He nods.

He can see the excitement in her eyes. 'Let me come with you. *Please?*'

'I'm not sure this is something you should get mixed up in.'

'Bit late for that.' She pauses. 'And I want to be with you, Ollie – If that's OK?'

'More than OK,' he says, thinking again how wonderful it is not to have to struggle with this on his own.

The city streets are quiet, a light drizzle falling on pavements littered with discarded drink cans and plastic food wrappers – evidence of the usual Saturday night jollies.

'So where is it we're going?' she asks, linking her arm through his.

'To someone who can help clear my name.'

'Don't know why you have to turn all mysterious on me,' she grumbles and for a moment he wonders if some of Hamish's cloak-and-dagger approach hasn't rubbed off on him. As they pass the Old Bailey, he half expects to catch sight of the diminutive figure striding ahead. *Dinna be late, laddie!* He still can't wrap his brain around the fact that the man has gone.

The alleyway is as he remembered: a shadowy area, dotted with dim shapes of litter bins, with the buildings on three sides towering above him. He wishes he'd advised Amy to wear trainers and now the click of her heels on the paving echoes round the enclosed space. Even in daylight, the place has an oppressive feel and he hurries towards the door at the end. He hasn't thought what he'll do if he finds it locked, but when he gives a tentative push, it opens. The entrance way is dark and when he clicks on the light switch, nothing happens. In the gloom, he can make out the door to the strange old woman's flat and the wires of the broken telephone dangling against the wall.

As he recalls the squalid room at the top, he turns to Amy. 'Maybe better if you wait down here.'

She gives a shiver, glancing over her shoulder. 'No way! I'm coming with you.'

He starts climbing the steep flight, trying not to breathe in the reek of cat piss. Behind him, Amy lets out a muttered: 'Phew – what a stench!' They continue on up until at last, they're at the top and there facing him is the door to Jimmy's room. He turns once more to Amy. 'If you think that smell is bad, just wait till you get a whiff of this.' He pauses. The excitement has vanished from her face and she looks at him, her eyes anxious. 'Stay back,' he orders, before turning and giving a rap on the door.

No answer. He knocks again and then cautiously turns the handle. The door swings open and he steps forward, aware of Amy craning over his shoulder. Then he remains quite still, trying to adjust to the scene in front of him.

The room is empty, stripped bare. Gone is the table with its grease-encrusted top, the rickety chairs and the bed with its pile of filthy blankets. The sink has been cleared of debris and the whole place smells of bleach and disinfectant. His stomach lurches with disappointment. He was banking – foolishly he now realises – on the boy being here.

'So where is this person you're looking for?' Amy whispers.

'No idea. But someone's gone to a lot of trouble to remove all traces of him.' He turns once more to Amy. 'We need to get back to The Strand and hope to God he's still using that doorway.'

'Doorway?'

'This is the rent boy Hamish was supplying with drugs in return for information. He kicked the shit out of Jimmy.' Ollie is surprised by how angry he feels. 'He wasn't fooled by all that House of Lords stuff. He knew what Hamish was really like.' He can see again the boy's white face and the way he cowered on the floor like some beaten animal. He pauses. 'I wish I'd stood up for him more.'

Amy squeezes his hand. 'But you told the police all this?'

'Yup.'

'And they believed you?'

He gives her a look. 'Of course they bloody didn't.'

They start clambering back down the stairs and have just reached the bottom when a door swings open. Standing inside it is the thin, old woman, in the same long skirt and tatty raincoat, a ginger cat pressing against her legs.

'Amelia!' he exclaims.

'Oh – it's you, young man.' Her upper-class accent once again takes him by surprise. 'No doubt looking for Jimmy.' She wipes watery eyes with a filthy handkerchief.

'Do you know where I can find him? It's very important.'

'You can search as hard as you like – it won't do you any good.'

'How do you mean?'

'He's gone.'

'Yes – but where?'

She taps her nose with a bent finger. 'Dead.'

Amy clutches his arm.

'My God,' he murmurs with a selfish stab of disappointment. 'But how?'

'The police reckoned it was an overdose.' She pauses. 'Well, what did you expect? Jimmy didn't have much going for him, did he?'

To his surprise, he feels tears well up. 'No one to care for him or give him a decent home.'

Amelia peers into his face. 'He said you tried to stop that obnoxious Scottish man from beating him up.'

'I didn't do nearly enough.'

'And now Lord Rosser's gone and got himself stabbed.'

'So you saw the news?'

She taps her nose again. 'I may be getting on in years, young man, but I can assure you that I am still in full possession of my faculties.'

A thought occurs to Ollie. 'So did you see him – Hamish, I mean – before he was killed?'

'Luckily for him, no. I'd have strangled him with my bare hands if I could. Although he denied it, I knew he was with those men – the ones who stole my money.' She gives a smile of satisfaction. 'I'm glad someone else got to him first.'

'The police think that *I* did it.' He swallows. 'I was hoping to find Jimmy so he could back me up – tell them what Rosser was really like.'

Amelia holds up a bony finger. 'Wait here!' she orders, before disappearing inside.

Amy shivers. 'This is such a creepy old place. Can't we just leave?'

He puts an arm around her. 'Let's hang on for a few moments. I need to see if the old bat has something useful to say.' Anything, he thinks, that might help.

She reappears, holding out a tattered notebook and a slim file. 'Jimmy asked me to keep these safe for him. Was terrified that Hamish fellow would come looking for them. The boy said you weren't a bad sort, so you may as well have them.'

He takes them from her, more out of politeness than anything else. Amy's spent hours trawling through those shipping manifests and is still no nearer to unravelling the mystery. 'Thanks. Well, we'd best be off.'

She looks at him with her sad, mad eyes. 'There must be thousands like Jimmy on the streets, left to scrounge for food, with no home to go to. This is meant to be a caring society, but caring for whom?' She pauses, the look of venom in her eyes making Ollie take a step back. 'I'll tell you for whom,' she continues. 'All those rich buggers. That's what this nation has come to and more shame on all of us!' Suddenly she turns and disappears inside her flat, the cat at her heels, the door banging shut after her.

'What a weird woman,' Amy murmurs, as they turn out of the cul-de-sac. 'You don't think she had anything to do with this murder, do you, Ollie? She seems to know more than she's letting on.'

'Mm.' He's only half listening, flicking through the notebook and scanning the sheaf of papers inside the folder. 'Sorry, Amy. I need to take a proper look at this when we're somewhere with decent lighting.'

They retrace their steps to the station and once on the train, he continues reading while Amy flips through her cell phone.

Then he looks up. 'I can't believe it!'

'What?'

He lowers his voice, although their carriage is virtually empty. 'This is the record of a prison sentence.'

'Hamish what's-his-name's?'

He shakes his head. 'But I think this is the story he was after.' Ollie waves the paper in the air. 'The prison sentence was given to a Sorina Theresa Logan.'

'Never heard of her.'

'You won't have because, according to this file, she's now known as Magdalena Leebury, the wife of Lord Arnold Leebury, a recently appointed Government minister.' And no wonder Magdalena was so frightened of Hamish, Ollie thinks. She had every reason to be.

'I still don't understand.'

'I'll explain it all later, but first I need to check some facts. And I'll have to discuss them with my editor.' Another thought strikes. 'Trouble is, Arnold Leebury seemed a decent sort, even if he is a lord. If this gets out, it will ruin him.'

'This is our stop.' Amy gets to her feet. 'But isn't it about bloody time you put us first, Ollie?'

He recalls the vast pile of Athelford Hall, the chauffeur,

the maid, and no doubt an army of other staff. Amy is right: the rich are well able to look after themselves. He pictures Magdalena Leebury, so assured and beautiful, gliding towards him across the room, and feels a twinge of disquiet at his own naivety. How easy it is to be taken in by someone like her. But as he knows from his dealings with Hamish Rosser, these people are experts in deception. So could Magdalena be guilty of this murder? She certainly had the motivation.

But if not her – then who?

THIRTY-ONE

MAGDALENA, SEATED IN HER BEDROOM WINDOW, pushes away her half-eaten croissant.

The rain continues to beat down and out in the park, a group of stags are clustered, their antlers a dark bundle of twigs against the grey February sky.

At moments like these, she hungers for lighted shops and the constant movement and noise of London. Here, everything seems drained of colour – made even more joyless by the recent change in her husband – that someone so kind and loving should now be treating her with such coldness. Obviously she miscalculated how much this government post meant to him but as she takes another sip of her coffee, she reminds herself that sometimes, wonderfully, fate can be on one's side. So now the Scottish man is out of the way, she'll be able to make things right.

As usual, Arnie has been up before her and, according

to the ever-reliable Marya, is dealing with paperwork in the library. Once she is dressed, she will go to him – put her arms around him. Tell him how marvellous this appointment is going to be – for both of them. There are bound to be plenty of dinners and formal occasions where to have her by his side will be an asset and of course she will support him in whatever way she can and –

A flash of yellow catches her eye. A uniformed officer is unwinding another length of crime scene tape – this time extending it further along the track. It's weeks since the murder and she would have thought the police would be finished with all that. So how much longer will they continue rooting about the place? She longs to find out what, if anything, they have discovered, but experience has taught her that it's always best to keep a low profile. And the police will soon be gone, she reminds herself, and no doubt the murderer will turn out to be some passing tramp. Or maybe, she thinks suddenly, whoever killed Hamish Rosser wasn't just some random lunatic. If he was planning to blackmail her, there may well have been others with a score to settle.

A knock makes her turn and she looks up to see the chauffeur in the doorway holding out the house phone. He pushes past Marya, covering the mouthpiece with one hand. 'Sorry to unterrupt, Madam.'

Magdalena sighs. 'I've told you before, Seamus – I never accept calls on the landline.'

He shakes his head. 'He's very insistent. Says he's from some newspapur.'

Magdalena's stomach twists. 'Did you not hear me? I said: "No!"'

But the chauffeur is not to be put off. 'He says he has important information. About the murder.'

Perhaps this is information that will persuade Arnie that she is not the one the police are looking for. 'Very well. Put the phone on speaker so that Marya can hear.'

'Who is this?' she says into the receiver.

'Lady Magdalena Leebury?'

'Yes.'

'My name is Jack Coslett, Lady Leebury. I'm the editor of The Dagenham Evening Post.'

'Dagenham?' she repeats, raising an eyebrow at Marya to indicate that this is just another ideeyot. 'I have never heard of that place.'

'I can assure you that it exists' A pause. 'Some information has come into my possession, Lady Leebury, and I was wondering if you've heard the name of Susanna Stepanov?'

She gives a sharp intake of breath. 'Of course not. Why would I?'

'Ten years ago, Susanna Stepanov, also known as Sorina Logan, served several years in prison for –'

Her mouth has gone dry. 'These people have absolutely nothing to do with me!'

'Oh, but I think they do, Lady Leebury.' Another pause. 'I think we both know they do.'

She's aware of Marya beside her, the consternation in her face mirroring her own. 'It is a stupeed lie. Where did you get these names?'

But already she's thinking: the passports. Were they what Hamish Rosser was after? Is that why he was killed?

And then the thought comes again: there may well have been others besides herself who wanted him dead.

'Lady Leebury?'

'I told you. This Susanna or Sorina, or whatever she calls herself, mean nothing to me.'

'So you are saying there's no truth in this report?'

'Of course there is not! Are you crazy, or what?'

'Not crazy, Lady Leebury, I assure you. In fact, I have in front of me a report giving details of your time in the women's prison in –'

'All false. All – how do you say? – fake news.' She draws in her breath. 'If you do not withdraw these stupeed allegations, I will get my solicitor onto you. I will get my husband onto you. He is an important man with much influence.'

'I have already spoken with Lord Leebury.'

She gives another intake of breath. 'If you had done so my husband would have informed me.' Or would he? She moves to the window, trying to put her thoughts in order. Suppose what this editor says is true? But then why hasn't Arnie said anything to her? Is this why he is being so cold? Aloud she says: 'And no doubt he will have told you where to put this ridiculous rumour.'

'I can assure you, Lady Leebury, that it is in your best interests to co-operate. This story is going out very soon. Better for you to be able to verify the facts – to make any necessary adjustments –'

'Oh – do what you fucking well like!'

'If that's how you want to play it.'

The phone goes dead and she looks up to see the

266

chauffeur in the doorway, his face expressionless. 'Anything else you need, Madam?'

'Thank you – but no.' She forces her lips into a smile. 'I know I can rely on your discretion, Seamus – to keep what you heard just now to yourself.'

He gives a slow nod. 'I'll be silent as the grave, Madam.'

The door closes behind him and Magdalena sinks into the nearest chair, covering her face with her hands.

In an instant, Marya is by her side. 'It is bad?'

She bites her lips to stop the tears. 'That man from the newspaper – he knows everything. And he says he's already spoken to Arnie. Whatever am I to do?'

Marya passes her a handkerchief. 'You must go to him. Get to him before Seamus tells him this editor has spoken to you.'

'But Seamus has promised not to tell Arnie.'

'That Irishman is not to be trusted.' Marya pauses. 'I never said anything before, but the night you and Lord Leebury went to that Christmas party – the night the Scottish man was killed – Seamus wasn't where he said he was.'

'How do you mean?'

'You remember that he was laid up with a virus and Arnold asked me to stay behind to keep an eye on him?'

'What of it?'

The maid swallows. 'After you left I went to check on him. It was a very wet night so I ran out to stable block and up the outer stairs to his room. I knocked on the door and when there was no answer, I put my head round.' She looks across at Magdalena. 'Seamus wasn't in his bed, or in the rest of the flat. I thought he must have gone into one of the garages or be somewhere about, but I wasn't going to go looking for him – not in all that rain.'

Magdalena stares. 'You eedyot, Marya! You know that Arnie suspects me of having something to do with this killing. So why the hell didn't you say anything about this before?'

'I thought it better to – you know – let sleeping dogs alone.' She bites her lip. 'Seamus is not someone to get on the wrong side of.'

Magdalena recalls the chauffeur's tall frame and muscular build, and nods. 'The world is filled with men like him – as we know only too well.' She wipes her eyes. 'But we'll come back to this later. More important for now is to work out what I say to Arnie. How can I possibly tell him anything about my past? He will never forgive me.'

'Better he hears it from you.'

Magdalena gets to her feet. 'You're right, and I need to catch him before he leaves for town.' She walks over to the wardrobe and tugs open the door. 'What to wear? Nothing too flashy, I think.'

'How about the Ted Baker trousers and silk shirt?' Marya suggests.

'Perfect, darlink. Now, we must be quick!'

A few minutes later, she's fastening pearls into her ears and with a quick spritz of perfume to wrists and throat, is heading down the stairs, Marya following behind.

In the hall, Edna is on her hands and knees wiping down the skirting-board, a dustpan and brush lying in the middle of the floor.

'Eedyot!' Magdalena shouts. 'I could have broken my neck!' Edna mutters something that Magdalena can't catch before dragging the dustpan to the side. Once things have been sorted out with Arnie, Magdalena decides, she will send Edna packing.

Marya takes her arm and as they walk along the corridor, she whispers: 'Stay close, darlink.'

The library door is closed and Magdalena gives a gentle tap before pushing it open.

Arnie turns from his desk and looks across at her, unsmiling.

'You are still here,' she says, trying to keep her voice bright. 'I thought you might already have left.'

He gets to his feet and she sees with a pang the new lines on his forehead. 'Close the door, Magdalena.'

She pushes it so it remains ajar, gesturing to Marya to stay perfectly still on the other side.

'Now,' Arnie continues, 'please tell me that none of this is true.'

'None of what, darlink?'

His eyes narrow. 'Don't come the innocent with me, Magdalena. I need to know.'

Her lower lip trembles. 'Did the chauffeur inform you that a newspaper man has contacted me?'

'No need for Seamus to say anything. This editor called me himself with some incredible story. I told him it was all a pack of nonsense, of course, but he seemed very confident of his information.'

'But why didn't you come to me, Arnie? Give me a chance to explain?'

Normally she has to will her tears to come but this time, to her surprise, his anguished look is enough to set them off.

'I was waiting for you to tell me yourself. As you're doing now.' He hands her his handkerchief. 'Oh, please don't cry, Lena. We have until midday to get back to him.'

Magdalena feels heartened by the use of that 'we.'

'Which is why you *must* tell me what on earth's going on,' Arnie adds. 'We need to stop these scurrilous lies in their tracks.'

So maybe it's not too late after all, she thinks, sinking into the chair he has drawn up for her. 'I am truly sorry, Arnie. I know I should have mentioned this to you before.'

'Mentioned what exactly?'

'I told you that my parents encouraged me leave our country, but I'm afraid that isn't true.'

The cold look is back in his eyes. 'So now what are you saying?'

She swallows. 'Six of us lived in two small rooms, sharing cooking and bathroom facilities with other families in the block. Despite the difficulties, we got by – until the war with Russia came.' She pauses. Should she tell Arnie that her father sold her to a paedophile in exchange for food? But no – it feels too shameful. 'That newspaper man,' she continues, 'has obviously found out about it. Goodness knows how.' The missing passports explain how she was tracked down, she thinks, but not how her prison record was obtained. But she will worry about that later. For now, her priority is to win back

Arnie's love – and protection. 'I can't pretend it wasn't tough,' she continues, 'and I don't think I'd have got through without Marya's help.'

'Well, thank God for her. But are your family still out there?'

'I was separated from them when I was nine and was told much later that there was a bombing raid. They were all killed – my parents, my two young brothers and my baby sister – as so many were in that war.'

His face is shocked. 'Oh, I'm so sorry, Lena. That must have been terrible for you.'

She nods. 'But I don't know where the newspaper got this other story from. They must be mixing me up with someone else.'

'And you give me your solemn promise that you have never served time in prison?'

'Of course I haven't.'

'You poor darling.'

She leans against him, trembling with relief.

'I wish you'd told me before.' He pauses. 'Obviously we'll need to issue an immediate denial. I'll get on to our solicitor straight away. Meanwhile, you must promise me, Lena, not to take any more calls from the press.'

'I promise.'

For the first time in what feels like an eternity, he kisses her on the mouth. 'I need to get going. I'm wanted up in London.' As he goes out of the room, he calls over his shoulder: 'I should be back early. Let's have dinner together.' He turns to Marya, who is still waiting outside. 'Thank you for taking care of my Lena.'

As he goes off down the corridor, Marya smiles across at her mistress. 'So – all is well.'

Magdalena doesn't reply straightaway. Then she says slowly: 'I have bought us some time, darlink – that is all. Let us just be grateful for that.'

THIRTY-TWO

'OF COURSE IT'S WONDERFUL TO HAVE FRANCES home,' Greg says, accepting the mug of coffee Mrs. Mehta hands him. 'It's just I hate to see her looking so frail.' He pauses. 'Do we need to get in more help?'

Mrs. Mehta shakes her head. 'She says she's happy for me to give a hand with her washing and dressing.' She pauses. 'And at least the house has lost its empty feel.'

Greg sips his drink, still trying to get his head around the bombshell Jason dropped two weeks' ago. 'The thing is, Greg, I've been signed up by this new agency, like. The money's ace so Poppy and I have, like, rented a flat – in Brixton. But thanks for everything.'

Too preoccupied with Frances's illness to mind how like a final brush-off this seemed, Greg is now left with a sense of being both used and useless.

He looks out to the rain beating down on the laurel bushes and running in rivulets along the driveway. If only there were some let up in this bloody weather – that sunshine over Christmas felt all too brief. He's aware also of how much Hamish Rosser's death still hangs over him. He barely knew the man but to be killed so brutally and still with no one arrested, is unsettling. As is the memory of his last meeting with Oliver Moorhouse, who was quite clearly panic-stricken. Did he go to the police as Greg advised? Should he have gone to them himself? But he has quite enough on his plate without getting mixed up in that whole nasty business.

'Do you mind, Mr. Jacobs?' Mrs. Mehta is saying. 'I need to roll out my pastry.'

'Of course.' He gets up from the table, embarrassed to have got in her way. 'I'll just see if there's anything Frances needs.'

He finds her lying, white-faced, on a sofa. She looks up and gives a weak smile. 'I know I'm putting you out,' she murmurs.

He takes the chair beside her. 'Let's have no more such talk. You know what the doctor said: plenty of rest and good food.'

'Thanks to Mrs. Mehta. Whatever would I do without her – and you!' She gives another smile.

'The boot's on the other foot,' he hears himself saying. 'What I mean is' – he hesitates – 'that it's a privilege and pleasure to help. And I intend to be here for you, Frances. Always.' There! He's said it.

She reaches out her hand and he presses it in his

own, enjoying the soft feel of it in his palm. Since her illness her hair has thinned, hanging in limp clusters, her sunken cheeks making the grey eyes too large for her face. A sneaking thought occurs: this illness makes her less attractive to men her own age. Although of course this is none of his business. Frances is like a daughter – the daughter he never had. That is all.

'Talking of the doctor,' she says. 'Those three friends from my course have texted and would like to call in again this afternoon. If that's OK?'

'No need to ask. You know they're always very welcome.'

They have visited several times now – Carys, round-faced and cheerful, with a pronounced Welsh lilt, Felicity, thin and dark-haired, who is from Romania, and the bearded nurse, Ahmed, with his bunch of wilting flowers.

'Well, I'll leave you for now, but perhaps later on you'd like me to continue reading *Persuasion*?'

Unlike most of her generation, Frances doesn't spend hours on her laptop or phone but prefers reading physical books, their shared love of Jane Austen further evidence of the growing bond between them.

Another smile. 'That would be really lovely, Greg.'

In the study that afternoon he clicks on his phone and dials a number. 'Hello, Arnold.'

'Who's this?'

'It's me – Greg.'

'Oh, yes.' No surprise the response is unenthusiastic. He's been intending to call but what with Poppy and Jason moving out and the scare over Frances, he hasn't got round to it. 'So – how are things?'

'Fine. Everything's fine.' The tone, tired and strained, is so unlike his usually cheery friend that Greg frowns. 'Still no arrest?'

'No – just letting the police get on with it.'

'But you must be excited about this government post, Arnold. Congratulations again.'

'Thanks.'

A pause.

'And Magdalena?'

'She's fine too.'

'How about linking up for a quick drink? Perhaps when you're next in town with time to spare.'

'I am rather busy at the moment, Greg. Maybe in a few weeks?'

As Arnold rings off, Greg feels a wave of dejection sweep over him. He misses not having a man to talk to and was hoping to pick up the friendship. But obviously Arnold is not himself, and how terrible it must be for him knowing the murderer is still out there, ready to target God knows who.

Greg's thoughts are broken into by the sound of voices. Frances's fellow students have arrived. He gets up from his desk and goes into the hall to greet them.

'How is she today?' Ahmed whispers.

'A little brighter.'

'That's good.' He smiles. 'We'll try not to tire her.'

Greg gives a nod of approval. 'I'll ask Mrs. Mehta to bring you some tea.'

'Her scones are nearly as good as my mam's,' Carys declares.

'Well, don't let Mrs. Mehta hear you,' Greg says. 'Not until after you've eaten them.'

Ahmed lets out a roar of laughter.

'Well, must press on.' He waves away their thanks before returning to his desk. There are still accounts to be gone through and now that Hamish Rosser, poor man, is out of the picture, Greg needs to find replacement sponsorship.

He's so engrossed in his work that the sound of the grandfather clock striking five takes him by surprise. He goes out into the hall. All is quiet so the visitors have obviously gone. He puts his head round the sitting-room door. 'How are you doing, Frances?'

She hesitates. 'Fine. It was good of those three to visit.' She sounds subdued.

'But something's wrong?'

'You always read me so well, Greg.'

He nods, settling in the chair beside her. 'You know you can talk to me about anything. Have your friends tired you?'

'I do feel a bit wiped, but that's not it.' She pauses. 'I wanted to ask you something.'

He leans forward and, on impulse, takes her hand in his. 'Of course.'

'It's just that Carys and Felicity are in a relationship and are wondering whether to get married. They keep asking *my* advice. Should they go for it? Should they have a cooling-off period – at least until they've finished their training? As if I've any experience in these things!' She hesitates. 'Maybe if

I'd been brought up by parents I would know more.'

Poor girl, he thinks. No wonder she's confused.

'But I'm also thinking about myself. Suppose for instance you're at close quarters with someone and you feel you love them, but you've not known them all that long. Is it OK to say something?' She pauses, blushing. 'I've never been very good with all this women's lib stuff...'

He can feel the pulse in his throat. 'That's a tricky one. But if I were this certain young woman then, yes – I would certainly tell the person concerned.'

'Even if it leaves one ...?' her voice tails away again. 'I'm sorry, Greg – I feel so embarrassed admitting how I feel.'

'I'm just very glad you've brought it up.' He squeezes her hand. 'Because I've been wanting to talk to you also.'

Her eyes widen. 'You have?'

'I was going to wait until you felt stronger.' He tugs his ear, suddenly nervous as a teenager. 'Ever since you've come into this house, Frances, I've known you were very special.'

'As you are to me.'

'And the fact that you're so bravely initiating this subject is proof of that.' He presses her hand once more. 'I've felt things between us develop and now, with this illness of yours, what I want most in the world is look after you.'

'But you already do, Greg! And I can't tell you how grateful I am.'

'But I'm not just speaking of gratitude, as I'm sure you realise.' He swallows. 'So now we both feel the same way, how about taking things further?'

She stares at him blankly. 'Further?'

God – how clumsy he's being! 'I realise this may all be a bit quick for you, so if you'd prefer to wait...' His voice tails away.

'But are you saying –?'

'Yes, Frances, I am!' He strokes her cheek. 'Can't you see how right this is? Obviously, you'll need time to get well, but maybe later in the year, we could start planning?'

To his consternation, she starts to cry, tears trickling down her thin cheeks.

'Oh, my darling.'

'But that's just it, Greg!' She reaches for her handkerchief. 'I'm not.'

'Not what?'

'Your darling.' She struggles upright. 'I'm so sorry. You know how much I owe you for all you've done. Taking me in – and Poppy and Jason too, of course. But if I've understood you right, we're not thinking along the same lines. I've told you how fond I am of you, but I don't mean in *that* way.'

He stares, trying to take in what she's telling him.

'I love you, Greg, because you're kind and generous – like the father I never had.'

'But...' He struggles for the right words. 'You've said how much you enjoy being with me, how special I am to you –' He breaks off, feeling increasingly foolish.

'What I've been trying to say, Greg, is that I've met someone. And I think I'm in love with him.'

He recalls the spring in the fellow's step as he entered

the house, that roar of laughter, the bearded face that seems to wear a perpetual smile. 'It's Ahmed, isn't it?'

She gives a miserable nod. 'We really clicked – right from the very first moment. Once I'm well enough, he wants us to move in together. That's what I needed your advice on.' She reaches for his hand. 'I'm so sorry, Greg. The last thing I want is to hurt you. It's just I had no idea…'

He stares into the red eye of the wood-burner. What is it that he's feeling? Disappointment? Humiliation? Fury? None of them come near it.

'This would never have happened without you, Greg.' Frances murmurs. 'Ahmed and I really owe you.'

He gets up abruptly and makes for the door, pulling it open and standing for a moment, as if paralysed. All his life, he thinks, he will remember Frances as she is now, looking up at him, her eyes filled with a look of mute appeal.

He should be telling her how glad he is for her, offering the fatherly advice she's obviously so desperate to hear– but he simply cannot bring himself to do so. And what makes this whole situation even worse is the knowledge that Ahmed is a thoroughly kind and decent young man. Well deserving of her.

He turns on his heel, steeling himself not to slam the door shut behind him.

Back in the den, he clicks on his laptop and sits, staring at the screen like a blind man.

THIRTY-THREE

MAGDALENA IS TAKING AN AFTERNOON NAP AND from high up in her bedroom, Marya keeps a watchful eye on the various comings and goings. After an absence of several weeks, the police are back, poking about the place, searching for God knows what. A uniformed figure passes below and even this brief glimpse of an official makes her recoil. Far more disturbing, however, is the figure accompanying the police officer – the chauffeur, Seamus, striding along in his usual arrogant way. However he has managed it, he appears to be on easy terms with the police. *Watch yourself with that one!* Marya longs to tell them. Now, recalling the bunched muscles in the man's shoulders and the veiled hostility in the dark eyes, she shudders. What would he do when he learns that Magdalena has discovered he was not in his bed on the night of the murder?

Arnold has informed the household that continuing illness and the on-going laboratory strike means it will be at least another week before the DNA results are through. Information that has reduced Edna to a trembling heap. Marya can spot a guilty conscience a mile off and, not for the first time, longs to advise Edna to tell the authorities what she's hiding from them.

But these domestic niggles are the least of Marya's worries. What causes her stomach to churn and her head to toss on the pillow throughout these long nights is the change in her mistress. Ever since reassuring Arnold Leebury that *of course* she has never been in prison – 'don't be so ridiculous, darlink!' she seems diminished – as if, Marya thinks, some light has been switched off inside her and all that ravishing beauty has been replaced by a faded version of itself. As usual that fat fool, Arnold Leebury, seems neither to notice nor care. The realisation makes Marya want to weep. That and the knowledge that if those passports have fallen into the wrong hands, it will be the end of life at Athelford Hall – for both of them.

The jangle of a bell pulls her from her thoughts. Her mistress has woken and is now downstairs.

She finds the Leeburys in the front room standing a few feet apart. They look across at her uncertainly, as if waiting to be told what to do. The fire has been lit but the logs give off only a feeble warmth and the room feels chilly. One of the projects Magdalena has been working on is the installation of a modern central-heating system. But that plan, along with so many others, is now on hold.

'Ah, Marya,' Magdalena says, speaking as if with an

effort. 'I could do with some coffee.' She turns to Arnold. 'For you also, darlink?'

'What's that? Oh, no. Whisky, please.'

Marya moves to the side table and lifts a decanter from its silver salver. All her movements are slow – she wants to listen to as much of their conversation as possible.

'As I've already told you, Lena,' Arnold is saying, 'the DNA results should be through any day.' He nods thanks as Marya hands him his glass. 'Though I don't know why you should be so concerned about them.'

'It's just all this waiting around. And must you go to London today?'

'Yup.' He gulps his drink. 'I did warn you that this new post is going to take me away more.'

'Having the police back here is unsettling, Arnie. Surely you can understand that?'

'They're only doing their job and I'm sure they won't be bothering us much longer.' He drains his glass. 'And once I'm established in this post, I'll have more time for you, Lena. I promise. And –' He breaks off as his mobile rings. 'One moment.' He checks the screen. 'Our solicitor. I need to take this.'

Magdalena stands motionless.

'Colin!' Arnold is saying. 'Thanks for returning my call. Yes – I'm at the Hall. Yes' – he glances across at Magdalena – 'she is here. O.K. Go ahead.'

After a few moments, he lowers himself into the nearest chair, the phone pressed to his ear. The solicitor is obviously in full flow because apart from the occasional 'yes,' 'no' and 'I see,' Arnold remains silent. Every so often he stares across at Magdalena but not as if he's seeing her, more as if he's a man in a dream. And she remains rooted to the spot watching, as Marya does, the expressions of disbelief, shock and anger chasing one another across his face.

'I'll get back to you, Colin,' Arnold says, clicking off the phone and hauling himself to his feet. He turns to Magdalena. 'As you'll have gathered, that was Colin Newcombe. He has quite a story to tell, but – surprise, surprise – it bears no resemblance to the version you've given me.'

She throws him an anguished look. 'If you'd let me explain –'

'Explain?' He steps towards her, arm raised, and she recoils. Next moment he seizes the empty whisky glass and hurls it across the room, where it lands, splintering shards of glass into the grate. 'Explain?' he repeats. 'Like you did the last time when you swore you were telling me the truth?' He swings round. 'Do you know what our solicitor has just told me? No –' as she goes to speak – 'for once let *me* do the talking. It seems that several passports and documents have found their way into the hands of the press. Oh, don't ask me how – and don't look so innocent, Magdalena! These passports contain your photograph and are most likely forgeries but that's not the worst of it. There is a written record that has now been verified showing that you have served several years in jail – and obviously not for some minor misdemeanour.' He pauses. 'That is the truth, Magdalena. Isn't it?'

She gives a miserable nod, looking across at Marya, the appeal in the grey eyes making Marya blink back tears.

Arnold starts walking up and down the room. 'Christ

in heaven! Have you forgotten how I brought you to the Hall, gave you free run of the place, provided you with anything you wanted? I thought you were so perfect, Lena. That life was so perfect. So how in God's name could you not have told me at the start whatever it is you've done?' He covers his face with his hands. 'This will obviously be the ruination of me – politically and personally. Who's going to want to touch me after this?'

'I am so sorry,' she whispers. 'I didn't mean –'

He swings round to face her. 'Didn't mean to marry me under false pretences? Didn't mean to lie to me all these years? Didn't mean to destroy my chance of a parliamentary career? Pull the other one!'

'I had no choice.'

'Everyone has a choice, Magdalena!'

'Living in your cosy little bubble, Arnold – you have no idea how the world really works!' Marya catches the flash of anger in the eyes.

'Maybe so. But what I do know is that I believed you loved me for who I was. Instead of which you have used me as a cover for whatever crime you have committed. What was it? Drugs? Fraud?' He hesitates. 'Murder? Don't you think you at least owe me a proper explanation?'

'I've wanted to, Arnie! Truly I have.' She takes a tentative step towards him. 'It's just I was too ashamed – and afraid – you wouldn't understand. When I was very young, my father sold me to this man and –'

'You know what, Magdalena? I don't want to hear yet another version of your life story. How can I believe a word you say?'

'I do realise how upsetting this is for you, Arnie, and especially as you're worried about your government post. But we still have each other. We still –'

'– for as short a time as I can possibly make it.' He narrows his eyes. 'I shall ask Colin to draw up divorce papers.'

She bites her lip. 'You can't mean it?'

'I assure you that I do.'

'You really want to leave your Lena, Arnie?'

'No, Magdalena.'

She looks at him, her eyes filled with hope.

'*You* are the one who will be doing the leaving. I can't force you out, but I suggest you book into a hotel as soon as possible– preferably one well away from this area.' He picks up his mobile and taps in a number. 'Seamus? Bring the car round straight away, please.'

'He did it, you know.'

'Who? Did what?'

'Seamus. He was the one who killed Hamish Rosser.'

'For God's sake, Magdalena! Haven't we had enough of your histrionics for one day?'

'But it's the truth. Ask Marya.'

They turn towards her and Marya sucks in her breath.

'Well?' Arnold says.

She hesitates, taken aback by the hostility in his eyes.

'I'm waiting, Marya.'

'It's j-just the night Scottish man was murdered,' she stutters, 'and you went out to that Christmas party, Seamus told the police he was too ill to leave his room.'

'That's right. The fellow was in a bad way.'

'You asked me to keep an eye on him but when I went to take him a hot drink, he wasn't there.'

'Well, maybe he was in the bathroom.'

'I checked. The whole flat was empty – I swear it.'

'And don't you think it suspicious,' Magdalena chimes in, 'that he seems to know so much about the workings of the government…?' Her voice tails off as Arnold gives her a look indicating both disbelief and contempt. 'Of course Seamus has a great deal of information under his belt– he used to work as a driver for the Foreign Office. It's one of the reasons he was given the job here.'

'But he has lied to you!'

'And who am I most likely to believe? Him or you?' He shakes his head. 'The man has passed all the security checks and has impeccable references. And tell me this: What possible motive could he have for the murder?'

'That I do not know, Arnie.'

He moves to the door before turning to face her once more. 'While we're on the subject, perhaps you could enlighten me on one other thing, Magdalena.'

'Yes?'

'Did *you* kill Hamish Rosser?'

Her hand goes to her face. 'How could you even think that?'

'Well, you've lied about everything else.' He pauses. 'I've been such a blundering fool – why on earth didn't I see it earlier?'

She takes a tentative step towards him. 'See what, Arnie?'

'That underneath that surface gloss is a very selfish

woman and – even worse – someone without a heart.' He pauses. 'When I get back, I expect you to be gone.' He waves a hand towards Marya. 'No doubt she's been in on this all along, so I want her away from here as well.' He pauses. 'Do you understand?'

'*Please,* Arnie. Couldn't you just –?'

'Couldn't I what? Pretend all this has never happened? Pretend that I'm not married to someone whose criminal record will be splashed all the press? No, Magdalena. I could not!'

The door slams shut after him and Marya looks across at her mistress, who stands, twisting a strand of hair between her fingers. With a pang, Marya is struck once more by the change in her appearance – the flawless skin is drawn and sallow, and the light has gone from her eyes.

'Oh, Marya!' she cries, 'if only I could make him understand.' She stares around her. 'Sometimes at night I dream I'm back in that bombed-out flat with the shells thudding around us, my mother lying on her blood-stained mattress. And that fat stranger in the doorway. 'Be a good girl and go with him,' my papa is saying. 'He is our friend.'

Marya moves to the side table and pours a large whisky that Magdalena accepts, hands shaking. 'And Arnie is wrong. Experiences such as ours do not take away our heart – they take away our soul.'

'It was destroy or be destroyed, my love.'

Magdalena gulps her drink. 'But do you think he will change his mind?' Her voice is sad.

Why, Marya thinks with a familiar stab of jealousy, she

really cares for that lump of a husband. She shrugs. 'Who can tell?'

'You are right. The milk is already spilt. And we have been in some tight spots before, have we not?' Magdalena wipes away her tears. 'How many years since we were in that prison?'

'Twenty-five,' Marya hesitates. 'But now we leave here?'

'Naturally.'

Marya is swept by a wave of gratitude. Once more she will have her darling to herself. And whatever is facing them now can't be as bad as what they went through all those years ago.

THIRTY-FOUR

'IT'S THAT MAN AGAIN, MR. JACOBS.'

Greg looks up from a mess of paperwork. He's spent the morning having a general clear-out, trying to shake off his anger and hurt pride. What a fool to have imagined that Frances could have the same feelings for him as he does for her! And she and Ahmed are coming over for a meal later. How on earth will he be able to cope with seeing the two of them together?

'Mr. Jacobs?'

'Sorry, Mrs. Mehta. What were you saying?'

'Oliver Moorhouse – the one they accused of Hamish Rosser's murder. Shall I tell him you're busy?'

He shakes his head. He'll be glad of something to distract him from his thoughts. 'I should have been more sympathetic – turns out he was innocent all along.'

'You were only protecting yourself – and this

household.' She pauses. 'You're always thinking of others, Mr. Jacobs. Maybe too much so.'

If only she knew. 'Never mind that. Now he's here, I may as well see him.'

As Oliver Moorhouse is ushered into the study, Greg is immediately struck by the change in his appearance. That shabby, defeated look is gone and there's a new air of alertness about him.

'I'm so grateful to you, Mr. Jacobs,' he says, giving Greg's hand a firm shake, 'for encouraging me to go to the police. It was tough going at first but, thank God, they now realise I was telling the truth all along.' He holds out an envelope.

'What's this?'

'Take a look. I thought you were the best person to have them.'

'Have a seat then.'

Greg shoves his papers to one side and extracts two typewritten sheets from the envelope. He reads slowly, before looking up at his visitor. 'This is unbelievable! You're sure they're authentic?'

'I know it's an incredible coincidence but it *is* her, isn't it?'

'Oh yes,' Greg says. 'It certainly is.' An idea is creeping into his mind.

'The originals are there, along with two copies. Up to you what you do with them.' He pauses. 'I don't want to be the one bringing unhappiness into yet more people's lives.' He gets to his feet. 'I'd better get back. I've promised my girlfriend I'd take her to the latest spy thriller.'

'Enjoy yourselves,' Greg says. 'And thanks.'

Greg finds Mrs. Mehta in the front room. Once again, he experiences a jolt, half expecting to see Frances curled in an armchair turning towards him with one of her wide smiles.

Mrs. Mehta puts down polish and duster. 'You seem a bit brighter.'

'Sorry– I've been a bit of a grouch lately.'

She sighs. 'Takes getting used to – not having Frances around, although I'm glad she and Ahmed are settled into their new place.'

'They're due around seven.'

'I'm making Chicken Jalfrezi – Frances's favourite.'

He thinks again of the information Oliver Moorhouse has given him. 'After we've eaten, I'd appreciate a quiet word with them.'

'Of course. It'll be so good to see her. And what a nice young man. Thoroughly reliable. You said he's just got his nursing degree, so at least they'll have his salary to live on.'

Greg knows that even a few weeks ago he'd have been offering financial help to tide the couple over until Frances qualified. But surely he's done more than enough? And maybe she'll be back under this roof sooner than anyone imagines.

He returns to the den and, pouring a whisky to steady himself, stares at the envelope from Oliver. With a feeling of guilt, he catches himself thinking. What would Anne have made of it all? He lifts her photo out of the drawer. Thirty years since his first sighting of her and, despite the devastating loss of Billy-boy and Greg's own depression, a happy enough marriage.

'I'll never forget you, my love,' he whispers, 'but you'd be the first to tell me that we can't stay stuck in the past.'

He replaces the photograph, face-down, in the drawer and drains his glass.

'Greg!' Frances flings her arms around his neck. For a moment, he feels taken aback by her exuberance. 'Good to see you,' he murmurs, pressing her to him.

'And it's so great to be here – and for you and Ahmed to get to know each other better.'

'Come on through,' Greg says, extending a hand to forestall the hug Ahmed seems about to give him. 'I thought we'd eat straight away. Mrs. Mehta will be joining us.' He'll be glad to have her with him – isn't sure how he'd cope having to make polite conversation when he's awash with such a potent mix of feelings – anger and humiliation, but also delight at seeing Frances once more.

They settle at the table. 'This is like coming home,' Frances declares, accepting the plate of curry Mrs. Mehta hands her.

So it won't be hard for her to adjust to being back, Greg thinks. 'Wine?' he offers.

Ahmed smiles, his teeth white against his beard. He's a good-looking chap, Greg grudgingly admits to himself. And *young*.

'Water will be fine,' Ahmed says.

'For me also,' Frances adds.

Her cheeks are a better colour and, despite being still

on the thin side, she's become more – Greg searches for the word – "alive."

'And you've passed your course, Ahmed,' Mrs. Mehta says. 'Well done!'

He gives another of his irritating smiles. 'It's been a bit of a long haul, but worth it. And we've got an announcement to make: Frances and I have decided to get married.'

'That's wonderful!' Mrs. Mehta says.

Greg should be offering his congratulations, but no words will come.

'We thought we'd go for a date in June,' Frances says.

Ahmed squeezes her hand. 'No point hanging around.'

'And it's not as if we've any relatives to consider,' Frances continues. 'Although' – she looks across the table – 'I think of you as family, Greg. And Mrs. Mehta also.'

'So you're from Syria, Ahmed?' Greg manages to get out.

He nods, his smile fading.

'The rest of your family still out there?'

'No – they didn't make it.'

Frances strokes Ahmed's cheek. 'Drowned in the Med, my poor love.'

'Oh, I'm so sorry,' Mrs. Mehta says. 'That must have been terrible for you, Ahmed.'

'Yes – but I've found the best way of coping is by giving something back. So I feel very lucky to have been allowed to settle here – and to have met this wonderful girl.'

'And we're going to build a wonderful life,' Frances

says. 'All thanks to you, Greg.' But like the twist of a knife in his gut her look of warmth is no longer for him.

He listens as they discuss the arrangements for their wedding and how they will juggle their different shift hours. Even harder than their excitement is the way Ahmed keeps fondling the back of her neck and laughing into her eyes. And as Greg sees how she leans against him, the total trust she puts in him, he thinks: they are lovers. Well, what did he expect?

At last a pause in the conversation allows him to move things on. 'That young chap came to see me earlier.' He tries to keep his voice casual.

'Who do you mean?' Frances asks.

'He visited with Hamish Rosser. You remember, Frances? You kindly brought us our tea.'

She frowns. 'Since having Covid, my brain's gone a bit scrambled. But it's terrible about that Scotsman being murdered.'

'You never told me about this, sweetheart?' Ahmed's forehead creases in concern.

'He was killed at the home of a close friend, Arnold Leebury,' Greg explains. 'He's really upset over the whole business.'

'Greg took me to meet the Leeburys,' Frances says. 'Their house is amazing – more like a palace really.' She smiles. 'They were both so kind. Said they'd love to see me again.' She strokes Ahmed's arm. 'Perhaps we could go down together so I can introduce you. With Greg of course.'

'Maybe allow time for the dust to settle,' he says,

wondering if he could arrange a visit when Ahmed was working a shift.

'But they still haven't found the killer, Mr. Jacobs?' Mrs. Mehta asks.

'Unfortunately not. Oliver – Rosser's assistant – was under suspicion but he's now in the clear.' He pauses, looking across at Frances. 'But he also told me something that concerns you.'

She frowns. 'I don't understand.'

'If we've all finished eating, perhaps you and Ahmed would come through to the next room and I'll explain.'

The young couple settle on the sofa, arms wrapped around one another. Ahmed looks across and gives a warm smile. How satisfying, Greg thinks, that in just a few moments he'll be wiping the grin off that bearded face!

'See we're not disturbed, would you?' he says to Mrs. Mehta, who nods and with a final glance at the couple, is out of the room.

Greg's pulse throbs in his temple and his palms feel sweaty. But he's come this far and will blooming well see it through. He clears his throat. 'I'm very sorry to have to tell you this.'

Frances leans forward. 'You're not ill, are you, Greg?'

He shakes his head. 'This is nothing to do with me. But I'm afraid it is something that will affect both of you.'

Ahmed grips Frances's hand. 'Whatever it is, we just need to know.'

'Some information has come into my possession which–'

'Mr. Jacobs?' Mrs. Mehta is saying.

He swings round. 'I told you– no interruptions!'

'But –' she gets no further because, shaking the rain from their clothes, their faces flushed from the outside air, are Poppy and Jason. The boy winks across at Frances and Ahmed. 'Old man giving you one of his lectures?'

Before Greg can speak, the two young women have thrown their arms around one another and then the four gather in a circle, laughing and talking.

'Just look at that, Mr. Jacobs,' Mrs. Mehta whispers. 'You should be very proud.'

He swallows, struggling to adjust to what is happening.

Jason breaks away from the others. 'We just came by to say a quick hello, like, and to congratulate Frances and Ahmed.'

'And Jason's got a favour to ask you, Greg,' Poppy says. Although her pregnancy isn't yet showing, she's lost that wan, pinched look.

'Well, spit it out.' This must be to do with money. Do they really expect him to continue funding them while they drift through life doing God knows what?

Jason looks away, embarrassed – as well he might, Greg thinks.

'The baby – a boy – is due in the summer,' Poppy says. 'And we're going to call him Chester.'

'And we want his second name to be Greg, like.'

'After you,' Poppy adds unnecessarily.

Greg stares – blindsided, speechless.

'And we'd love for you to come to see us, Greg – when you can fit us in.'

He feels tears well up. 'Thanks very much, the pair of you.'

Greg gives Poppy's stomach a pat. 'We'll keep you posted, like, as to how Chester Greg is getting along.'

After Jason and Poppy have been waved off, Greg stands in the hall with the other young couple. 'So what was it you needed to tell us, Greg?' Frances is trembling and there are deep shadows under her eyes. Ahmed puts an arm around her and, as he looks at them, Greg feels the fight drain out of him. 'Nothing that can't wait.' His voice is gruff. 'And I think, Ahmed, it's time you took Frances home.'

Back in the den, he sinks into his chair and reaches for Anne's photograph, studying the fair hair blowing in the Cornish breeze and that quizzical expression, as if to say: *What now?*

His mobile buzzes.

'Greg – I'm so glad to have got hold of you. Oh, God! – I – it's just that...' Arnold is sobbing down the line, incoherent, and starts repeating his wife's name, over and over: 'Lena, Lena, Lena...'

The papers have been full of it, of course.

'I'm so very sorry, Arnold.'

'I could have understood her being convicted for drug dealing, robbery – even murder! But child trafficking..?' He breaks down, once more overwhelmed by sobs.

'Would you like to meet up?'

'I'm staying in town at my club.'

'So how about tomorrow morning, around eleven?'

'That's really good of you, Greg. See you then.'

Greg sits back in his chair. Arnold's call has disrupted

his earlier train of thought and it's an effort to focus.

He moves over to the filing cabinet and, extracting a page from one of the folders, places it on the table with the document Oliver Moorhouse gave him earlier – the prison record of Sorina Theresa Hofer, aka Magdalena Leebury.

And beside it, Frances's birth certificate: *To Sorina Theresa Hofer, a daughter, Frances Matei. Born: London August 14th, 2003. Father unknown.*

Lady Leebury's criminal past may be common knowledge, but what is known only to Oliver Moorhouse and Greg himself is that Magdalena is Frances's mother.

And better it stays that way, Greg thinks, getting to his feet and putting the documents through the shredder.

THIRTY-FIVE

M ARYA FOLDS THE RED LACE EVENING GOWN INTO the suitcase and pushes down the lid. 'That's the last one,' she declares.

'Excellent, darlink,' Magdalena says, inching her chair closer to the electric fire – the Hall's only source of heating since the radiators packed up.

Two days since Arnold Leebury ordered them out but, despite all Marya's urgings, Magdalena remains adamant. 'Why should we have to slink off to some hotel? Once our flights are confirmed, we will leave with our heads held high. And anyway, who is to know?'

Certainly not that stupid husband, Marya thinks, hauling the suitcase over to join the pile by the door. He informed them he was moving into his London club, and Mrs. Acheson and Edna have also gone – without a word of a goodbye. Not that Marya misses them, or that pig of a chauffeur, who is presumably staying up in town also. But still she's anxious to be away from here. Any moment the story of Magdalena's prison sentence will be bringing reporters and, God knows who else, to the door. And suppose the police come knocking with further questions about the murder?

Yet a further cause for unease is the memory of the items Magdalena has removed from the safe: banknotes, diamond jewellery and a Faberge egg that was a wedding gift from Arnold's father to his bride. 'If Arnie didn't mean me to have them, he would have changed the combination,' Magdalena declared. But Marya is not convinced – can imagine him bursting in on them with a look of outrage and a couple of uniforms at his heels.

'You worry too much,' Magdalena says now. 'The taxi will be here in a couple of hours so how about you brew us some fresh coffee?'

As Marya makes her way down the wide stairs, she's struck by how quickly the place has taken on the desolate feel of an empty house: dead ash piled in the fireplaces and dust shivering in the draft from under the doors. In the hall, a spider dangles from the marble bust. Edna's bucket and dusters are heaped by the skirting-board and on impulse Marya picks up a cloth and drapes it over the head, glad not to have those blank eyes following her around.

She climbs down the narrow flight to the kitchen, where she is greeted by a blast of hot air. She's never learned the workings of the Aga and the heat accentuates the stench from unwashed dishes, overflowing bins and stack of greasy containers. Since Mrs. Acheson's departure, they have been living on takeaways – with all the money she and Magdalena now have, Marya's days of clearing up other people's mess are done.

She wipes a line of sweat from her forehead before moving over to the kettle. The heat of the kitchen feels tropical and she is swept by a wave of vertigo. The past two days of sorting and packing has got to her. Her joints ache and the thought of the flight ahead fills her with fear. Enclosed spaces still make her panic – a reminder of what it was like being trapped in that container all those years ago.

She closes her eyes and, with a jolt, is back once more, standing beside Jacques on that dockside, waiting for the last cargo of the day to load.

It was a relief to feel the burning heat of the day ease. Soon, thank God, it would be time to return to the room she shared with three others to collapse exhausted onto her bunk.

She watched the black van draw up, on schedule as always, and the same woman, still in her drab clothes, climbed out, followed by some two dozen young girls, dressed in a rainbow of pinks, oranges and blues, chattering away like a flock of exotic birds.

'Wouldn't mind getting in amongst that lot!' Jacques whispered.

The man might be repulsive but Marya understood his reaction. As the girls drew closer she could see how pretty they were: slim-waisted with flawless skin and shining hair. And how naïve, she thought, tempted for a moment to warn them. But even if she did, they probably wouldn't have believed her. And also it would be at the price of her job, her life, the first rule of which was that it was everyone for themselves.

The woman held up a hand for silence before pointing the group towards the waiting ship. Night came suddenly here and as the darkness fell, the dockside lamps clicked on.

The woman led the way up the lighted gang plank, with Marya behind and Jacques bringing up the rear – the three of them on hand to forestall any hint of rebellion from the girls. At the top, a container stood apart from the others. The woman flashed her torch inside to reveal mattresses, buckets and several air vents cut into the far wall.

The girls fell silent.

'The journey will only take a couple of days,' Jacques assured them. 'Your luggage will be waiting for you at your accommodation, which will be first class.' He gave the nearest girl a shove. 'So get in there.'

As the group stepped inside, two stevedores moved forward. Like all the dock workers, they were well paid for their co-operation – and their silence.

'Time to leave,' Jacques ordered and the woman, with Marya behind her, started their descent down the gangplank. They were almost at the bottom of the ramp when the wail of a siren wafted towards them. Marya and the woman froze. Jacques jumped onto the dockside. 'Fucking hell,' he called up, 'make a run for it!' The sirens grew louder and four police cars came careering across the concrete, drawing up with a squeal of brakes.

Marya watched the uniformed figures leap out and go running after Jacques and the other figures that were emerging from the darkness.

The entrance gates were blocked by police and already Jacques was being wrestled to the ground. She turned to see the schoolteacher stepping into the container, yelling at the crew to seal the doors. Marya hesitated before running back up and flinging herself inside. She landed with a thud and the girls pulled back, startled.

'What are you doing?' the woman stood over her, arms folded across her chest. 'There's no room for you here.'

Marya looked up at her. 'Please,' she said. 'If the police don't get me, Jacques will.'

Her face contorted with fear. 'What do you think he will do when he finds both of us gone? Now get the fuck out!'

Marya ignored her, crawling onto the nearest mattress and when the woman made a grab, she kicked out, her shoe contacting flesh.

'Little bitch!' The woman backed off, rubbing her leg. 'Do you imagine you're going to get work like these girls?'

Of course she was right. Who would want an ugly, middle-aged woman when there were these gorgeous young things on offer? So why leave the port for a life that might prove much worse? If she stayed, she'd spend only a few months behind bars while, with any luck, Jacques would get a long sentence.

Marya had plenty of practice in moving fast and now she was on her feet and lunging towards the doors. For any moment now the police would come charging up the gangplank to arrest the captain and impound the ship.

One of the girls, with a pretty face and dark hair who looked to be in her early teens, joined her. 'I've also changed my mind,' she called.

But they were too late – the doors slammed shut and she could hear the throb of the engines vibrating through the metal walls. The dark-haired girl burst into sobs while the rest of the group huddled together in silence, their giggles long gone.

The woman glared across at Marya. 'You have a kick like a mule.'

The container gave a lurch and Marya steadied herself against the metal side. Her shirt was soaked with sweat and she could feel the thump of her heart as if it too was trying to break free.

She could feel them being hoisted up until they hung in the air, swinging from side to side. Some of the girls began to scream. The woman sank onto a mattress. 'For God's sake,' she murmured, through closed eyes, 'stop your yowling and settle down'.

Marya moved from the doors, sucking on her bruised knuckles, and choosing a corner where she could keep watch on everyone. The girls posed no threat – barely out of the nursery, the little fools. But although the woman sat with closed eyes, some instinct told Marya to stay on her guard.

When, a couple of hours later, it was clear the harbour police were not coming in pursuit, Marya consoled herself with the thought that at least she'd got away from that bastard, Jacques, who with any luck would soon be rotting in some prison hell-hole. And when the ship finally docked, the waiting gang would have no use for her. So, that would be the moment to disappear. But how to do that without money or help?

They were now out on open water, the ship tipping violently from side to side. From the group of girls came cries followed by the splatter of vomit on the metal floor.

'Use a fucking bucket!' the woman shouted.

But even if they'd done so, it would have made no difference. The air reeked of puke and diarrhoea. As Marya knew only too well, fear turned most people into cattle.

A couple of the girls – twins by the look of them, with the same blonde curls and turned-up noses – began crying again. Marya expected the woman to restore order but she was bent double, clutching her stomach. Suddenly she sprang up, reaching one of the buckets and vomiting copiously into it. When she finished, she began hunting through her handbag, before coming up empty-handed and sinking onto the mattress once more.

Marya hesitated before getting up and holding out a crumpled handkerchief. The woman took it from her and wiped her mouth. 'You didn't have to do that. But thanks.'

'Water?' Marya asked.

She nodded, taking a swig from the bottle Marya handed to her. 'Fucking sea. I've never cared for it.' She looked up at her. 'You obviously have a strong stomach.'

'And a mule's kick.'

The woman's face softened into a smile.

'Name's Theresa,' she said, pressing the handkerchief to her nose.

'Marya.'

She jabbed a finger towards the girls, some of whom were curled on mattresses while others queued for one of the buckets. 'Didn't think I'd end up in here.'

Marya couldn't mask the anxiety that crept into her voice. 'But what will happen when we reach port?'

'I'll get the crew to ship you back.'

Marya hesitated. 'And if I don't want to return?'

'That's up to you.' She paused. 'I saw the way Jacques was pestering you.'

'If it's not him, it'll be someone else.'

'Not very good at looking after yourself, are you?'

Marya felt a wave of anger. 'I was seven years old when my parents upped and left, taking my brothers with them. As the only girl, I was of no use to them.' She paused. 'I've been taking care of myself ever since.'

Theresa looked at her. 'The captain might be able to arrange for you to be taken to wherever it is you want to go.'

'But won't he be arrested?'

She gave a smile. 'Rudy is well able to look after himself.'

'But I've no money.'

The woman patted her handbag. 'Plenty here.'

Everything came at a price, Marya thought. Aloud she said: 'Why would you do this?'

'Having you here gives me courage.'

'To leave the port?'

Theresa hesitated again. 'To leave Jacques.' She pointed to the girls. 'Ten years ago I was fourteen and just like them. Jacques took a fancy to me, paid a week's wages to the gang organiser and has kept me as his mistress ever since.'

'Oh.'

'So what we need to do now is to see the girls are handed over without any scenes or panic. Then we will ask my friend, Rudy, for help.' She patted the mattress. 'Room here if you want it.'

Marya sank down beside her, and as Theresa's head nodded onto her shoulder, she felt unexpected warmth towards this stranger, who seemed to be offering an escape from her miserable existence. She took it with a pinch of salt, of course, but still the apparent kindness moved her.

Hours later she woke to the grinding of machinery followed by loud thumps. She looked up to see that Theresa was already on her feet. 'That's us docking now, girls. Form a queue – and no pushing. I don't want your new employers to think they are paying for the services of an ignorant rabble.'

'But how will they want us to clean and cook for them looking like this?' one of the fair-haired twins wailed. Her hair was matted and her dress streaked with vomit – and the rest of the group were no better.

Theresa nodded. 'First of all, you will be taken to a hotel – five star, of course – to be cleaned up. Hot showers, a change of clothes, make-up and perfume. Whatever food you wish.'

In an instant the girls were all smiles, forming an orderly line, and once more chatting together. Poor little fools, Marya thought.

Then came the same swinging sensation of the container being winched up and the thud as it landed on the deck. 'I will lead the way, girls,' Theresa said, as they heard the bolts being drawn back. She turned to Marya. 'Stay close.'

Marya was only too pleased to obey and when she finally stepped onto the gangplank and drew in deep breaths of the salty air, she wondered when she had last felt so happy – and so free.

'There's Rudy.' Theresa pointed to the dockside where a group of figures, dressed in navy uniform, stood staring up at them. 'He will fix everything.'

They began their descent and when they reached the quay, Theresa paused to root in her bag and spray herself copiously with rose water, the scent of it helping to mask the stink of vomit. Then she moved forward, holding out her hand to a stocky, red-bearded man, looking to be in his late forties. 'Rodolfo!' She smiled up at him. 'Bet you didn't expect to see me!'

He remained silent.

'This is the one?' a second uniformed figure asked.

It took just a few moments for Marya to realise that the uniformed figure at his side was not a harbour official but a police officer.

THIRTY-SIX

TWO POLICE CARS AND AN AMBULANCE, ITS warning lights flashing, were lined up on the quay and, like a punch to the gut, Marya realised: the captain was being dragged away.

A second uniformed officer prodded the two women forward. They passed the group of young girls, who were being offered blankets and hot drinks. One of the blonde twins gave them the finger. Marya treated the girl to a cold stare. Little fool didn't know how lucky she was, she thought enviously.

'You must listen to me,' Theresa, stumbling in front of her protested. 'I was forced into that container.'

The police officer gave her another shove. 'Save your sob story for the boss.'

Marya followed Theresa and the rest of the crew into a brick building, its floor covered in cracked tiles and the walls stained with traces of blood and bodily excretions. They joined a line of those waiting to be processed by the bored-looking official behind the desk. From there, they were transferred to a police station and herded into a cell with seven other women: blacks, Chinese, a frail-looking Indian, bent double with curvature of the spine, and a younger European with shaved head and nose rings who launched a gob of yellow spittle that landed at Marya's feet.

'Caddisflies!' Marya muttered, looking around for her friend.

She was crouched in a corner of the cell, her skirt creased and stained and her mousy hair plastered to her cheeks. She looked up at Marya with panicked eyes. 'For God's sake – get me out of here!'

Marya didn't know what impulse made her reach out and stroke the woman's face. 'You'll get used to it,' she whispered.

She gave a disbelieving laugh. 'At least with Jacques, I had a home and decent food.'

Marya waved a hand at a large, brown cockroach scuttling across the floor. 'There's something for us to chew on.'

Theresa shook her head. 'What if the bastards here won't listen to me?'

She searched for words that would comfort. 'What is the worst that could happen? A prison sentence? For sure. But maybe only for a few years, and –'

Theresa clutched Marya's arm. 'You must understand. There's no way I would survive that.'

Marya gazed at Theresa's matted hair and snotty nose and felt that same urge to protect and, more than that, a strange tenderness. She squeezed Theresa's hand. 'We will get through – together.'

She gave the ghost of a smile that lit up Marya's insides in a way that was pleasurable but confusing. She had only had close dealings with men so perhaps what she was feeling was maternal love? After all, Theresa must be a good two decades younger. But having someone other than herself to care for gave her a sense of sunshine reaching inside her.

After weeks of waiting, their case came to trial and they were given a five-year sentence. The prison compound, its brick walls topped with rolls of barbed wire, consisted of four three-storeyed blocks, centred around a muddy, rectangular courtyard, where they were allowed to exercise for an hour each day.

Compared with Marya's childhood experience, the life here seemed almost luxurious. The food – polenta, tripe soup and cabbage – was adequate, they were allowed a cold shower once a week, and best of all, she and Theresa were housed in a cell with two Nigerian women in their forties, who spoke only to one another in their own language – Hausa or Yoruba, according to the guards. This suited Marya, who wanted nothing to distract from her task of ensuring that Theresa swallowed down the prison food and walked with her round the courtyard each day, often in bitter winds and driving rain. It took nearly a year before she started eating with any appetite. 'Whatever would I have done without you?' she said. Best of all, sometimes at night Theresa would allow Marya to climb into her bunk to stroke her back and plant kisses on the smooth breasts. Once or twice she reached down, for the soft place between Theresa's legs. Inevitably, her hand would be pushed away, leaving Marya to climb back into her own bunk. And as she lay pleasuring herself in the dark, she clung to the thought that one day Theresa would return her love – a precious gift that she longed to share.

Yet now Theresa was stronger, there was a new source of worry: the looks the guards gave her as she passed. 'These men are animals,' Marya warned, but that did not stop Theresa casually tucking a strand of hair behind her ear or walking with a suggestive swing of the hips that left Marya weak with desire – and unease. Gone were the efficient schoolmistress and the woman with dead eyes and in their place was someone who moved with the assurance and stealth of some wild creature.

The following year, as a reward for good behaviour, they were given a cell to themselves. If there was trouble from any of the other women – fights were frequent – Marya was well able to deal with them, protecting Theresa from flailing fists and delivering well aimed blows that ensured they were left alone.

They were assigned to different workshops – Marya to the laundry where she spent long hours scrubbing sheets and towels in a mixture of soap flakes and caustic soda that left her hands raw and bleeding. Theresa had an easier time in the kitchens, chopping potatoes and cabbage and clearing up after the evening meal. She would return to the cell a good hour after Marya, often carrying a bag of food

– soft bread and salami, oranges or a container of good coffee – as well as luxuries like shampoo and scented soap. 'What did you have to do to get these?' Marya would ask. 'You're happy enough to enjoy them' was the reply. 'And if you're scared of wolves,' Theresa added, 'then don't go into the woods.'

One evening, at the end of a tough day's work, Marya lay dozing on her bunk until the clang of doors alerted her: they were being banged up for the night and Theresa had not returned.

A guard appeared in the doorway. 'My cell mate's not back,' she called, trying to keep the panic from her voice. 'What have you done with her?' He shrugged, shutting the door with a slam.

'Where is she!' Marya called through the vent.

'Shut the fuck up or I'll have you in isolation!'

Marya buried her face in her hands. Punishments for breaking the curfew were severe: weeks in the slammer or a deferment of the release date. But even more terrible than these options was the dread that her beloved friend was lying injured – perhaps wounded by an inmate or guard.

The night dragged on and then, at first light, the cell door was unlocked and Theresa appeared wearing a curiously satisfied look.

'I thought you'd been attacked or killed!' Marya cried.

'No need to get so worked up. I've been busy – planning our future.'

'How do you mean?'

Theresa smiled. 'The governor is a generous man.'

Just the thought of Octav Matei made Marya shudder. Middle-aged and overweight, with thick, red lips and greying hair, he emerged from his office each New Year to give the inmates a speech underlining the virtues of self-restraint and obedience.

'How can you stand it?' Marya whispered, as the two women lay in their bunks for what remained of the night. 'Being pawed by that man and – you know...' She couldn't bear to think of it.

Theresa reached out and stroked Marya's arm. 'What's a little fuck here and there, when it will get us what we want?'

Marya quivered under the rare touch. 'What *we* want?'

'You will see.'

A week later, Theresa arrived back in the cell. 'It's paid off!' she exclaimed. She dug in her pocket, lifting out bank notes along with a bundle of papers that she waved in the air. 'Passports and plane tickets!'

'But where are we going?' Marya asked, although she didn't care as long as they were together.

'To make a new start.'

They landed at Heathrow on a breezy afternoon in late March. The flight was bumpy and, as they stood together in Central London, Marya felt profound gratitude for having survived the experience of being hurtled through the air at God alone knew what speed, with only a thin sheet of metal between her and oblivion.

Theresa was left queasy and as they sat in a cafe in Piccadilly, she picked at a salad. Marya, however, was enjoying the best meal of her life: a beefburger crammed with real meat, a mound of fries, and apple pie swimming in yellow cream.

She enjoyed seeing the chattering crowds inch their way past the window while opposite, a wall of coloured advertisements shifted in a kaleidoscopic display. It was a miracle to have made it this far, so was it too much to hope that in this wonderful new country, her love might be reciprocated?

Theresa pointed to the advertisements. 'See that blonde woman in the racing car? Just by looking the way she does, she convinces the world to buy anything – to do anything.'

Marya scooped up the last mouthful of pie. 'You will go blonde?'

Theresa smiled. 'Maybe a nice shade of chestnut. And with proper clothes and makeup, I shall reinvent myself. But first, we have a problem.' She gave her stomach a pat. 'Why do you think Octav was so keen to get rid of me?'

Marya put down her spoon. 'You don't mean you're…?'

'I was offered an abortion but you know what those butchers are like. And if I try for one here, I'll get deported.' She sighed. 'So I'll just have to go through with the birth.'

Marya reached for Magdalena's hand. 'You mustn't worry about anything. I will look after you.'

They found work as night-time office cleaners and, as Theresa's pregnancy advanced and she became too tired to manage more than a couple of hours, Marya covered for her, vacuuming and polishing at speed and ensuring that Theresa was on her feet when the supervisor came round to inspect.

Five months later, on a humid August morning, Theresa's waters broke. An ambulance rushed her to hospital and when Marya visited the maternity unit the following day, she was relieved to find her friend sitting up in bed, the baby in the cot beside her. 'Thank God you are all right!'

'An official is coming tomorrow to take my details,' Theresa said, 'so I need to get out of here. You've bought a change of clothes?'

Marya nodded. 'What about the child?'

'I will pin her name to her cot – Frances, after a neighbour who was kind to me, and Matei, after my friend the governor.'

'It's not too late to change your mind. We could still care for her.'

'And what kind of life could I give her?' She reached down and stroked the small head with its fluff of dark hair. 'She does have such tiny fingers and the softest skin – like a peach.'

'But you are crying!'

'She'll be better off without me.' Theresa wiped away a tear. 'And, anyway, the moment I'm fit for work, I plan to earn far more than I'll get as a cleaner.'

'But how?'

'The only profession open to us, darlink. The oldest one.'

Marya gazed again at the sleeping child and thought: As well we're leaving her. She has Matei's nose.

THIRTY-SEVEN

EARLY MORNING CALLS STILL MAKE OLLIE NERVOUS – a reminder of those times when Hamish Rosser would ring to demand another meeting or to ask for information that Ollie simply didn't have.

The buzz continues, as persistent as a wasp. 'For God's sake, answer the blooming thing!' Amy mutters, pulling the duvet over her head.

He clicks on the phone and next moment is off the bed.

'We need to speak, Ollie. OK to call into the office – soon as you can make it?'

'Be with you by seven,' he says, registering with satisfaction the new note of compromise in Jack's voice.

Forty minutes later, Ollie is stepping into the open-plan room, where a couple of colleagues are at their desks.

Nick waves a hand. 'Thought you were still banged up, sunshine!'

Jack is ushering him into his office. 'One hell of a story this Lady Leebury business!'

'And there's more.'

'Excellent!' Jack peers at his screen. 'My contacts at the Met are proving useful and ITV want to run an in-depth report. So I thought we should review what you've got.' He holds up a hand. 'And I'm happy for you to take the lead on this. Since the story broke, our circulation's gone through the roof.'

Ollie can hardly admit that, without Amy's help, he could never have got this far. 'That's great,' he manages to get out.

'And you've got the remaining documents?'

Ollie spreads them on the desk. 'The manifests show a shortfall in the load – contents not accounted for.'

'The contents being?'

'White goods – mainly refrigerators and washing machines.'

'And the shortfall?'

'A container is being used to traffic underage girls to the UK.'

'Good God! But the proof is definitely there? These figures and columns may not be enough.'

'Not on their own.' Ollie finds himself speaking with growing confidence. 'But the police have the originals, as well as letters written on parliamentary notepaper – and the photographs, of course.' He looks across at Jack. 'It's clear from these that Hamish Rosser was blackmailing members of the House of Lords.' Ollie jabs a finger at the manifest in front of him. 'Some of the girls were being supplied to his colleagues.'

'Christ! A parliamentary paedophile ring. So where does the youth – Jimmy, wasn't it? – fit in?'

'He was a rent boy, whom Rosser used to gather information.' Ollie recalls the letter with the House of Lords logo stamped on the top. 'Jimmy stole photographs and documents from his clients' homes and in return Hamish supplied him with drugs.'

'And the boy's death was suspect?'

Ollie pictures the chalk-white face and the arms scored with needle marks. 'The inquest ruled he died from a heroin overdose.'

'Heroin supplied by Rosser?'

'Yes, although now he's dead, it would be hard to prove. But knowing what we do about the man, it's highly likely he was also threatening to expose Magdalena Leebury.'

'Because of her prison record?'

Ollie nods. 'Which wouldn't sit well with her husband being a newly-appointed government minister.'

'And which gives her a strong motive for Rosser's murder.' He tilts back his chair. 'Wonderful, by the way, that you were able to get hold of her passports and prison record. I won't ask how.'

Ollie hesitates. 'One thing I'm still not clear on. And that's how Rosser obtained the security code for the safe.'

'Ah – I can help you there. According to my source, a cleaning woman – Edna Cox – has admitted to the police that Rosser paid her for the information.'

'God – he had everything worked out, didn't he?'

'Apart from how not to get himself murdered. Where *is* Magdalena Leebury by the way?'

'I imagine still with her husband at Athelford Hall.'

'And he a peer of the realm.' He pauses. 'Great for sales. Talking of which, Ollie, you've obviously been hiding your light under the proverbial bushel.'

'I don't know about –'

'Stop being so fucking modest! You've cracked this case single-handed, and I'm sure there will be others. So I'd like to offer you a post of roving crime reporter. A month's trial and see how it goes?'

He stares, speechless. This is hardly the time to admit that, after his dealings with Rosser, he has no taste for this kind of work, let alone the competence to carry it out.

'That's settled then. We'll obviously need to keep a close eye on things. This story still has a lot of legs.' He smiles. 'Great work, Ollie. Anything else I need to know?'

He's certainly not about to tell Jack that one of Greg Jacobs' young proteges is the daughter of Magdalena Leebury. After all, the girl is hardly to blame for her mother's actions. Ollie pictures Magdalena – her full lips, those incredible grey eyes. 'I can't help feeling sorry for the Leeburys. Arnold Leebury struck me as a good man.'

Jack gets to his feet. 'Good people don't pay our bills. Talking of which – I've arranged for back salary to be transferred to your bank and of course you'll be getting a raise.' He extends a hand. 'See you at next week's editorial meeting.'

Still bemused by the turn of events, Ollie takes the lift

to the ground floor and there coming towards him is Nick, accompanied by a strong waft of vinegar.

'Fancy a chip?' he offers, holding out a brown paper bag.

'Bit early for me.'

'So what are you doing here? Persuading Jack to put you back on full-time?'

'Not exactly. I –'

'He's a stubborn sod, but now you're off the hook police-wise, I could have a word in his shell-like.'

Ollie nods. 'How are things with you?'

'That radio job never came off and with so many matches cancelled because of flooded pitches, I'm back covering bloody local planning.' He sighs. 'And the exes are still a big drain on the old finances.'

'Sorry to hear that.'

'We must go for that drink when there's space in the old diary. I'll give you a bell.'

'I meant to say that I owe you.'

He turns. 'How do you mean?'

'Helping me out over that Mercedes.'

'Think nothing of it, mate. Just wish I could have done more.'

'No worries. I can understand you didn't want to get too involved.' He pauses. 'But in fact it's all turned out pretty well. Jack and I are working together on this big scoop.'

He stares. 'You and Jack? A scoop?'

'The one our front page has been covering. It's in all the nationals.'

'The story about that Leebury woman? You crafty sod! How in hell did you manage that?' He steps closer. 'Tell you what – with a bit of luck I should be able to fit you in later in the week. So how about that drink?'

Ollie smiles. 'I've quite a lot on, so why don't I get back to you. When there's space in the old diary. Okey-doke?'

THIRTY-EIGHT

THE ROOM IS POORLY LIT AND GREG PAUSES IN THE doorway to get his bearings. The frock-coated doorman points ahead. 'In the far corner, sir. Lord Leebury has asked for you not to be disturbed.'

Arnold sits slumped in a high-backed chair, a jug of water, a half-empty whisky bottle and two glasses at his elbow. 'How are you doing?' Greg asks, settling beside him. Yet one glance at the shrunken frame and the eyes, red-rimmed from alcohol and tears, says it all – and is also an unwelcome reminder of the terrible time after Anne's death when Greg too lived in a state of semi-drunken despair.

'Thanks for coming.' Arnold's words are slurred. 'Fancy a snifter?'

'Just water.'

He reaches for the jug, his hand shaking. ''Fraid I'm not

fit for much these days.' He pauses. 'Not fit for anything, to be honest.'

Greg looks around the room. Its dark furniture and portraits of men in military uniform can hardly be helping his friend's mood, although it makes perfect sense that Arnold would choose a club like this. The whole atmosphere is strikingly similar to that other deadening place – Athelford Hall.

Arnold tops up his drink. 'Christ in heaven, Greg! How can this have happened?'

'The story may be in all the headlines but it will blow over.'

'That's not the point, is it?' Arnold's chin trembles. 'Even though my parliamentary career – such as it was – is finished, I still have to live knowing I married someone convicted of the worst of offences.' He gulps his whisky, his hand trembling. 'I feel such a fool – to have let myself be taken in. First, by Magdalena and then by Rosser.'

'I'm sorry,' Greg mutters, wishing there was something more helpful he could say. 'Is Magdalena still at the Hall?'

Arnold shakes his head. 'I told her I never wanted to set eyes on her again so she and that maid of hers will have taken off, God knows where.' He take another gulp of his drink. 'I couldn't stand staying on in the house on my own, so I've been holed up here ever since.' He pauses. 'Just as well, because I've lost my driver.'

'How do you mean?'

'Seamus handed in his notice just after Lena left. And the next day he was gone – no apology or excuse.' He takes another swig. 'I thought he of all people would stay loyal but obviously he couldn't wait to distance himself from the scandal.'

'You must let me know what I can do to help.'

'It's good of you to come but what can anyone do?' He pushes himself unsteadily to his feet. 'Must have a pee. Back in a tick.'

As Arnold shuffles his way to the door, Greg is left not just saddened but ashamed. However bad the loss of Frances has been, it's nothing compared with what his friend is going through. And of course it will serve no purpose to tell him that Frances is Magdalena's illegitimate daughter. The girl would only serve as a painful reminder of the wife Arnold is struggling to forget.

Arnold is back beside him. 'Sorry to be such a poor host. Coffee and sandwiches are on the way. Need something to mop up the alcohol.'

'But what are you planning to do, Arnold? Once you leave the club, I mean.'

'Leave?' A look of alarm spreads over the drawn face. 'Oh, no. I'm staying put, and in the longer term, I may even sell the Hall. Can't see myself rattling around the place on my own.' He hesitates. 'Now the young people have moved out, I don't suppose there's any chance of a spare room with you?'

Greg is saved from having to answer by the appearance of a waiter, who places a plate of sandwiches on the table, pours their coffee and retreats. The two men eat and drink in silence, which gives Greg time to think through Arnold's suggestion. Ever since their flat-sharing days they've got on well and over the years have kept up the contact. But now that Frances, Jason and Poppy have left, Greg needs to plan for the future– carry on the work that he and Anne started. There will be plenty of others desperate for the sort of help he can provide – help that Arnold doesn't need. But how to refuse his long-standing friend?

'So' – Arnold leans towards him. 'Where was I? Ah yes –' He breaks off. A tall figure in dark sweatshirt and jeans is coming towards them.

'What on earth are *you* doing here?' Arnold exclaims. 'If it's money you're after, you've had all you were owed.'

'Nothing like that, sur.' Seamus points to a chair. 'All right if I sit down?'

'If you must.' He pauses. 'You remember my friend, Greg Jacobs?'

'Indeed,' Seamus says, settling opposite. 'You visited the Hall in early January, Mr. Jacobs, along with your young friend – Frances, wasn't it?'

Greg nods, impressed and disconcerted by the man's memory.

Seamus fixes dark eyes on him. 'And if it's all the same to you, Mr. Jacobs, I'd appreciate a word with Lord Leebury – in private.'

Arnold shakes his head. 'You stay right here, Greg. Anything Seamus has to say can be said to the two of us.'

'Very good.' Seamus leans forward. 'I feel bad about the way I left Athelford Hall, sur. I can't imagine what you must have thought.'

'It was a bit of a blow.'

'But the truth is, I was called away.'

'"Called?" – how do you mean?'

'I hope this won't come as too much of a shock.' He hesitates. 'For some time now, I've been working undercover–'

'Undercover? What are you talking about?'

Seamus holds up a hand. 'Let me explain. I needed to get clearance from my superiors that it was OK to fill you in on some background to the operation.'

'Operation? So you were spying on me?' Arnold looks indignant, as he has every right to be, Greg thinks.

'If you want to put it that way.'

'Well, what way would *you* put it?'

When Seamus doesn't answer, Arnold adds with a sigh: 'It's to do with Magdalena, I suppose?'

Seamus gives an emphatic shake of his head. 'No, sur. It's to do with you – and Hamish Rosser.'

'I don't understand.'

'We've had our eye on the man for some time. And I can tell you now that he was mixed up in some very unpleasant stuff.'

'What sort of stuff? Good God, man, Hamish Rosser helped me out. He was a friend!'

'Bitcoin fraud, drug dealing, blackmail, a paedophile ring linked to members of Parliament.'

'You're not serious!'

'Afraid so.'

'Was he working alone? Wait a minute – what about that young assistant who was with him? Oliver someone-or-other?'

'We believe Rosser to have been the sole operator.' Seamus pauses. 'But none of that need concern you, sur. What I'm here to talk about is your brother.'

'Rupert? What's he got to do with anything?'

'I don't suppose Rosser ever mentioned his son, Angus?' Arnold shakes his head.

'The two of them were very close. Anyway, a few years back, Angus was celebrating his 50th birthday in Vegas and was thrashed by your brother in a poker game. Angus lost everything and the humiliation was too much. Angus's wife left him – they had no children – and two months later he hanged himself.'

'Good God!' Arnold mutters.

'We believe, sur, that Rupert's death on the ski slopes was no accident. Nothing that the police could prove, although we do know that Rosser flew into the resort two days beforehand and left the day after the death.' Seamus pauses. 'According to a reliable source, Rosser swore to destroy, not just Rupert, but you as well.'

Arnold leans forward. 'This makes no sense! Look at the strings he pulled to get me that ministerial job.'

'But don't you see? Once you accepted the post, your eventual downfall – by the disclosure of your wife's prison sentence – would be all the more terrible.' Seamus pauses again. 'The target was never Magdalena. It was you.'

Greg leans forward. 'But for a man to go to all those lengths – it's unbelievable.'

'He wasn't just ruthless, Mr. Jacobs. He was vindictive – and cunning. It's very hard to get close to a man like that. So the moment we discovered he was targeting you, I joined your household in the hopes of gathering enough evidence about his various criminal activities to bring him to justice.'

329

'But someone got to him first.'

Seamus nods.

'And the murderer's still out there?' Greg asks.

'Unfortunately, yes. But the DNA results are now through so an arrest is expected very soon.'

'But hang on a minute, Seamus.' Arnold leans forward. 'Magdalena said you weren't in your bed on the night of the murder. So perhaps you saw something?'

'Can't help you on that.' Abruptly, he's on his feet. 'I must be on my way.' He looks down at Arnold. 'Strictly off the record, sur, I have it on good authority that your parliamentary career is still open to you – if you want it.'

Arnold stares after his retreating back. 'I suppose he's to be trusted?'

'He did seem genuinely keen to help,' Greg says. 'But what a bombshell! I'm still struggling to get my head round Hamish's criminal activities.'

'To say nothing of the coincidence of his being responsible for Rupert's death.'

'Small world,' Greg says, thinking of that other coincidence – that Frances should be Magdalena's daughter. But Magdalena has also been used, he thinks, and but for the Scotsman, she and Arnold might well have continued to live happily together. Aloud he says: 'Would you ever be able to forgive your Lena – further down the line, I mean?'

'Don't think it hasn't crossed my mind.' Arnold's voice is sad. 'But how could I ever trust her again? So no – I think a clean break is best.'

Greg pushes back his chair. 'I'm afraid I need to press on.'

'Of course. Any chance of linking up again, say, in a few days' time?'

'I'll check my diary and get back to you. And Arnold –'

'Yes?'

'It looks as if you still have your ministerial post.' He pauses. 'And don't you think that Hamish Rosser's done enough damage?'

Arnold gives a slow nod. 'You're right. The man may have brought about Magdalena's downfall but I'll be blowed if I'll let him destroy me.'

THIRTY-NINE

A T HALF FOUR IN THE MORNING, THE AIRPORT terminal is bustling. Marya has chosen a table overlooking the entrance, so she can watch for the first sightings of press or the police who have plenty of reasons for coming after them.

Yet crowds provide welcome camouflage, she reminds herself, as she watches a party of backpackers shoving their way through the busy concourse below.

'Do try to relax, darlink.' Magdalena arranges her Burberry over the back of her chair. 'A couple more hours to kill and we'll be on our way.' In cream jacket and skirt, with a red bucket hat perched on waves of silken hair, she looks for all the world like someone heading for a formal lunch or a wedding.

But Marya, in shabby raincoat and scuffed shoes, round eyes constantly scanning her surroundings, will not rest easy until they are both safely on board. She clears her throat. 'I've something I need to –'

'How about a glass of bubbly to steady the nerves?' As always, the smile warms Marya's insides and as she queues at the bar, she watches her scan her phone, seemingly oblivious to the stares she is attracting. It's as if she has some inner magnet that draws people to her. Of course, no one could have guessed at this ability if they'd seen her all those years ago, sitting in that London cafe, her mousy hair and sallow skin not due just to having been cooped up in gaol for years but because morning sickness was still taking its toll.

They never spoke of the baby again and with the birth safely behind them, found jobs washing dishes in a West End restaurant, returning in the evening to their shabby bedsit in Earls Court. All spare cash was put aside for make-up and clothes for Theresa, who had the knack of plucking a bargain off a rail and making it appear like a designer outfit. The years went by and whilst Marya remained on the wash-up, Theresa went to night school to improve her English and, having renamed herself Magdalena – 'to go with my new image, darlink' – worked her way up from waitress level to Front of House Manager. Soon she was attracting a string of male admirers, who took her to the cinema and night clubs, to dinner and dancing. She would return before dawn to find an anxious Marya pacing the small room. 'Try not to worry, darlink. These men are like Octav, focussed only on what they can't keep in their trousers. But they pay well, so now we just need to wait.'

But for what? Marya thought, fearful that her

unpredictable friend might abandon her for one of these rich clients. Just the thought turned her stomach cold.

And then came an evening when Theresa, elegant in black dress, heeled shoes and gold earrings – dragged Marya from the pot she was scrubbing and pointed to the corner of the dining area. 'That one,' she whispered.

Marya viewed the customer with surprise. He was so ordinary-looking – in his fifties, perhaps, with plump cheeks, thinning hair and an apologetic stoop to the shoulders. Even more of a surprise was how, as the weeks passed, Magdalena seemed genuinely to warm to him, dropping her other male escorts and accepting the gifts with which he showered her. A couple of months later, Marya was introduced and only gradually did the two women discover that not only was Arnold Leebury willing to take both of them into his home, but that he was also offering them a lifestyle they could hardly have dreamed of. Although as far as Marya was concerned, the trappings of Athelford Hall meant nothing as long she and Magdalena could be together.

'To our new beginning!' Magdalena says, raising the glass of champagne Marya has placed at her elbow. 'But why the long face?'

'The thing is…' Her voice wavers.

'A dose of the cold feet? You'll feel differently once we are away from this dreary British rain and the even drearier British people.'

'About the Scottish man –.'

'Forget him, darlink. Soon the person responsible will

be arrested. And I wish I could see Arnie's face when he realises all those suspicions about his Lena were so much hot air.'

Marya gulps her champagne. She's never liked the sour taste of the stuff and puts her glass down with a click. 'Remember the night of the Christmas party?'

'But I doubt he'll ever forgive me for ruining his dreams.'

Marya tugged Magdalena's sleeve. 'You must listen. Seamus said he was unwell so Arnold asked me to stay behind to keep eye on him.'

She sighs. 'What of it?'

'About an hour after you left, I was on my way down to the kitchen when I saw headlights coming towards the house. I thought you or Arnold must have forgotten something.'

Magdalena is studying the departure board. 'Shouldn't our flight have been called by now?'

'The car didn't pull up by the front but drove on round to the courtyard. So I ran down to the kitchen to see who the visitor was. When I looked through the window I saw Rosser's green car pull up – I'd have recognised it anywhere – and that caddisfly assistant climb out of the passenger seat. I could tell from the way he was creeping about that he was up to no good.'

Magdalena shifts her gaze from the departure board. 'So you went out to ask what the hell he was doing?'

She shakes her head. 'I hid in one of the storerooms.'

Magdalena smiles. 'I didn't think you scared so easy, Marya. But whatever did he want?'

'Let me finish. I listened to him opening the back door and switching off the alarms. He made quite a racket, I can tell you.'

'And you didn't stop him? But wait a minute!' She stared across at Marya. 'It must have been him who stole the passports. And you've known this all along! Why the hell haven't you said anything before?'

'I didn't know at the time. How could I? As I followed him up the stairs, I had no idea of what he was after. But then, through the front window, I saw the Scottish man's car driving up the rise and stopping under the trees, still with its lights on. And then it came to me.' She pauses, licking lips sticky from champagne.

Magdalena leans over the table. 'What did?'

'I pulled on my raincoat and shoes and let myself out of the house. It was a terrible night – blowing a real gale. I made my way up the track and as I got near the car, I saw a figure under the trees.'

'The murderer?' Magdalena whispers, all her attention now on Marya.

She shakes her head. 'The Scottish man. He had his back to me.' She paused. 'So I moved behind him – he never heard me in all that wind and rain – raised the knife I'd taken from the kitchen, took aim, and –' She banged her hand on the table, making the champagne glasses jump. 'Seconds later he was on the ground.'

'You're saying you killed him?'

She nods.

'But why, for God's sake?'

'I did it for you, my darling.' She leans over and grips

336

Magdalena's hand. 'He was out to destroy you and I couldn't allow that to happen – not after all we've been through.' She pauses. 'I propped him against the nearest tree, jammed his hat back on his head and ran back to the house to change out of my wet clothes.'

Magdalena looks away, biting her lip.

'You are pleased, aren't you? Even at the time I kept thinking how proud you'd be of your Marya.'

'Proud?'

'For remembering details like not just throwing the knife away.'

'So, what did you do with it?'

Marya smiles. 'I put it in the dishwasher. Edna would have replaced it in the block after the next cycle.'

'But the DNA results will link you to the killing.'

'That's why I'm telling you now because we'll need to go into hiding until the police stop searching for us.'

'For us?' Magdalena stares down at the table. 'If you are caught, the police will believe that I had a part in the murder.'

'We will take care not to get caught.'

She gives an emphatic shake of her head. 'They will find you, Marya – no matter how far you run.'

'But I will tell them I acted alone.'

'They won't believe you. And don't you see, darlink, that after the life I've had with Arnie, to be locked away again would finish me.'

Marya feels her insides turn cold. 'So what is it you're saying?'

She hesitates. 'That maybe it would be best for us to

337

travel separately. That way we'll attract less attention. So I will catch this flight as planned.'

'And I will take a later plane?'

She nods. 'We have our mobiles and when things have calmed down, I will message you where to meet.' She glances at the departure board once more. 'That's my flight being called.'

'My ticket, Magdalena.'

'What?'

'I need to exchange it.'

She fiddles with the clasp of her bag. 'I think that perhaps it's not a good idea after all.'

'What are you saying? How can I join you without it? And I have no money.'

Magdalena opens her bag and shoves a handful of notes across the table. 'These will keep you going for a bit.'

Marya is swept by a rage that has her on her feet, spitting out her words. 'Who was it who stopped you finishing yourself off in that prison? Stood by you all those years in London? Has lied and killed for you!'

Magdalena studies her nails. 'Of course I'm grateful, darlink, and –'

'I don't want your fucking gratitude!' Marya yells, as those around them turn to stare. 'I want my ticket!'

Magdalena bites her lip. 'I must make a move.'

'I won't let you do this!' Marya swipes her hand across the table, sending the glasses flying into the air.

'Watch out!' someone calls as they crash onto the floor.

Marya grabs Magdalena's arm. 'I must have it!'

'Let go of me!'

A small crowd has gathered and a broad-shouldered man in tracksuit and trainers steps forward. 'You all right?' he says to Magdalena.

The grey eyes fill with tears. 'I'm afraid I'll miss my plane.'

Marya tightens her grip, staring into the faces around them. 'Take a good look. This tight-arsed cunt is only out for herself!' She waves the fistful of notes in the air. 'She's spent years in prison – is on the run from her husband – has a bag stuffed full of stolen cash!'

The man steps between them. 'You need to calm down,' he says to Marya. And to Magdalena: 'You know her?'

'She used to work for me and is a little bit upset because I no longer require her services.'

'Well, if I were you, I'd get going.' He drapes Magdalena's Burberry over her shoulders. 'You don't want to miss that flight.'

'You fucking whore!' Marya shouts, as two security guards in pale blue shirts appear at her side. 'I've always looked out for you, you selfish bitch! Would never have betrayed you!'

'You'd better come with us, love,' one of the security guards is saying.

Marya's energy has drained away and it feels as if some light has been switched off inside her. She peers over the heads of the crowd for a last sighting of the red bucket hat disappearing into the distance.

FORTY

OLLIE IS LOADING THE DISHWASHER WHEN HIS mobile buzzes. Over the past couple of weeks he and Amy have swapped roles and the new arrangement is working well. She now spends her spare time looking up crime reports for him to follow up on, while he keeps himself busy on the domestic front, relieved to have a sense of pressure off.

He dries his hands on a tea towel and clicks on the phone.

'Greg Jacobs here,' the voice at the other end says.

'How are you doing, Mr. Jacobs?'

'Fine. I'm ringing about those documents you gave me. The ones linking Magdalena Leebury with one of my charges, Frances.'

'Oh, yes.' Ollie hopes there's not going to be yet another twist to the story.

'Anyway,' Greg Jacobs continues, 'I just wanted you to know that I've shredded the lot. No point raking over the past.'

Ollie is swept by a wave of relief. 'Exactly my feeling.' He pauses. 'You saw on the news that the maid at Athelford Hall has confessed to the murder? And that Magdalena Leebury's done a runner?'

'Poor Arnold. I phoned the moment I heard. He's been completely gutted.'

Ollie pictures the man – kind-faced and unassuming. Perhaps what has happened is for the best, he thinks, although how hard it must be to detach oneself from someone as stunningly beautiful as Magdalena.

'I had dinner with him last week,' Greg Jacobs continues. 'Thankfully, his colleagues are being supportive and he tells me he's going to throw himself into parliamentary life.'

'And the daughter, Frances, still has no idea who her mother is?'

'None at all. And best it stays that way. She's getting married in the summer.' A small laugh comes down the phone. 'I'm busy brushing up on the-father-of-the-bride speech.' A pause. 'I'm also about to become an honorary grandparent – the other couple who lived here are expecting their first baby.' Another pause. 'It's all been a bit sudden.'

'You must miss them,' Ollie says, recalling what it was like to return each evening to an empty house.

'I can't pretend it's been easy, but corny as it sounds, when one door closes... I've got three more young people moving in next month and I'm going to try and see the old lady, Amelia, right.'

Just to hear the name brings back the reek of cat piss, and Jimmy's arms scored with needle marks. 'That's good of you,' Ollie manages to get out.

'Well, all the best.'

Ollie clicks off the phone and moves into the front room to find Amy bent over the day's newspapers. 'Who was that?'

'Someone called Greg Jacobs. It wasn't important.'

She looks up at him. 'Babe?'

Her tone immediately puts him on the alert.

'I've got something to ask you.'

'Yes?'

'Would it be OK if I moved in – permanently, I mean?'

He stares. 'Mind? Of *course* not!'

'It's just my mum's pregnant.'

'How old is she, for God's sake?'

'Well over forty. Think she's a bit shocked too. Her partner's a nice enough guy but I don't want to be around after the birth. Because guess who'll be landed with the baby-sitting?'

Ollie fights off a moment's disappointment. So Amy's decision is not because she can't live without him.

'Just look at your face, Ollie Moorhouse!'

'What do you mean?'

She reaches up and strokes his cheek. 'I do love you, you pillock!'

'And I – what I mean is – you –' He still can't get the words out.

She rolls her eyes at him before turning her attention to the newspapers once more. 'I think I may be onto something. There's a man in the Oxford area accused of stalking two housewives. Stands outside their homes for hours, follows them to the supermarket – all that sort of thing.'

'Oxford's not exactly my patch, is it?'

'No – but one of the women lives half a mile from here. You could try for an interview? Maybe at the weekend.'

'To be honest, I was looking forward to our having a quiet time at home.'

'Sunday's clear. We could go together?'

If he's to keep in with Jack, he can't afford not to follow up a lead like this. Aloud he says: 'Fine.'

'And I've been thinking, Babe. If you continue taking on more household stuff, I could go part-time at the store? We could then put a story like this one together?'

'Worth a try.' He still hasn't told her about the money stashed away in the wardrobe which is going to give them so many more options. And best of all is the knowledge that it hasn't played a part in her decision to move in.

He nuzzles her ear. 'I've got some good news on the financial front. Let's go to the pub and I'll tell you about it over lunch.'

Ten minutes later they pause together on the front step of the house, listening to the water dripping off the gutter onto the concrete path.

Amy takes his arm. 'Let's get going.'

He points to where a watery sun floats above the roof tops. 'Can you believe it?' he says. 'It's stopped raining.'

ABOUT THE AUTHOR

E. J. PEPPER HAS AN M.A. IN CREATIVE WRITING from Chichester University. She has published two previous novels. *The Colours of the Dance* (historical fiction) won the First Novel Prize, and *Flight Path* (contemporary fiction) was winner of the Exeter Novel Prize.

She lives with her husband in Southern England.